Dark Power Untamed

THE CHILDREN OF THE GODS
BOOK FIFTY

I. T. LUCAS

Dark Power Untamed is a work of fiction! Names, characters, places and incidents are products of the author's imagination or are used fictitiously and are not to be construed as real. Any similarity to actual persons, organizations and/or events is purely coincidental.

Copyright © 2021 by I. T. Lucas

All rights reserved.

No part of this book may be reproduced in any form or by any electronic or mechanical means, including information storage and retrieval systems, without written permission from the author, except for the use of brief quotations in a book review.

Published by Evening Star Press

Cassandra

"Look at that ass," whispered the guy standing in line behind Cassandra. "I want to sink my teeth into those fleshy cushions."

She rolled her eyes but didn't react. It wasn't the first time guys had made lewd comments behind her back, and most times she pretended not to hear them and did not engage.

"I want to sink something else between them," his friend said, without even trying to lower his voice.

Her hands fisted at her sides.

It was one thing to whisper vulgarities to a friend. It was another thing to make sure that she heard it. It was rude in the extreme and a call to battle.

One the jerks would not win.

Her temper rising, Cassandra considered her options. She could turn around and lash out at the buttheads, releasing some of the negative energy that had built up and preventing it from reaching an explosive level, or she could pretend that she hadn't heard them. The problem with that was if her anger kept building, she would lose control over it.

Bad things happened when she allowed the pressure to accumulate without releasing at least some of the steam. At best, electronic devices around her malfunctioned, inanimate objects toppled and shattered, or glass cracked and exploded. At worst... she didn't want to think about that. Letting herself dwell on it would ruin what had been so far a relatively decent day.

The artwork for the next Surprise Box launch was finally done, which was why she'd allowed herself a small break and had gone out of the office to grab a cup of coffee. But instead of enjoying a few moments of peace, she had some jerks standing behind her and talking about what they would like to do to her ass.

"That's a really fine piece of ass," said a third one as he joined her club of admirers.

Out of the three, his comment was the least offensive, but it was the last straw.

Turning around, she glared down at them. "You know that I can hear you, right?"

Her intimidating pose had the pimply teenagers take a step back. With the three-inch heels she had on, Cassandra was over six feet tall and towered over them.

Combine that with her hard glare, and the little jerks were probably shaking in their fashionable sneakers.

The boys were sixteen or seventeen at the most, and seeing how young they were, some of her anger dissipated, enough to significantly reduce the danger of things exploding in her vicinity.

Still, they should know better than to trash talk about a woman, especially one who was old enough to be their mother. Well, only if she had had triplets at seventeen, but still, if they were hers, they never would have dared to talk like that.

She blamed their parents. They had done a piss-poor job of raising them.

One of the three lifted his hands in a sign of peace. "We meant no disrespect. It's just guy talk."

As the other two took another step back and cowered behind the leader, she leaned down to level him with one of her deadly stares. "How would you like it if a bunch of girls commented on the shape of your butt and what they wanted to do with it?"

He smirked. "I would love it."

She had to give him points for guts. Her glares had grown men cower before her, and yet the skinny, pimply boy looked her straight in the eyes and kept smirking.

"What if a bunch of pimply whelps made comments like that about your mother or sister?"

His smirk melted away. "I wouldn't like that."

"There you go. A word of advice that will save you a lot of grief in the future. Don't say anything that you wouldn't want others to say about the important women in your life."

"Yes, ma'am." He lowered his eyes.

"Cassy," the barista called. "Your usual?"

She turned around and smiled. "How are you doing, Dylan?"

"I'm good." Leaning sideways, he peered at the three boys, who were keeping a proper distance from her. "Were they bothering you?"

"They needed a lesson in manners."

He chuckled. "I bet you gave them one to remember."

"I hope so." She handed him her card. "One venti mocha Frappuccino, please."

"A venti? Are you celebrating?" He swiped it and then gave it back together with the receipt.

The thing was probably a thousand calories, but she'd earned the right to indulge. "Yeah, I'm celebrating having a few moments to myself."

"Good for you. Every minute that is not miserable is worth celebrating."

"Amen to that." She collected her drink and waved at Dylan. "I'll see you again tomorrow, and if not, have a great weekend."

"You too."

Outside the wind had picked up, whipping the few strands of hair that had escaped her messy bun into her face, and as she crossed the street back to the office, it started raining. Cassandra ran the rest of the way, careful not to spill her drink or slide and land in a puddle. That would certainly ruin the rest of her day.

Once inside, she climbed the stairs to the second floor and opened the glass double doors. Striding through the firm's large common room, she ignored the unfriendly glares some cast her way, and the indifference of others, as well as the fake smiles of those who thought to gain favor with the firm's VP.

Cassandra had almost made it to the sanctuary of her private office when Kevin's personal assistant waved her down. "Cassandra! The boss was looking for you. He wants to see you in his office."

"Crap," she muttered under her breath and turned to walk in the other direction.

She loved Kevin, but the guy liked to talk, and right now she didn't have the patience for his so-called brainstorming, which was mainly about him throwing ideas around and using her as his sounding board. She planned on leaving at a reasonable time today and not taking work home with her. Perhaps she would even humor her mother and join her to watch that mini-series she was obsessing about.

"You wanted to see me?" Cassandra walked into Kevin's sprawling office, pulled out one of the fancy Art Deco chairs, and plopped tiredly onto it.

Whoever thought that the job of a creative director was glamorous didn't know how difficult it was to be in charge of ten unmotivated snowflakes, who for one reason or another kept dropping the ball on her left and right. Picking up the slack, she was working sixteen-hour days, taking work home, and barely making it in time for the monthly mystery boxes rollouts.

Kevin flashed her one of his charming smiles. "I hope you don't have any plans for Saturday evening."

"Why?" She narrowed her eyes at him.

"I need you to accompany me to the charity gala." When she opened her mouth to protest, he lifted his hand to stop her. "Josie can't make it. She has a concert the same night, and I need a stand-in."

If his wife had a performance scheduled, he would have known about it months in advance.

Cassandra wouldn't be surprised if Josie just wasn't in the mood to do the whole dog and pony show again. The woman was a saint for tolerating being paraded around and presented as her husband's muse, the inspiration for the company's *Fifty Shades of Beauty* cosmetics line.

Kevin was a businessman to his core, and he used every advantage available to him, including his beautiful wife who was a world-renowned cellist. He loved telling the story of how he'd been inspired to create foundations to match every skin tone because of her. When Josie couldn't find the right one for her dark olive complexion with reddish undertones, he'd had an aha moment.

In reality, that moment had been more about realizing the marketing potential of a unique angle than formulating a perfect shade for his wife.

"And you find out about it now? What the hell, Kevin?" Cassandra pushed to her feet. "Find someone else to go with you."

Who else had turned him down that he waited until the last moment to ask her?

Besides, Cassandra's days of posing for the camera were over. She still looked good, but she couldn't compare to the young girls they used to model their cosmetics. Kevin could ask any of them, and they would be thrilled to attend the gala with him and have their pictures plastered all over social media.

"Cassy, please, sit down. I need you to do this for me."

Damn him and his pleading tone. She hated when he did that, but after all that Kevin had done for her, she couldn't refuse him, and the bastard knew it.

"I don't want to be a stand-in for Josie. What are you going to tell the crowd? That you created the line for me?"

"I did."

She rolled her eyes. "You hired me after that. Besides, your wife is famous, and everyone knows what she looks like. I can't pretend to be her."

"I'm not asking you to." Leaning back, he crossed his arms over his chest. "Since even now you are wearing my foundation on your beautiful face, I can slightly alter my regular speech and say that I created it for you." He smirked. "Just not exclusively."

Ugh. Being paraded around by Kevin, her face stretched in a fake smile for hours, was Cassandra's personal definition of hell.

She probably wasn't going to win the argument, but that didn't mean that she was going to stop until she had exhausted every excuse possible to wiggle out of the damn event.

"Take one of the models. They all use your cosmetics, and they would love to hobnob with the rich and famous at a posh charity gala."

Assuming a sheepish expression, Kevin raked his fingers through his thinning hair. "I can't take an eighteen-year-old to the event. The media would eat me alive. The damn gossip magazines would publish articles about me taking advantage of the young women working for me, or worse, that I'm cheating on my wife with them. You are my vice president and the company's creative director, and other than Josie, you are the only one I can take. Besides, just like my wife, you embody the type of woman I created the line for. Strong, successful, and absolutely stunning."

Finally, she realized what he was after. He was going to use her to promote their best-selling foundation shade.

He was such a greedy, manipulative prick, but he paid her generously and gave her near-complete autonomy over the marketing creatives.

She owed him.

"I get it. My spice latte skin tone is a perfect match for your bestselling foundation. You want to show me off to promote it."

He didn't deny it. "Come on, Cassy, say yes."

Huffing out a breath, she uncrossed her arms and picked up her Frappuccino. "I don't have anything appropriate to wear."

"Take a day off tomorrow and use the company credit card to buy everything you need. Dress, shoes, jewelry, the works."

She arched a brow. "Budget?"

"Up to ten grand." He smiled. "But knowing you, you'll find stuff on sale at a fraction of the cost. You just can't stomach wasting money."

"That's because I didn't grow up with a silver spoon in my mouth."

"Neither did I, but I worked hard for what I have, and I don't mind spending it on the things I like."

She shrugged. "It's your money. You can do with it as you wish. But I'm not going to treat it any differently just because it doesn't come out of my own pocket."

"I know. But do me a favor and don't buy a dress at a thrift store. For this Saturday evening, you represent the company. Get something that will have the media photographers chasing you around like a bunch of rabid dogs."

She grimaced. "Calling them rabid dogs is uncalled for. Most are just trying to make a living like everyone else."

"I have a love-hate relationship with the media," Kevin admitted.

"Of course, you do. You want the free publicity when it suits you, but you don't want them around when it doesn't."

His mouth twisted in distaste. "Some of them are nasty bastards."

"Regrettably, that's true."

Cassandra had met some slimy photographers, but even as an eighteen-year-old model, she'd known how to deal with them. If they pissed her off, their pricey cameras had suffered irreparable damage.

Kevin shrugged. "I want your picture plastered over all the beauty magazines."

"I get it. You want to generate free publicity, and my story is interesting." The model turned executive who'd helped *Fifty Shades of Beauty* grow exponentially.

Kevin smirked. "Precisely."

"You are aware that the entire staff is going to hate me even more for this."

"Refusing to come is not going to make them like you better. You have a nasty attitude, and they are resentful because I let you get away with it. But mostly, they are just jealous of your success."

"That's why I don't bother trying to be nicer. It's not going to help anyway, and I'd rather they feared me."

The staff had a lot of reasons to hate her. She'd joined the company at eighteen as a model, but Kevin had recognized her talent early on, and he had promoted her ahead of people with college degrees and much more experience in the field. When he'd made her his VP and raised her salary to a quarter of a million, two other senior staff members had quit.

Her bitchy attitude didn't win her any popularity contests either, but she wasn't about to apologize for that. Cassandra demanded from others a fraction of what she demanded from herself, and yet they routinely failed to produce even that.

What did they expect? Praise?

Not from her.

Kevin was the politician, the one who smoothed things over and calmed the hysterical snowflakes after she'd melted them with the heat of her wrath.

Several petitions had been submitted to have her fired, and when Kevin had refused, they had started whispering that she was his lover. Some even went as far as saying that she had him bewitched.

Given what she was capable of when her temper flared, she might indeed wield dark magic, just not the kind that could bewitch a guy into loving her. If she could do that, she wouldn't be single at the ripe old age of thirty-four.

Besides, Kevin was happily married, and her relationship with him was purely professional.

Well, that wasn't entirely true. He and Josie were also her friends, and Cassandra valued that no less than the incredible break they had given her professionally. Just like her, the two of them had risen from nothing and had worked their fingers to the bone to get to where they were today.

"Do you really care that they'll become even more resentful?" he asked.

"No, I don't. Just don't complain to me when you receive the next petition demanding my dismissal."

He laughed. "Agreed."

Onegus

After reading the changes Bridget had made to his speech, Onegus shook his head. "The language is too strong for this type of event. The rich and famous come to these charity events to mingle, to be seen, and to have a good time. They don't want to have the horrors of trafficking shoved down their throats."

The parts Bridget had added had been taken from the speech she'd delivered in front of the clan's big assembly. Her no-nonsense blunt words had struck a chord with the retired Guardians, motivating most of them to return to the force and join the war on trafficking. But motivating rich humans to donate to the cause required a more diplomatic approach.

Thankfully, the doctor didn't seem offended. "I thought that was what Kian wanted me to do. Your speech lacks the punch to the gut that will make them pledge generously to the cause."

He chuckled. "I'm afraid that your verbal punch would just sour their stomachs and induce nausea. Trust me, I know what I'm doing. Talking about the transformative power of the rehabilitation we provide to the victims will put a positive spin on the ugly subject that the donors will feel comfortable rallying behind."

Leaning back, Bridget crossed her arms over her chest. "I trust your instincts. Feel free to remove the entire opening paragraph. What about the other changes I made?"

"Those are good. I'll keep them." Onegus collected the pages they'd worked on and put them in his briefcase. "Any chance that I can convince you to accompany me to the gala? I need a shield against the socialites. They swarm all over me at these events."

"That's the price of being so handsome," Bridget mocked.

"Yeah, right. They think that I'm the rich philanthropist in charge of the international conglomerate that runs the charity organization."

Bridget laughed. "You'll survive. You can pretend to be nasty, and maybe they'll leave you alone."

"Are you kidding me? That will only make them bolder. Besides, I'm there to solicit donations, which means that I need to be charming and smile at everyone."

Her expression turned apologetic. "I don't like going to events without Turner. It just feels wrong to get all dolled up and not have him by my side. When you find your one and only, you'll understand."

"Fat chance of that." He let out a breath. "Always the groomsman never the groom, which is fine with me. All my head Guardians are mated, and it's making things difficult. I can't send them on out-of-town missions because they can't stand being away from their mates. A military organization can't function like that."

"Most of our missions are local." Bridget glanced at her computer screen. "We've been running an average of fifteen missions a week for months now, and we haven't made a dent in the local problem. I don't see us venturing out of the Los Angeles area anytime soon, and if we do, it would be farther south, to San Diego, which is only three hours away. Being so close to the border, the city is a major hub for traffickers."

Onegus was well aware of that, and he had even contemplated approaching Kalugal about using his men to expand the operations. The guy would most likely refuse, and Kian wasn't keen on the idea either, but it was a possibility.

In the meantime, though, Onegus had the Kra-ell problem to deal with.

"Kian wants to send Arwel with a couple of Guardians to China, and to do that, he needs to convince Jin to go as well. That's just wrong. She's a civilian, and she has no business going on a reconnaissance mission that might get dicey."

Bridget shrugged. "Eleanor is a civilian as well, and yet you had no problem letting her go on a reconnaissance mission."

"That was different. First of all, Eleanor has experience in undercover work. Secondly, she's training with Kri and is in top physical condition. And thirdly, infiltrating a cult on US soil and investigating its leader was a very low-risk assignment, especially given Eleanor's compulsion ability. We had no way of knowing that Emmett was an immortal, or rather a long-lived distant relative of ours. Not only was he immune to her compulsion, but he also was much too strong for her to fight off."

Bridget winced. "Eleanor was lucky that he didn't kill her. She was powerless against him."

Onegus nodded. "So was Peter, and he's a trained Guardian. The Kra-ell are dangerous, and we need to find out what their plans are." He tapped his fingers on her desk. "Emmett is not a bad guy, but his people sound no better than the Brotherhood. They keep humans enslaved in their compound, using them for breeding hybrids and as a source of nourishment. They also treat the hybrids as second-class members, and their leader sounds like a ruthless tyrant."

Bridget sighed. "They have a different set of values and beliefs, and their social structure is very different from ours. That doesn't make what they're doing acceptable, but it also doesn't make them evil."

Onegus raked his fingers through his short hair. "That's an old philosophical dilemma. The fact that they don't think of themselves as evil doesn't mean that what they do isn't wrong. I don't accept cultural or religious beliefs and practices as an excuse for mistreating people, their own or others. I also don't care if their own people think that's the way it should be because it was drilled into their heads that it is. If their actions cause suffering, then those actions are unacceptable. End of story."

"I agree. But it's not our job to go in and forcefully change things for the better. Our job is to provide information and nudge humanity toward equality and democracy." She leaned forward. "Navuh and his scores of warriors are a much bigger problem than Emmett's people, and we haven't made any meaningful progress dealing with that threat, and not for lack of trying. Frankly, I don't understand why Kian is freaking out about the Kra-ell. Their numbers are insignificant, and they haven't caused us any trouble yet."

Bridget was brilliant, and she ran the rescue operations efficiently, but her lack of military background was evident.

"Navuh is a known adversary. We know what he wants, how he thinks to achieve that, and we also know how to thwart his efforts for world domination. The Kra-ell are an unknown. We don't know how many groups like Emmett's are scattered around the world, and we don't know what their agenda is."

Bridget pursed her lips. "That's where Jin's special talent might come in handy. She's the perfect spy, and she can blend in, provided that she masters Mandarin by the time they head to China."

Onegus shook his head. "She has no training, and she's hotheaded. I don't feel comfortable sending her out on a mission even with Arwel and a couple of other Guardians to keep her safe. She might endanger them all."

"It's true that Jin is a civilian with no combat training, but she has skills that are much more valuable than any Guardian's. The problem I see with that is her unwillingness to go. If she refuses, Arwel might turn down the assignment, and you will have to find someone else for the mission."

Onegus grimaced. "You see what I have to deal with? No other chief has to worry about his troops refusing to go out on missions because they can't be away from their mates."

"Don't forget that they are all newly mated," Bridget said. "Perhaps in a couple of decades, they will have no problem leaving their mates for weeks at a time."

"I don't have decades to wait, and besides, I doubt that the bonds will ever loosen. I have nightmares about the entire Guardian force being mated and having no one to work with."

Smiling, Bridget put her hand on his shoulder. "Have faith, Onegus. When the time comes, and everyone is mated, we will find a solution. We always do."

Bowen

"You really don't have to do that." Margaret stood next to the open front door, leaning on her crutches. "I will be perfectly comfortable on the bench."

"Right." Bowen lifted one of the armchairs and carried it out to the front porch. "You'll be more comfortable sitting on this." He set it down in a sunny spot near the railing, where she would be warm.

"Thank you." Margaret lowered herself carefully onto the seat and leaned the crutches against the wooden railing.

It was a beautiful day in the mountains. The sky was clear, the sun was shining softly, and the excited chirping of birds was announcing loudly that spring had arrived and it was time to mate.

Regrettably, he wouldn't be joining the mating frenzy anytime soon. He wanted Margaret, but she was off-limits. First of all, she was in a cast, healing from an injury. But even if she was perfectly healthy, it would be a bad idea. He'd befriended her, cared for her, and he could never treat her like one of his random hookups, enjoying her and then vanishing without giving it a second thought.

The situation Bowen found himself in was frustrating.

He couldn't have Margaret, and he couldn't go hunting for sex in the usual places where he found willing partners until he returned her to Safe Haven. Not that he was looking forward to the old, tired routine and the revolving door of sex partners. It reduced sex to a necessity like eating and drinking, stripping it of the emotions that made it so much more meaningful for mated couples.

For Leon, the chase was over, and even though Bowen was happy for him and Anastasia, he couldn't help but envy the guy.

Thank the merciful Fates, Anastasia had transitioned successfully and with no complications, was feeling great, and the couple was on their way back to the cabin, which meant that he'd better start on lunch.

Newly transitioned Dormants were not supposed to eat anything heavy, but Leon had already warned him that Anastasia was ravenous and craved hamburgers.

Lifting the long-necked lighter, he glanced at Margaret. "Are you sure the smoke is not going to bother you?"

If the smell made Margaret nauseous, she wouldn't eat, and he wanted to fill her belly with meat. She needed to get stronger.

"I like the smell." Margaret smiled up at him. "And I also like watching you grill."

"You do?" He lit the barbecue.

"You're so meticulous, and you take pride in it. You enjoy doing things well."

He could think of several things that he did exceptionally well, but they had more to do with licking and fondling than with cooking.

"Yes, I do." He couldn't help the nearly full octave drop in his voice.

Getting his meaning, she lowered her eyes as if he'd made her uncomfortable, but the slight scent of her arousal said otherwise.

Damn. He needed to get a grip. The poor woman had suffered enough. She didn't need to pine after a guy who couldn't return the sentiment no matter how much he wanted to.

"I'm going to get the meat." He walked back inside.

In the kitchen, Bowen loaded a tray with the steaks that he'd left marinating in the fridge overnight, a pack of seasoned hamburgers, a beer for him, and a bottle of water for Margaret.

After putting the tray down on the wooden cart he'd placed next to the grill, he took the bottle and walked over to Margaret. "You need to stay hydrated." He handed it to her.

"Thank you." She took it without lifting her head from her phone.

After finally learning how to use the search function, Margaret was surfing the internet like a pro, collecting articles for her workshop and saving them to a note application he'd downloaded for her.

Bowen was happy to see her doing what she enjoyed, but it was also a reminder that she would be going home soon, and he would probably never see her again.

When the gate opened and Leon pulled the car up in front of the house, Margaret reached for her crutches. "They are right on time. Are the steaks about ready?"

"They are." Bowen helped her down the stairs.

As the passenger door opened and Anastasia got out, he was taken aback. He'd expected her to look exhausted, but she looked radiant and beautiful. If he hadn't known that she had just been through a difficult transition, he would have thought that she'd been to a beauty spa instead.

"You look amazing," Margaret echoed his thoughts. "Are you sure it was food poisoning?"

"Yeah." Anastasia hugged her friend. "I wonder whether the doctor put some magic elixir into the IV that I was hooked up to."

Good one.

Evidently, Anastasia had learned from Leon how to twist words around, so she didn't actually lie but didn't tell the truth either.

"I hope you're hungry." He started loading the steaks onto a platter. "I made enough to feed a small army."

Inhaling deeply, Anastasia closed her eyes. "They smell divine, and I'm starving."

"Then let's eat." Leon took the platter from Bowen and headed inside.

"I wish we had a table on the porch." Margaret followed Anastasia. "It's such a nice day."

Bowen closed the door behind them. "We can have one delivered."

Margaret let out a soft sigh. "I'll be going home soon, and I guess that the three of you will leave as well." She looked at Anastasia. "I assume that you are not coming back to Safe Haven with me?"

"I'm not. But I'll come to visit you whenever I can. I'll probably go back to school and finish my law degree. I'm thinking about switching to nonprofit organizations."

"Good for you." Margaret waited for Bowen to pull out a chair for her. "Is there a chance that you'll visit me too?"

"Of course." He forced a smile.

Probably not. It was going to be difficult enough to say goodbye without dragging it out. A clean break would be best.

Kian

"Mother." Kian bent nearly in half to embrace Annani's petite frame. "How was your trip?"

"Pleasant." She kissed both his cheeks before pushing him away to open her arms to Syssi. "And how is my favorite daughter-in-law?"

"I'm your only daughter-in-law." Syssi chuckled. "But I'm doing great."

Their embrace was a bit awkward given the big pregnant belly Annani couldn't wrap her arms around, and then it started moving this way and that as Allegra responded to all the excitement.

"Oh, wow." Annani released Syssi to put her hands on her belly. "That was one mighty kick, little one. Have mercy on your poor mother."

"I don't mind," Syssi said, her voice tender with love for their daughter. "When she's active, I know she's okay.

Sometimes, I get anxious when she sleeps, and I poke her awake to make sure she's okay."

Alena put her hand on Syssi's shoulder. "I still remember each of my pregnancies and the irrational worry that gripped me whenever the baby was inactive for a while. But thank the merciful Fates, they were all born healthy."

"You're a pro." Syssi smiled. "Let's move the party to the dining room. I'm sure you're hungry after your trip."

As Kian followed the procession, he wondered about his eldest sister's miraculous fruitfulness. She'd had all of her eleven children in relatively quick succession and then stopped. It had been many centuries since her last daughter had been born.

Had she been actively avoiding pregnancy? Or had her body decided that eleven children were enough?

Alena had done her part ensuring the clan's future, and no one expected her to keep on producing babies. As it was, she deserved the title of Clan Mother no less than Annani.

"Are Amanda and Dalhu joining us for lunch?" Alena asked.

Kian pulled out a chair for his mother. "Amanda had a faculty meeting this morning that she couldn't get out of, but she'll join us for dinner."

"Thank you." Annani gathered the long skirt of her gown and sat down. "Any new developments with our newest dungeon guest?"

Kian hadn't spoken with her since Saturday, but he had no doubt that she was on top of things and had heard about the latest developments from Syssi and Amanda.

"How much do you know?" he asked.

His mother smiled indulgently. "The last time we spoke, you had not interrogated Emmett yet, and you were entertaining the idea that he might be a confused or insane immortal. Is that still a valid hypothesis?"

Kian shook his head. "Regrettably, it's not likely. If it was, I could have put the entire thing behind me and concentrated on the upcoming celebrations. Stella came forward with a story that confirmed Emmett's. It's still not a hundred percent conclusive, but it seems that Emmett is telling the truth. In addition, I suspect that his group is not the only one, and that there might be many more of them."

"Syssi told me about Stella's confession." Annani sighed. "Poor woman has kept the secret of who fathered her son for over twenty years. It must have been eating away at her." Her eyes smiled as she looked at him. "I am surprised that you are not angry at her."

"She vowed on Vlad's life never to reveal who his father was. It was the only way she could convince the Kra-ell hybrid to let her go. I can understand her fear of breaking such a vow. In her shoes, I would have done the same. Just as there are no atheists in a foxhole, I bet most parents would not be willing to gamble on their children's lives even when it's only a superstition."

"What are you going to do about the Kra-ell?" Alena asked. "Are you going to search for them?"

He nodded. "Emmett provided us with the exact location of their compound, but chances are that they are no longer there. After he escaped, they probably moved locations so he couldn't sell them out. And if they hadn't moved back then, they certainly did that after receiving his email about us. That being said, we might find clues that will lead us to them, which is why I want to send a team to investigate."

"What if they didn't get the email?" Syssi asked. "They could have sold the company, and whoever opened the email might have sent it to the trash folder, thinking it was junk mail or a prank."

"That's possible. If we are lucky, they didn't, and we'll find them where Emmett left them."

"Who are you planning to send?" Annani asked.

"We have no one who speaks the language fluently and knows the local customs. Turner is providing us with a human team that has worked in China before, and I'm supplementing it with several Guardians. I want Arwel to lead our team. His empathic abilities will be useful, and if Jin agrees to accompany him, her tethering ability could be invaluable to the mission."

"Did you speak with them?" Syssi asked.

"Not yet. I plan to call Arwel later today or tomorrow."

Annani eyed him sidelong. "I thought that you would take me to see Emmett later today."

Of course she did.

"Tomorrow works better for me, and you need to rest after your journey."

"I do not." She huffed. "But if you are busy, I will find ways to pass the time productively."

Was that an implied threat?

He narrowed his eyes at her. "What are you plotting already?"

"I want to talk to Stella. Did she tell Vlad about his father?"

Kian shrugged. "I don't know. But just in case she didn't, I suggest that for the time being we keep quiet about it. I don't want the rumor to spread and for the kid to hear about it from someone other than his mother."

Vlad had enough on his plate as it was. Kian didn't know whether he was still planning on visiting Wendy's father and getting him to confess what he'd done to the mother, and he didn't want to know.

Personally, Kian supported Vlad's quest for answers and even his need to avenge the wrongs that had been perpetrated against his mate. But as regent, he couldn't do that.

It was against clan law to thrall humans for personal gain.

There were only a few instances in which it was allowed, and Vlad's investigation wasn't one of them.

Vlad

Despite moving out of his mother's house many months ago, Vlad still felt awkward about knocking on the door of what used to be his home. His mother wouldn't mind if he just walked in, but she had a mate now, and the fact that Richard used to be Vlad and Wendy's roommate and probably wouldn't mind didn't make it okay either.

Richard was still at the construction site, though, and he wouldn't be home for another couple of hours.

His mother opened the door. "You don't need to knock. No matter where you live and how old you are, this will always be your home."

"I love you too, Mom." He leaned and kissed her cheek.

She looked tense, and Vlad wondered what was going on. It wasn't unusual for her to call him and ask him to stop by on his way home. He would bring a tasty treat from the bakery, and they would have tea together. Today though, she'd sounded anxious on the phone, saying that there was something she needed to talk to him about.

The only thing that came to mind was that Stella and Richard were having a baby, but that shouldn't make her so nervous. Vlad wouldn't mind having a baby brother or sister. In fact, he would love it.

Except, maybe it was about his plans to pay Wendy's father a visit?

Richard might have said something, or maybe Wendy had.

"I brought muffins." He lifted the brown bag. "Blueberry, your favorite."

She smiled tightly. "I'll make tea."

He followed her to the kitchen. "What's going on, Mom?"

Her shoulders slumped. "I need to tell you something, and I hope that you won't be too upset."

He let out a relieved breath. It didn't seem like anyone had told her about his plans, so it had to be a baby.

"Why would I be upset? Perhaps I will be happy for you?"

Her forehead furrowed. "Happy for me? What do you think this is about?"

Vlad pushed his bangs back. "Apparently not what I expected."

"What did you expect?"

Now that he was about to say it out loud, it seemed silly. His mother and Richard hadn't been together long enough to have a baby. Then again, neither had Kalugal and Jacki, and they were expecting.

He chuckled nervously. "I thought that you and Richard were having a baby, and I got excited thinking about a little brother or sister."

Her eyes softened. "Fates willing, one day we will, but that's not what I need to tell you." She poured boiling water into the two mugs she'd prepared and handed him one. "It's about your father."

Vlad had never given much thought to the human who had contributed his genetic material to create him. He had been just an unknowing sperm donor. Vlad didn't even know that his mother had kept tabs on the guy.

"What about him? Did he die?"

She shook her head. "Not as far as I know. Your father wasn't human, so it's unlikely that he died."

Vlad's blood turned cold. Unless his mother had broken the taboo of having relations with another descendent of Annani, her only option for an immortal lover was a Doomer. "Was my father a Doomer?"

"No. He was Kra ell."

That was it. His mother had officially lost it. She was confusing reality with the Krall virtual adventure she and Richard had experienced.

"The Krall are not real people, Mom. They were invented by Syssi for the Perfect Match virtual studios. I know that the virtual adventure felt like real life, but it wasn't."

Stella leaned over and put her hand on his chest. "Syssi is clairvoyant, Vlad, and the Krall aren't a figment of her imagination. She saw them in a vision. She got some of the details wrong, and her imagination filled in the gaps, but the real Kra-ell are very similar to her fictional Krall. Did you hear about the cult leader who kidnapped a Guardian?"

Vlad's blood went from cold to boiling in an instant. "I didn't hear anything. How did it happen?"

Richard was getting inside information from Kalugal, who was getting it from Kian, and Stella had heard about it from Richard. That didn't mean that the entire clan knew about it.

"The cult leader is one of them, I mean the Kra-ell, and he's also a powerful compeller who can compel other immortals. The Guardian was rescued, and Emmett Haderech was captured and is locked in the keep's dungeon, so that's over, but his capture opened up a whole new can of worms."

"Like what? And how does it affect me?"

"I hope it doesn't. You got the immortality gene from me. The Kra-ell are long-lived but not immortal, and other than your incredible strength, it doesn't seem like you have inherited anything else from your father. You don't crave or need blood for nourishment."

"They are really like the Krall? Are they vampires?"

"In that regard, they are. But according to Emmett, they never drain their victims. Also, their main source of blood is animals, not humans, and they don't drain the animals either. They only take what can be replenished in a few days."

"Or so he claims. Did the one who fathered me claim the same?"

"Vrog didn't tell me much about himself or his people. My first thought was that he was a Doomer, but he didn't know what I was talking about, so I assumed that he belonged to an unaffiliated group of immortals, maybe the descendants of other survivors."

She pushed a strand of hair behind her ear. "I should have paid closer attention to what he said. He told me that he wasn't immortal, only long-lived, but I thought he only meant that immortals were not impervious to catastrophic injuries. He also told me that his people were ruled by a ruthless female who treated the males as her personal slaves, but again, I thought she was just a bitch, and that he was a fool for not leaving. I even offered him the option to join the clan, but he had made a vow never to betray his leader and couldn't leave."

"Where did you meet him?"

"In Singapore. Until he bit me, I thought that he was just an attractive human."

"Did he drink your blood?"

"I don't know. I blacked out." She smiled sheepishly. "It was my first venom bite."

"Yeah, that's too much information, Mom."

She lifted her hands, her many bracelets jingling. "You asked."

"I know. How come you never told me about him?"

His mother's eyes misted with tears. "Somehow, Vrog knew right away that we'd created a life, and he was terrified of what his leader would do if she ever found out. He wanted me to get an abortion. I was alone, in a foreign country, and Vrog was incredibly strong. I needed to come up with something to persuade him to let me go, and since he took vows so seriously, that's what I did. I vowed on the life of my unborn child that I would never reveal his secret."

Vlad wasn't a big believer in the power of vows, but his mother was superstitious. "You kept your vow for nearly twenty-two years. How come you broke it now?"

She sighed. "Richard figured it out after our Krall adventure, but I wanted to believe that didn't count as vow breaking. And then Emmett was caught, and Kian thought that he was making the entire story up after participating in a similar experience at one of the Perfect Match studios. I couldn't keep quiet and let him think that. Emmett had sent an email to his leader telling her about us and how our males could activate their Dormants. That was why he kidnapped Peter. He wanted to use him for that. Without the ability to activate their Dormants, they are facing extinction. They would do anything to get their hands on our males, and Kian needs to safeguard our people, which he wouldn't have done if he still believed that Emmett had made the story up."

"Wasn't Emmett's need to consume blood evidence enough?"

"They thought it was a fetish. But even if Kian eventually believed that the Kra-ell were real, there was another complication. Since according to Emmett, the Kra-ell females have fangs and venom, they were all talking about the connection to Mey and Jin, and how their peculiar traits could be explained by a Kra-ell father. It was only a question of time before they figured out that you weren't a typical immortal male either. I didn't want you to find out about it from someone else."

His eyes widened. "Jin and Mey were also fathered by a Kra-ell?"

"Isn't it obvious? Otherwise, why would they have fangs?"

"Damn. They might be my cousins."

Stella smiled. "Their mother must have been a Dormant, our kind of Dormant, but she wasn't Annani's descendant. So yeah, they might be your cousins on your father's side."

"Did you get to see Emmett?"

"I did."

"What do you think of him?"

"He's arrogant, and he has a penchant for theatrics, but he doesn't strike me as evil."

"Can I talk to him?"

She tilted her head. "Why would you want to?"

"To find out more about the blood coursing through my veins."

"Emmett is imprisoned in the keep. You'll need to ask Kian."

Kian

Kian pulled out two new earpieces from his pocket and handed them to Annani. "You need to put these in."

She looked at the devices as if they were a couple of worms. "You said that Emmett is in chains. Why do I need to put these in? If he tries to compel me, Arwel can stop him with the push of a button. I would rather go in without them and test my compulsion on him."

"He could compel you to order everyone to stand down, and then Arwel wouldn't be able to do anything. I'm not willing to risk it."

She rolled her eyes. "Arwel is wearing his earpieces, so he will not be affected by my compulsion any more than he will be by Emmett's." She pushed his hand away. "I am going in without them."

"You promised me that you would wear them."

She looked down her nose at him. "I changed my mind. I need to test Emmett's susceptibility to my compulsion."

Annani was right, but Kian hated to put her in danger even if it was minimal. Not that he had much choice in the matter. Given her stubborn expression, his mother was not going to back down.

"How are you going to test it?"

"I will ask him to tell me everything he knows about his people."

"We have no way of verifying whether it's true, and even if it is, he might reveal the information voluntarily." Kian chuckled. "Given how terrified he is of his leader, he might be too scared to lie to you."

"That is possible." Annani turned to Arwel. "You have spent some time with Emmett. Is there anything he holds dear that I can ask him to reveal and it can be verified?"

"The wealth he's accumulated over the years seems to be more precious to him than anything else. You can ask him to tell you the numbers of his offshore bank accounts. We can verify those."

"Excellent idea. Thank you, Arwel." Annani turned to Kian. "Any more questions and instructions before we go in?"

"I think we have it covered." He looked at Arwel. "Set the remote to stun. The moment he tries anything, zap him."

"Understood."

Kian put his earpieces in and activated them.

As Arwel engaged the door mechanism, Kian put his hand on his mother's slim shoulder. "Wait until I say it's okay to go in."

"As you wish."

If only she could be so agreeable more often.

When the door swung all the way out, Arwel went in first, followed by Kian.

Emmett was seated in the same armchair as before, chained, and Alfie stood across from him with his hand on the gun. But unlike the other times Kian had visited him, Emmett didn't complain about the shackles or pretend nonchalance.

The guy looked nervous, which wasn't really surprising. He was about to meet the goddess, and given what he'd told them about his leader, he had good reason to fear his visitor.

Emmett lifted a worried pair of eyes to Kian. "Shouldn't I be on my knees?"

"The Clan Mother doesn't demand obeisance. Keep your tone respectful, and you should be fine."

"Of course."

Kian stepped back outside. "He's ready for you, Mother."

"Thank you, my son."

It was disturbing to hear his mother through the devices, sounding like a male. William had promised to work on a new design that would adapt to the speaker's voice, but he hadn't been successful yet.

Perhaps Annani was right about the low risk of Emmett trying anything.

Discreetly, Kian removed the devices from his ears and put them back in his pocket. For once, his longish hair would be useful for something other than pleasing his wife. It would cover the fact that he wasn't wearing the compulsion-blocking earpieces.

As Annani glided into the suite, Emmett sucked in a breath and bowed his head. He remained frozen like that, not moving a muscle and not saying a thing.

"You may gaze upon my face, Emmett." Annani lowered herself regally into the armchair across from him. "It is not forbidden."

Very slowly, Emmett lifted his head. "It's an honor to be in your presence, Clan Mother."

She nodded. "Tell me about your people, Emmett. Everything you know."

As Kian felt the soft caress of her compulsion, he wondered how Emmett's and Kalugal's felt. Luckily, he'd been spared from enduring either, but he was sure they felt nothing like Annani's.

"There were twenty of them to start with," Emmett said. "I don't know where they came from, but I was born in a rural area outside of Beijing."

It was difficult to tell if Annani's compulsion was working on Emmett. Kian paid attention as the guy repeated the same things he'd told them already, poised to catch any inconsistencies.

By the time Emmett had left, he said, the community had grown, but not significantly. Six purebloded children had been born to the original settlers, two females and four males. Twenty-four hybrids had been born to human mothers and Kra-ell fathers, of which only two were females and the rest males. Children born to hybrid males with human females had been born human, and Emmett didn't know whether the hybrid females took human lovers.

Annani lifted her hand to interrupt him. "If you are like us, which I suspect you are in many ways, the children born to Kra-ell hybrid fathers and human mothers do not carry your longevity genes. Only the female hybrids can pass it on to their children, who can be activated with venom. You were fortunate that we captured you before you delivered Peter to your leader. He would have been useless for activating your second generation of hybrids, and she might have ended your life for bringing her a false promise." Annani smiled sadly. "My understanding is that she is not a forgiving female."

Emmett swallowed. "I was so excited to find a possible solution that I didn't pause to think it through. Peter told me that only the females transmitted the immortal gene." He looked at her with pleading eyes. "Can you tell me more about my origins? My father and the other purebloods refused to tell us anything. They considered us second-class members of the community."

She nodded. "My parents were the same, and I am not a hybrid, and I definitely was not considered a second-class anything either. I was born a pureblooded goddess, the daughter of the leading couple and the chosen heir to my father's rule. I suspect that their past was shameful, and they wanted a fresh start free of the taint of past deeds. They wanted the next generation to believe the gods were benevolent, only wishing to help humanity evolve into a free, democratic society like their own. It was a noble goal, one which I took upon myself to propagate after the demise of my people."

Emmett tilted his head. "If the gods were benevolent and taught their children well, how did your enemies, the Doomers I believe they are called, come to be?"

Annani smiled sadly. "How do you think the gods' era ended? The thirst for power is corruptive. It is poison. One ambitious god wanted to run things differently and rule over the other gods. He turned against them, and when he attacked, he perished alongside them. His son continues his evil legacy to this day. My clan and his followers have been fighting over the future of humanity for thousands of years."

"Who is winning?" Emmett asked.

Was it a genuine question? Or was it meant as sarcasm?

By now, Emmett must have figured out that Annani wasn't a terrifying tyrant, and he might have felt emboldened.

Annani lifted her chin. "Despite their superior numbers, we are winning, but it is not a smooth progression. There are setbacks, and sometimes the Brotherhood manages to thwart and even undo our efforts, rewinding humanity's progress by hundreds of years. Still, we keep pushing forward. Without us, humans would still be in the Dark Ages and probably enslaved to the followers of Mortdh."

For the first time since Annani's arrival, Emmett turned to look at Kian. "The followers of Mortdh have been actively working against you for thousands of years, and you are worried about my people being your adversaries? They don't even know that you exist, let alone bother you."

"Not yet. But they might."

"Unlikely," Annani said. "Given their social structure and the scarcity of females, the Kra-ell cannot multiply at the rate the Doomers do, and their numbers will remain insignificant."

"I agree that number-wise they are not a threat," Kian said. "But the days of needing brute force to take control of people are over. With today's technology, a small group of people with compulsion ability and advanced technological knowhow could take over the world."

Annani nodded and then turned to Emmett. "How advanced were your people?"

"Frankly, they did not strike me as more advanced than humans. We didn't have any interesting gadgets or weapons. I don't know that for sure, but I think that they obtained the knowhow needed to start Kumei telecommunications from compelling humans to give it to them."

Annani looked at Emmett skeptically. "How is it possible that people who traversed the universe to get here have no advanced technology?"

Kian crossed his arms over his chest. "We don't have the technology or ability to build an interstellar ship either, and yet, our ancestors got here somehow. Being passengers on a ship doesn't make them engineers. They might have been dropped off on Earth, for whatever reason, and their ship returned home."

Or was still orbiting the Earth, hidden by a cloaking device, or simply hiding behind the dark side of the moon.

Annani adjusted the folds of her long skirt. "The technology could depend on materials we do not have on Earth. The gods did not build anything technologically advanced either. Whatever they had, they must have brought with them, and the devices slowly deteriorated over time. We only had a few flying machines, and the same was true for the tablets. I remember my Uncle Ekin, who was the only one among the gods I knew with technological knowhow, working on inventive solutions using what was available in the world back then. I guess the Kra-ell were faced with the same difficulty." She looked at Emmett. "One last question before we part. Please tell us the bank location of your largest offshore account, and recite the number along with your personal access code."

This time, the compulsion she used was not a gentle caress. It was more like a chokehold, so oppressive that Kian felt the mental pressure even though it hadn't been directed at him. It was a struggle to pull out his phone and get ready to write down the information Emmett was about to reveal.

Looking as uncomfortable as Kian felt, Emmett did as she commanded, wincing with every letter and number leaving his mouth. When he was done, sweat beaded on his forehead. "You are a powerful compeller, Clan Mother."

"Indeed." She smiled apologetically. "Do not worry, no one is going to take your money. This was just a test to make sure that I can compel you."

As access was granted, Kian whistled. "You have done pretty well for yourself, Emmett. Is that all from running the Safe Haven retreats? Or did some of your community members bestow their inheritances on you?"

"I'm a savvy investor, and I had a long time to do it."

Kian put his phone back in his pocket. "No doubt by compelling people to give you insider information."

Emmett shrugged. "Are you going to hold that against me as well?"

"It's immoral, and it's a crime, but it's not a crime against the clan."

Besides, Kalugal had done the same thing and was probably still doing it, and yet Kian had invited him to join the clan.

Annani pushed to her feet. "It was a very interesting meeting, Emmett. Good day."

He bowed his head. "Good day, Clan Mother."

When they were at the door, Annani paused and turned around. "One last thing before I go, Emmett." She walked closer to him, halting several feet away from the prisoner, and unleashing her godly power on him. "You will never attempt to compel any of my clan members, and you will not do anything to harm them physically or otherwise. You will not attempt to escape, either."

Once again, Annani's compulsion felt like a vice around Kian's throat even though it had been directed at Emmett.

The guy must have felt it tenfold, and yet he took it without averting his eyes or slumping in his seat.

When the power winked out, both Emmett and Kian let out a relieved breath.

Annani smiled sweetly. "Goodbye, Emmett."

Arwel

When the interview ended, Kian motioned for Arwel to follow them outside. "After you move Emmett back to his cell, come to my office. Annani and I will wait for you."

Arwel arched a brow. "Does it have anything to do with my prisoner?"

"In a way. Finish with Emmett first." Offering his arm to the goddess, Kian started toward the elevators.

She smiled up at her son. "The last time I visited your old office was under similar circumstances. It was when I came to see Lokan."

Anandur and Brundar followed behind mother and son, and as the four entered the elevator, Arwel opened the door and walked back into the suite.

Alfie had already unlocked Emmett's leg shackles, and as he tossed them on the floor, Emmett's eyes followed, his mouth curling with distaste.

"You did well." Arwel clapped him on the back.

"I didn't expect the Clan Mother to be so powerful, or so kind, or so beautiful."

The order of adjectives was telling. Emmett wasn't as impressed with beauty as he was with power and kindness.

Emmett stretched his arms over his head. "Do you have a book about the history of your clan that I can read?"

After the initial shock and awe of seeing the goddess, the guy had gone back to his usual act of a bored, harmless intellectual.

"We don't."

Edna kept records, but they weren't in story form, and they weren't accessible even to clan members. If anyone wanted to go through the records, they needed to ask Edna's permission and give her a reason for the request.

"That's a shame. I would have liked to learn more about you. Any other books that you can lend me? I'm bored."

"You can watch television." Arwel walked Emmett out into his own cell. "Or play video games."

"I enjoy reading more. I would really appreciate some books."

"I'll see what I can do. What do you like to read?"

"Anything that's well written. Fiction and non-fiction."

"Did you read *Game of Thrones*?"

Emmett grimaced. "It was too cruel and bloody for my taste. I read to relax."

Arwel arched a brow. "A pacifist bloodsucker? That's a contradiction in terms."

"I'd rather avoid conflict when I can. I guess I inherited my peaceful nature from my human mother."

Arwel wanted to ask Emmett more about his experience growing up as a hybrid in the Kra-ell compound, but Kian and Annani were waiting for him.

"I need to go. We can talk more when I come back."

Emmett nodded. "I'm looking forward to it. Our little talks are the highlight of my day."

Even with his empathic ability, Arwel wasn't sure whether that was meant as a compliment or as sarcasm. Emmett was a natural actor, and sometimes it was difficult to tell the difference between what was an act and what was real, probably because the lines were as blurred for Emmett as they were for his audience.

The guy was a condescending prick and a know-it-all, but the truth was that Arwel enjoyed their talks as well. Emmett had a good grasp on human nature and on politics, and he'd even read the works of all the major philosophers.

Nevertheless, if Kian had a new assignment for him, Arwel would jump on it. Jin was tired of the dungeon, and so was he.

As the elevator doors opened and Arwel stepped out on the office's level, he saw Anandur heading his way.

"I'm going up to get coffees from the vending machines. Do you want anything?"

"No thanks." Arwel grimaced. "Living here, I've had too much of the café's limited selection already."

As he walked into Kian's office, his boss motioned to the chair next to him. "Take a seat, Arwel."

"How are you enjoying your post here?" Annani asked.

Arwel sat down. "Emmett is not a difficult prisoner, but I'd rather get out of the dungeon."

She tilted her head. "I thought that you preferred living underground. It filters the human emotions that bother you topside."

"It does, but living in the village is better. Immortals don't broadcast their emotions nearly as much as humans, and I'm exposed to humans only when I go out on missions, which is tolerable. My quality of life has improved significantly since we moved out of the keep."

She smiled indulgently. "I am sure that having a mate has a lot to do with it as well. How is Jin taking all this? Has she met with Emmett?"

"Jin expressed no desire to do so."

Annani looked surprised. "Is she not curious about her father's people?"

Arwel shrugged. "She saw Emmett on the surveillance feed, and I told her everything I learned listening to the interrogation and also from talking to him. At first, we were worried about the Kra-ell shorter lifespans and how it might impact Jin and Mey if they are related to them, but since their mother must have been a Dormant, that's no longer a concern."

Huffing out an impatient breath, Kian was done waiting out their small talk. "I want you to be in charge of the China team," Kian said. "Your empathic abilities might be useful on an information-gathering mission."

Arwel was the right guy for the job, but that was not the kind of mission he'd been hoping for. Leaving Jin behind would be tough. Hopefully, he wouldn't have to be gone for more than a few days.

"Who else is going?"

"Turner is supplying a human team that is familiar with the local culture and knows the language. I want you to work with them, and you can take as many Guardians as you deem necessary. But since this is a reconnaissance mission, less is probably better."

"How long do we need to plan to be there?"

"A couple of weeks." Noting Arwel's barely stifled grimace, Kian tapped his fingers on the table. "What do you think about taking Jin with you?"

"As my companion or as a spy?"

"Both."

Arwel shook his head. "She doesn't want to use her ability for spying."

"I know, but the results of this investigation have direct implications for her and Mey. Aren't they curious about their biological parents?"

"The father or fathers who discarded them as if they were garbage? I don't think so. They consider the Levins their parents and rightfully so."

"I get it about the biological father or fathers, but the mother didn't have a choice. She was forced to give them up. If she's still alive, and we don't have a reason to think that she's not, she would be overjoyed to see how well her daughters have turned out."

"I can ask Jin."

Kian nodded. "Good. I want you to hire a tutor to teach you and your chosen Guardians Mandarin. It will be faster than learning from an audio course."

Arwel pulled out his earpieces. "We can use these to translate what is said to us, but it would be beneficial to be able to speak it. Do we have anyone in the village who speaks it fluently?"

"Stella does," Annani said. "But I do not know if she is fluent. You might want to check with Morris. When he is not flying the clan's jet, he translates flight manuals into different languages. Perhaps one of them is Mandarin."

Arwel chuckled. "We should include Carol in the class. Isn't she supposed to accompany Lokan to China?"

"She won't come back for that," Kian said. "She's staying in a hotel in Washington until Lokan is ready to leave. She refuses to be apart from him."

"Can't blame her." Anandur walked in with two cardboard trays filled with paper coffee cups. "She and Lokan can use a Rosetta Stone to learn." He started distributing the drinks. "And so can Arwel and his team."

Arwel shook his head. "Unlike other immortals, Jin is not good with languages. It's probably because she transitioned as an adult. It would appear that the ear for languages develops at a young age. If she agrees to join me on the mission, she'll need a one-on-one tutor."

Onegus

"Is that the tux?" Connor's eyes lit up as Onegus walked in with the garment bag slung over his shoulder.

The tux had been ordered a month ago with input from his roommate, who considered himself a fashionista and would no doubt want to examine the finished product.

"It is." Onegus sniffed at the aromas coming from the kitchen. "What's cooking? I don't recognize the smell."

Connor was gracious enough to cook for both of them, but his repertoire consisted of six recipes that he cycled throughout the week. Not that Onegus was complaining. If not for Connor, he would have been subsisting on sandwiches and pastries from the café.

As the chief, Onegus was entitled to a house all to himself, but he preferred to share it, just not with one of the Guardians. His position created a natural distance between him and those he was in charge of, and cohabiting with one of them would have been awkward.

Connor had been a good choice. He was a composer and worked from home, while Onegus spent most of his waking hours in his office or traveling as Kian's representative.

"I'm trying one of Callie's recipes," Connor said. "She posted it on the clan's website last weekend."

"Then I'm sure it's delicious." Onegus headed to his room.

"I want to see you in the tux," Connor called after him.

"You'll see it tomorrow."

"I need to get one for myself, and I want to check the craftsmanship."

Onegus stopped and turned around. "What's the occasion?"

Connor was an excellent score composer, but he hadn't gotten nominated for an Emmy or an Oscar yet.

"It's not a nomination, if that's what you were thinking. Regrettably." Connor sighed. "I've been invited to speak at an event." He cast Onegus an accusing sidelong glance.

Was he offended that Onegus hadn't invited him to be his pretend date?

He'd jokingly asked Brandon and had made the mistake of telling Connor about it.

"Fine. I will try it on for you." Onegus ducked into the bedroom.

When he emerged a few minutes later, Connor whistled. "That's one hell of a well-tailored tux. You look dashing." He chuckled. "Good luck with the gold-diggers."

"I'll be fine. It's not my first rodeo, and I've refined the technique of brushing them off politely."

"Oh, yeah? How?"

"I pretend not to notice that they are flirting with me. I just smile and keep talking about how important the charity is and how much the contributions collected at these events help us rehabilitate more rescued trafficking victims. Eventually, they get bored with me and move on to the next eligible bachelor."

"What do you do when they just flat out proposition you? You can't pretend not to get it."

"You'd be surprised. I tell them how flattered I am but that I have so much work and can't possibly make time for pleasure."

It wasn't a complete lie. He worked insanely long hours.

Amusement dancing in his eyes, Connor cast him a pretend stern look. "Tell me the truth, Onegus. When they get really pesky, aren't you tempted to push them away with just a smidgen of a thrall?"

"Tempted, yes. Do I do that? No. I'm the chief. If I break the law or even bend it a little, how can I demand compliance from you civilians?"

Connor smiled. "Come on. No one would know. It's not like a little thrall can do much harm."

"I would know." Onegus ran his fingers through his short hair. "I need to get a haircut."

"Don't. It's short enough. Just gel it. If you want, I can do that for you."

"Thanks. It will save me a trip to the barber."

The look of disdain on Connor's face was comical. "A barber? That's who cuts your hair? No wonder it's a mess."

"What's wrong with it?"

"Everything. You need a stylist, not a damn barber."

"Well, since I don't have one, the job is yours."

Cassandra

"Cassy? Are you home?" her mother called from downstairs.

"I'll be down in a moment." Cassandra unzipped the garment bag, pulled out the dress she'd bought, and laid it on the bed.

At first glance, it might not have looked like much to the untrained eye, which was probably why she'd gotten it at a bargain price, but Cassandra had known it was the one the moment she'd laid eyes on it. And when she tried it on, it looked as though it had been custom-made for her.

The color was a very dark purple, nearly black, the dress was sleeveless and had sheer panels that precluded wearing a bra, but that wasn't a problem. Her breasts were small and perky enough to get away with it. The dress was sophisticated and daring without being too showy or trashy.

Kevin would be furious if he found out that she'd gotten it at a boutique specializing in used designer attire, but hopefully he wouldn't check the receipts from her purchases.

She just hadn't had the heart to spend a fortune on a dress for one night. So what if some celebrity had worn it once? It was absolutely gorgeous and had been dry cleaned.

Everything else she'd gotten was new, and the shoes had cost twice as much as the dress. Opening the box, she pulled out the black velvet Louboutins and gazed at the masterpiece of craftsmanship.

"Hello, gorgeous." She pulled them out, slipped them on her feet, and walked over to the full-length mirror attached to the back of her bedroom door.

Wearing only a pair of skimpy bikini bottoms, a lacy bra, and the shoes, she looked hot if she said so herself, and she couldn't resist striking a pose and admiring herself in the mirror.

Not bad for a thirty-four-year-old.

It was a shame, though, that she didn't have anyone to model for. Not in her underwear anyway. The last time anyone had seen her without her clothes on had been over a year ago.

With a sigh, she turned around, lifted the dress off the bed and pulled it on. As evening gowns went, it was very comfortable. The fabric was stretchy, and it molded to her body perfectly.

"Cassy?" Her mother knocked on the door. "Can I come in? I want to see what you got."

Smiling, Cassandra opened the door. "What do you think?"

Her mother's hand flew to her chest. "Oh, Cassy, you look so beautiful. I wish your father could see you like that."

She stifled the urge to roll her eyes.

Cassandra had never met her father and didn't even know who he was. Her mother's stories about him changed according to her mood. Sometimes he was a surgeon whom she'd met while recovering from an injury in a hospital. Other times he was an astronaut in training she'd met in a bar, or an ambassador from Ethiopia whom she'd met on the beach, and so on.

Her mother had always lived in a fantasy world, and yet she'd somehow managed to raise Cassandra well and provide her with everything she needed. They had lived in a one-bedroom tiny apartment, but it had been in a good area with decent schools. Cassandra had never felt like she lacked for anything.

Now that she was making excellent money, she'd bought a house and was taking care of her mother.

"Who is he this time, Mom?"

"What do you mean?"

It was pointless to challenge the stories, but sometimes she just couldn't help it. "Never mind. Aren't you going to your book club meeting tonight?"

Cassandra doubted that her mother's outings were always as innocent as book club meetings or bingo night with her girlfriends, especially since she often came home in the early hours of the morning.

She was a beautiful woman, who didn't look old enough to have a daughter Cassandra's age, and she was most likely more sexually active than her daughter.

Not that that was difficult to achieve. Cassandra didn't do hookups, and she'd broken up with her last boyfriend over a year ago. If not for her trusty BOB, she would have turned into a virgin again.

"It's tomorrow." Her mother sat on the bed. "Just look at you." She sighed. "I just wish you were going to the gala with a nice young man instead of your boss."

"I don't have time for dating."

"You work too hard."

"I work as hard as I have to. Kevin is not paying me a quarter of a million salary for a nine-to-five job."

Her mother leaned her elbows on her knees and rested her chin on her fist. "I know that you don't have time to go to clubs or wherever young people go to mingle these days. But what about those dating apps everyone is talking about? You could try those."

Cassandra had tried a couple, and her mother had known that, but Geraldine's memory was spotty, especially long-term memory, and she'd probably forgotten.

It was best to ignore it. Her mother got upset when anyone noticed her memory issues or commented on them, and she tried to cover up for the lapses by making up stories.

"I tried, Mom. It was a colossal waste of time. People lie on their profiles, post pictures that are a decade old or Photoshopped, and it was one disappointment after another."

"Perhaps you are too picky?"

"I'm not going to lower my standards. I'm not looking for a dashing billionaire, but I want a guy to be in reasonably good shape, have a paying job, and be able to hold an intelligent conversation for more than five minutes. I don't think that makes me picky."

There were other requirements as well. Like respect and fidelity. Cassandra had met a few players in her life, and she'd dropped them as soon as she'd figured out the pattern. If a guy only wanted to hang out around her place or his, didn't introduce her to any of his friends or family, and found excuses for not taking her out, it meant that he wasn't serious and was probably seeing other women at the same time.

The right guy also shouldn't mind that she still lived with her mother and had no intentions of moving out anytime soon. Or ever. Her mother needed to be taken care of, and she had no one other than Cassandra.

Geraldine had many friends but no relatives, or at least none that Cassandra was aware of. Her mother might have forgotten them.

All they had was each other.

"I just don't want you to end up alone, Cassy."

Neither did she, but what were the chances of her finding a man who checked off all her boxes?

Cassandra sat on the bed and wrapped her arm around her mother's shoulders. "I'm not alone. I have you."

Bowen

"Good morning." Leon saluted Bowen with his mug. "Coffee?"

"Definitely." Bowen pulled out a stool and straddled it. "Is Anastasia still sleeping?"

As an immortal, she would need no more than four hours of shuteye, but she was still recuperating from the transition.

"My mate is not an early riser, and I don't think that's going to change even when she's fully transitioned." Leon handed him a steaming mug. "I wish I could stay in bed with her longer, but waking up at dawn is a habit that I can't seem to break." He sat next to him.

"When she recuperates fully, I'm sure she'll need less sleep."

Leon smiled. "I hope so. I'm looking forward to early morning walks and other fun activities before our workday starts."

"You are one lucky bastard." He took a sip from the piping hot coffee.

"I know." Leon swiveled the barstool to face him. "But maybe you are too."

Bowen lifted a brow. "Meaning?"

"Eleanor made an interesting observation. On the face of it, Ana and Margaret have nothing in common. But despite the age difference and their very different backgrounds, they became best friends in no time. Eleanor thinks it might be affinity at work. Margaret might be a Dormant."

For a brief moment, his heart leaped at the kernel of hope, but then it dropped back down and sank low.

"I wish. But she doesn't have any paranormal talents. I know that not all Dormants have them, but it would have been helpful to have a big-ass hint like that. Margaret is fragile, and she went through hell before joining Safe Haven. I don't want to hurt her any more than she's already been hurt by giving her hope and then taking it away."

"Do you have feelings for her?"

"I think that's quite obvious."

Leon seemed to be mulling over something, but then shook his head and said nothing.

"What do you want to ask?"

"It's none of my business." He took a sip of his coffee.

"What's on your mind, Leon? We've been friends and partners for a long time. You are like a brother to me, and nothing you can say will offend me."

"I'll remind you of that when you swing a punch at me." He put his mug down and pushed it aside before turning back to face Bowen. "When I met Ana, all I could think about was making her mine. I was fighting it with everything I had, but she obliterated my resistance because she felt the same. I know that you and Margaret like each other, but I don't sense that overpowering need to get naked together from either of you."

"She's recuperating from surgery, and she has a cast on her entire leg. I can't think of her as a sexual being when she's hurting and so breakable. And as for Margaret, I think that she doesn't believe in her own appeal, so she's afraid of letting herself feel anything other than friendship toward me."

Seeing that no punch was heading his way, Leon lifted his mug and took another sip. "Unless you try, you won't know. Don't let Margaret return to Safe Haven without making sure. She might be your one."

Bowen shook his head. "How do you propose I do that?"

"Easy. Make love to the woman, just be gentle."

Bowen winced. "I'm afraid to touch her the wrong way and undo all the progress she's made. Besides, I know nothing about wooing a woman, romancing her. All I know is how to seduce women for hookups."

Leon pulled out his phone. "I'm sending you a link."

Bowen chuckled. "What for? Dating advice?"

"How to make love to a woman whose leg is in a cast."

"Don't tell me there is an instructional YouTube about that."

"It's an article written by a woman who had surgery on her knee just like Margaret, and how she managed to have sex safely despite the cast. She gives a lot of practical advice."

Arching a brow, Bowen crossed his arms over his chest. "Did you actually research that?"

"Anastasia did on the way here."

"Oh, that's just great. You two had nothing better to do than to plan how to get Margaret and me in bed?"

"Ana is really excited about the possibility of her best friend being a Dormant. She's already making plans for how the two of them will live in the village and get to hang out together."

"It still doesn't solve my problem of how to approach Margaret. I've been playing the role of the Good Samaritan. How do I switch to being a romantic interest?"

"You can start by asking her out on a date. Margaret would love that. And then you seduce her. Come on, Bowen, you're not a kid. I don't need to explain the birds and the bees to you."

Bowen groaned. "If she's a Dormant, I don't want to induce her transition without her consent, and I can't ask her consent before I'm sure that she's the one for me."

"You said that she's easy to thrall."

"So?"

"Use condoms until you are sure of your love for her and her love for you, and then get her consent before going bareback."

"I don't have any."

Smirking, Leon rose to his feet. "Lucky for you, you have a friend who thinks of everything. Ana and I stopped at a Walgreens on the way, and I got you enough condoms to last you a couple of weeks." He headed for the bedroom he shared with Anastasia. "I'll get them for you."

Bowen shook his head. "I don't know if I should be mad at you or thank you."

"Thank me. You are definitely going to thank me."

Onegus

Onegus tossed the key to the valet. "Take good care of my baby."

"I will." The young guy eagerly sat behind the wheel of Onegus's borrowed black Porsche and drove away.

Onegus had a room reserved at the hotel, but he still hadn't decided whether he was going to spend the night there. The drive to the village wasn't long, and staying in the hotel was more a safety precaution than a convenience. The paparazzi would certainly try to follow him, and some would lurk in the vicinity throughout the night, but there would be fewer of them tomorrow, and losing them would be easier during the day, using Turner's mall parking lot trick.

Fixing his bow tie, Onegus strode through the front doors and headed straight for the podium. As the official host of the event, he was the first speaker, and therefore had arrived early, but he wasn't the first one there. About a quarter of the guests were already sitting at the tables, the men in black suits and tuxedos, the ladies in evening gowns and sparkling jewelry.

Waiters in white jackets and black bow ties circled between the tables, taking drink orders and serving hors d'oeuvres.

As people turned to look at him, Onegus flashed them his signature broad smile, waved at those he recognized, and scanned the faces of those he didn't for potential trouble later on.

So far, it seemed like not many young socialites had made it to the event, but he knew he wouldn't be that lucky.

"Onegus." Brandon waved him over. "Meet my very dear friend Mrs. Warbleton."

"Enchanted." Onegus leaned and took the matron's gnarly hand, brushing his lips over the back of it.

"I'm sure." She flashed him a smile full of pearly white teeth. "I'm looking forward to hearing your speech." She leaned closer. "I hope it's not too long."

"It isn't. I promise."

"Good. When you're done, come back to my table. I want you to meet my granddaughter. She's a lovely young lady, and she's single." The matron winked.

He forced a smile. "It would be my pleasure."

Great. The evening hadn't started yet, and he was already getting propositioned.

Well, at least the woman's granddaughter wasn't a gold-digger. Mrs. Warbleton was one of the richest women in the country, but not many knew her by her married name, which was how she preferred it.

At the podium, Onegus pulled out his notes and read over them one more time. By now, he had them memorized and could deliver the speech without looking at them, but it never hurt to keep them at the ready.

When he was done, he lifted his eyes to scan the crowd again, glancing at Mrs. Warbleton's table to see if her granddaughter had arrived. Perhaps if he flirted with the woman, her grandmother would make a larger contribution.

Onegus didn't like the idea of pimping himself out, but he could stomach a little innocent flirting for a very deserving cause.

The matron's table was filling up, but none of the guests was a young woman, and he moved his eyes to the next table over.

Now, that was a woman he wouldn't have minded doing more than flirting with. Tall and willowy, she had a model's body and posture but not the vacuous stare so many beautiful women wore. She looked regal, confident, and a little bitchy, which he didn't mind in the least.

A gorgeous woman like her was probably accustomed to fending off overzealous male advances, and the sneering expression was her defense against unwanted attention.

She reminded him a little of Rihanna, just minus the curves, and she was taller, towering over the guy she was with. She was all sharp angles, except for her ass. It was small, but perfectly rounded.

The woman was simply spectacular.

The top of her dress had sheer panels, but it wasn't immodest, just a little daring, her hair and makeup were impeccable, and her jewelry perfectly matched her outfit. She either had an exceptional stylist or great taste.

He recognized the guy she was with, the founder of a cosmetics company that had been growing exponentially over the last several years. He'd attended the gala last year, but Onegus couldn't remember who his companion had been. It certainly wasn't the stunning beauty he'd brought this time.

Onegus would have remembered her.

The only reason he remembered the guy was the generous contribution he had made last year, and the name of his company that was a clever play on those books that had been all the rave a decade ago—Fifty Shades of Beauty. The name was easy to remember, not only because of the books bearing a similar name, but also because of the monthly boxes full of his company's cosmetics that had been arriving like clockwork at the sanctuary and the halfway house ever since last year's gala.

Was she his wife? His lover?

She smiled at something the guy had said, and then turned to the woman sitting on her other side and struck up a conversation. It was hard to tell whether the two were romantically involved.

Onegus was staring, and at some point she must have felt his eyes on her and turned, pinning him with her intense dark eyes.

He flashed her one of his practiced charming smiles, but she didn't smile back. Her eyes lingered on him for a moment longer, and then she turned back to her companion as if Onegus wasn't worth her time.

Damn, it hurt.

Usually, women undressed him with their eyes and salivated over his good looks, even when they were with someone else.

Onegus wasn't used to being ignored.

Perhaps she was in love with the cosmetics guy, which would be a damn shame.

Cassandra

Wow, talk about a punch to the gut.

Cassandra averted her eyes to sever the sizzling electrical current the guy's smile had sent straight to her core.

He was seriously gorgeous, but when he smiled, he was devastating.

She leaned toward Kevin. "Who's the guy on the podium?"

"That's Onegus McLean. The head of the 'Save Them' charity foundation."

She'd heard about him from Kevin. The elusive billionaire who only showed his face to the public to solicit donations for the charity his international conglomerate had started.

Except, the guy didn't look like any billionaire she'd ever seen on television or in the news. Elon Musk was handsome, but he had nothing on Onegus McLean. Billionaires who looked like that could only be found on the covers of romance novels.

Kevin smirked. "Handsome fellow, isn't he?"

"I guess." Cassandra pretended indifference. "Since when is the charity called Save Them? What happened to Save the Girls?"

"Some of the trafficking victims are boys, so they changed the name to Save Them."

"They could have called it Save the Girls and Boys. 'Save Them' sounds weird."

Kevin arched a brow. "Are you putting your foot in your mouth again, Cassy? That's not PC. What if some of the victims don't identify as either?"

"Right." She crossed her arms over her chest. "They need to reinvent the language and call everyone they and them. As is it now, it's too damn confusing."

Cassandra was only thirty-four, but she was already too old to understand the new generation and its new rules of propriety. Half of her altercations with her employees and coworkers were over perceived offenses. At least she was spared being called racist, but it was only a matter of time before someone found a way to pin that on her as well.

Kevin, who was more than a decade older than her, had a good grasp on all that PC stuff. She wondered if he had secretly researched the latest guidelines or was just better at absorbing them than she was.

"Distinguished guests!" Onegus's rich baritone sounded over the loudspeakers. "It's a great pleasure for me to be here today."

He looked straight at Cassandra as if he was addressing her alone.

"First, I want to share with you the tremendous difference your contributions have made in the lives of the rescued victims of trafficking. Without your help, we would have been forced to limit the number of residents in our sanctuary and in the halfway house, sending these young people back into the world before they were ready. Instead, they can stay for as long as they need to, allowing time for healing and recovery. The support we provide is so much more than just a temporary shelter. We are providing them with the tools necessary to not only survive, but also to flourish, so when they are ready to spread their wings, they can do more than fly away. They can soar."

There was a round of applause, after which Onegus told a few personal anecdotes, and how he had been inspired to help trafficking victims after a friend's daughter had been lured into a trap but saved in the nick of time.

He finished with a couple of jokes and then encouraged the guests to donate lavishly, pledging to match each contribution to double the evening's proceeds.

The guy was charming, funny, compassionate, and looked like a movie star. The audience was eating it up, and Cassandra wasn't immune, catching herself gazing at him dreamily and imagining what it would be like to have a man like him.

Except it was all a show, and the guy was probably a spoiled playboy who hadn't worked a day in his life. The international conglomerate most likely belonged to his family, and he was just the pretty face that they used for public speaking.

She was willing to bet that all that charm was an act, and that in real life, the guy was a stuck-up snob with a stick up his ass the size of a flagpole.

When he was done and people rose to their feet and applauded him, he bowed his head politely, and smiled that panty-melting smile of his.

"Thank you." He dipped his head again.

As Onegus stepped down, someone else got up on the podium. "Let's give it up one more time for Mr. Onegus McLean."

Everyone clapped again, and then it was Kevin's turn to give his speech.

"Come on, Cassy. Do your part."

Plastering a smile on her face, she followed him up to the podium and struck a pose. That was her damn part. To be Kevin's prop for the evening, and for her so-called Cinderella story to provide him with free publicity.

"You owe me big time for this," she hissed.

He kept on smiling while the photographers went into a snapping frenzy. "Whatever you want, it's yours. You're worth it."

Onegus

Onegus pretended to listen to Kevin Brunswick's speech, smiling politely and clapping when everyone else clapped, but his entire focus was on the stunning lady standing next to the guy.

When Kevin turned and smiled at his companion, though, Onegus snapped to attention.

"I would like to introduce my Fifty Shades of Beauty creative director, Cassandra Beaumont."

Everyone clapped again.

"Cassandra started in my company as a model, but she soon proved to be so much more than that. If there is one person I should credit with my company's rapid success, it is my beautiful and incredibly talented vice president. Give her a round of applause."

As the guests clapped and the photographers snapped away, Cassandra forced a smile and dipped her head.

"Thank you," she said to the microphone and then moved aside, giving the stage back to her boss.

She was comfortable in front of the cameras, striking a well-practiced pose and turning her head to just the right angle so they would get her best side. Still, Onegus could tell that she didn't like being up there and was struggling to hide how pissed she was. Her smile never reached her eyes, and she glared daggers at her boss.

Evidently, she hadn't been on board for his little publicity stunt. A beauty rising from rags to riches thanks to hard work and extraordinary talent made a good story, and the free publicity Fifty Shades of Beauty would get out of it was priceless.

He had her name now, and she wasn't just a pretty face, a piece of eye-candy on Kevin's arm. She was a creative director of a large cosmetics company and Kevin's vice president. Pretty impressive for such a young woman.

No wonder she radiated confidence.

Cassandra wasn't a kid, though. Onegus estimated her to be in her late twenties or early thirties, which made her absolutely perfect. He liked his women to be more mature and to have a mind in addition to looks.

And as an added bonus, she wasn't at the gala to snatch a rich husband or a sugar daddy.

Not that he had any objections to being the latter, but she didn't need his money. He had no doubt that the position Cassandra held in Kevin's company came with an appropriate salary.

The only question was whether she was taken.

Several rings adorned her long, elegant fingers, but none looked like a wedding or an engagement ring. Except, that didn't mean a thing these days. She could be married and not wear a wedding ring, or she could be cohabiting with a partner.

Onegus had a rule against seducing married women, and that included those who had live-in boyfriends.

When all the speeches were done and everyone had made their pledges, dinner was served, and after that the mingling part of the event finally arrived. Usually that was the part of the evening he hated the most, but not tonight.

Excusing himself from his dinner companions, Onegus beelined straight to where Cassandra and Kevin were standing and talking with several of the other guests.

"Good speech." He clapped Kevin on the back and smiled at Cassandra.

"Yours was too." The guy offered Onegus his hand. "How much was collected tonight?"

"I have no clue." He offered his hand to her. "It's a pleasure to make your acquaintance, Ms. Beaumont. I'm Onegus McLean."

"I know who you are, Mr. McLean."

She reluctantly put her slender hand in his, and it was like getting zapped with a high-voltage current, but not in a sexual way.

"Wow." She pulled her hand out of his. "Static electricity." She smoothed it over the side of her dress. "It must be the fabric. Or maybe the shoes."

As she stuck one dainty stiletto-clad foot out from under the long skirt, Onegus had the absurd urge to kneel on the floor, wrap his hand around her ankle, and remove the shoe.

Why?

He had no clue. It wasn't as if he had a shoe fetish, and he'd never gotten excited over a woman's foot, but hers was just so perfectly shaped, and her skin so perfectly smooth that he wanted to lick it all over.

"If you'll excuse me." She smiled nervously. "I need to powder my nose."

Onegus stifled a chuckle. That used to be a polite way for ladies to say they needed to use the bathroom, but nowadays it had a very different meaning that had to do with a certain drug that was in powder form. He wondered whether Cassandra knew that. She was too young for the old expression, but perhaps a little too old to realize what the latest generation of young humans used it for.

In Cassandra's case, though, it was probably neither. For some reason, she wanted to get away from him.

Perhaps the curious sparks between them had unnerved her.

She arched one perfectly shaped brow. "What's so amusing? Did I miss a joke?"

He leaned closer. "I'll tell you when you return from powdering your nose."

As her lush lips thinned out into a stubborn expression, he expected her to insist that he tell her now and not later, but she must have thought better of it and forced a polite smile before turning to start toward the bathrooms.

Damn, she had a fine ass. And that runway walk was causing him all kinds of trouble.

With an effort, Onegus tore his eyes away from her sashaying hips.

He had no intentions of letting her escape. She couldn't run off without Kevin, who was most likely her ride home, and Onegus planned on keeping him engaged until Cassandra's return.

Perhaps while she was gone he would coax more information about her from her boss, specifically whether she was married or had a steady boyfriend.

Cassandra

As Cassandra turned away from the infuriatingly handsome billionaire, she let out a muted relieved breath. Walking toward the restrooms, she could feel his heated gaze on her back, and the contrary part of her decided to give him something worth looking at, a version of a runway walk that would leave him panting for what he couldn't get.

Damn, the guy was hot. If he made a move on her, it would take all her formidable defenses to keep him at arm's length.

And what in the name of the devil was that electrical current that had arced between them?

Cassandra was attracted to Onegus, so she'd expected some reaction when she put her hand in his large paw, but instead of a pleasant tingling or excited butterflies in her stomach, she'd produced an energy zap that had nearly knocked her off her Louboutins.

Hopefully, it wasn't her witchy power reacting to him. Or perhaps it was?

Other than being too handsome, too tall, too rich, and too charming, Onegus McLean hadn't done anything to aggravate her enough to cause such an instant spike.

It must have been her subconscious thought process that had caused her power to suddenly unleash, and now that she had allowed those thoughts to surface, her anger simmered close beneath her skin. It was good that she'd released some of it earlier, or she would have been in trouble.

The guy probably thought he could get any woman he wanted, but if he tried anything with her, he would discover that wasn't so. Cassandra didn't do hookups, and she didn't compromise on anything less than a man's full and dedicated attention, and a genuine effort to win her heart. Onegus was too smooth and too everything else to be anything other than a player.

It was a shame, and a tiny part of her hoped that she was wrong, but her rational mind knew better. If McLean ever had a serious relationship, it would be with an heiress, someone just as rich as he was. People like him didn't marry for love. They married for political gain or business advantage or both and had lovers on the side.

Prejudice much? A small voice in the back of her head whispered. Perhaps he was a perfectly nice guy who was looking for the love of his life?

Right.

Onegus wasn't freaking Prince Charming, and she wasn't freaking Cinderella.

It was true that she'd come from basically nothing, but Cassandra had made something of herself with hard work and dedication. If anyone was her Prince Charming, it was Kevin, and thankfully he'd done it not because he'd fallen in love with her, but because he'd recognized her talent and believed in her.

His gamble on her had paid off big time. From a small company that had been barely making it, Fifty Shades of Beauty had become a national brand, and it wasn't thanks to how great the products themselves were, but thanks to her cohesive branding and marketing.

After finishing in the restroom, Cassandra fixed her lipstick, checked her updo for any strays, and when there was nothing else to justify her prolonged stay in the ladies' room, she squared her shoulders and walked out.

Hopefully, Onegus had moved on to his next victim, and she could grab Kevin and tell him that she wanted to leave. Josie's concert should have ended a long time ago, and he was no doubt eager to go home to her.

No such luck.

Onegus and Kevin were still standing in the same spot she'd left them.

Cassandra huffed out an annoyed breath. So be it. She wasn't embarrassed about asking Kevin to take her home in front of their host.

Onegus must have sensed her approaching and turned around, flashing her that beautiful panty-melting smile of his. "Here you are. I thought that you got lost."

She arched a brow. "I'm surprised you're still here." It was rude, even she knew that, but he was pushing her buttons without intending to.

Onegus leaned closer, his breath tickling her ear. "I promised to tell you why powdering your pretty nose amused me, and I never break my promises."

"Really?"

"Really. Come dance with me and I'll tell you."

She crossed her arms over her chest. "Tell me now."

Kevin chuckled and then waved at someone. "I'm going to say hi to Bob Grinberg." The traitor walked away, leaving her alone with their host.

"Come on, Cassandra. Just one dance. I promise not to bite." He winked. "For now."

He was so full of himself. But to refuse was to admit that he scared her. Well, not that he was scary. It was her attraction to the bad boy billionaire that was frightening.

"Fine." She put her hand in his and let him lead her to the dance floor. "But just so you know, I have two left feet, and I don't know these kinds of dances."

He looked down. "Your feet look absolutely perfect to me."

Finding them a spot on the crowded dance floor, he put his hand on her waist while holding the other. "Just let loose and follow my lead."

The man knew how to dance, and he was being a perfect gentleman, not trying to bring her too close against his body or holding her too tightly, and after a minute or two she started to relax.

Well, she wouldn't call it relaxed when her body hummed with need, and she was reining in the traitorous rioting hormones with sheer willpower.

"Where did you learn to dance like that?" she asked just to break the silence.

"My mother taught me."

"Are you close to your mother?"

"We talk once a week, and I visit her at least twice a year. She lives in Scotland."

A man who cared about his mother couldn't be too bad.

"What about your father? Are you close to him?"

"He passed away a long time ago."

After leaving his fortune to his son, but still, the fact that Onegus hadn't pissed it away indicated that he was at least a decent businessman.

"I'm sorry."

He shrugged. "As I said, it was a long time ago. How about you? Are you close to your mother?"

Cassandra smiled. "Very. I still live at home." That usually cooled down most guys.

"That's lovely."

She eyed him from under lowered lashes. "I'm thirty-four."

"So?"

"So, most men find it strange that I still live with my mother."

"I see nothing wrong with a daughter taking care of her mother. I value family above all."

"How do you know that I take care of her?"

"You didn't mention a father, so I assume he is not around and your mother has no one else. Otherwise, you wouldn't have stayed. You are too strong-willed and independent for that, and it's not a financially driven decision either because you must be making a very good living."

"You don't know me."

"True, but no one achieves the level of success you have by being meek." He leaned closer. "I bet that you are supporting your mother, financially and emotionally."

He was either a very good judge of character, or what was more likely, he'd learned all of that from Kevin the traitor.

"I see that you had an interesting conversation with my boss. What else did he tell you about me?"

Onegus grinned. "Nothing that I didn't know already. He said that you are one of a kind and that he's very fortunate to have you. Then he threatened me with bodily harm if I tried to steal you from him."

Cassandra laughed. "He's so full of it." Kevin was in good shape, but he was tiny compared to Onegus who seemed to be built from solid rock. "Nevertheless, I love him for saying that."

Onegus

Onegus's good mood had gone straight to hell. "Is there anything going on between you and your boss?"

Her lips a thin line, Cassandra glared at him and then smiled wickedly. "A lot. We spend hours together nearly every day, our heads bent together as we whisper secrets to each other."

She was mocking him, taunting, but that didn't answer his question and he had to make sure. "Are you in love with Kevin?"

Cassandra tilted her head, her dark eyes so intense that he half expected to see flames in them. "You are lucky that you didn't ask if I was sleeping with him, because I wouldn't have deigned to answer and would have just walked away. But you asked whether I was in love with him, so I'll humor you. I love Kevin, and I also love his wife. They are like family to me. Kevin was already married when he took me under his wing, believed in me, and supported me when I doubted myself, and I'm grateful to him for it. But there were never any romantic feelings between us, and all he ever wanted from me was my talent and work ethic. Kevin thinks of me as his little sister and has never hinted at anything else."

Despite all her bluster, Cassandra was naive.

"Kevin seems like a good guy, and he might love his wife with all his heart, but unless he's known you since you were a little girl, I doubt that he can think of you as a sister. Males are just not built like that."

She shrugged. "What he thinks is irrelevant. His actions are what matters." She chuckled. "If I was held responsible for the thoughts running through my head, I would have been arrested on several counts of attempted murder. I feel like killing someone at least once a day, but since I don't actually do it, I'm still a free member of society."

"Very true, and talking about illegal activity reminds me that I haven't told you what powdering your nose means these days."

It took her a couple of seconds to figure it out, and then her eyes widened. "No way. Are you sure? I've never heard that before." Her beautiful lips twisted in a grimace. "But then I don't get out much. I'm all work and no play."

He nodded. "I'm afraid so. If you don't want people to think that you are going to the bathroom to snort cocaine, you need to find another polite expression for excusing yourself."

"That's so twisted." She shook her head. "I don't get this new generation. Perhaps it's because I skipped the last two years of high school and never went to college. I wasn't exposed to all those changes."

He was surprised. Cassandra was way too smart to drop out of high school. She must have opted for homeschooling and had acquired her marketing skills in other ways. There were so many online courses these days, some even from fully accredited universities, that attending a brick-and-mortar institution was no longer the only or even best way to get an education.

"What made you switch to homeschooling?"

She smiled. "I'm glad you didn't assume that I dropped out."

Her stiff posture softened, and as the song ended, Cassandra made no move to pull out of his arms. When the next one started, they resumed dancing.

"You're too smart for that." His hand on the small of her back, he drew her a couple of inches closer to his body, but not close enough so their chests were touching.

She didn't resist. "Thank you. We lived in a decent area of the valley, but the local high school was nevertheless overrun by a bad element. I didn't feel safe attending, and I told my mother that I preferred to finish the last two years at home. She agreed provided that my grades wouldn't take a turn for the worse. I graduated a year early with perfect grades."

"Why didn't you continue to college? Was it because you needed to take care of your mother?"

Onegus didn't have a high school diploma or college education either, but that was because those hadn't been available to him when he was a young lad.

His mother and his uncles had taught him what he'd needed to know, and the rest he'd learned on his own and was still learning. Knowledge wasn't a stagnant thing, and continuous education was a must.

Cassandra's expression turned thoughtful. "That wasn't the reason. I don't want you to get the wrong impression of my mother. She's not disabled. She just has memory problems from time to time, but she can mostly take care of herself. I couldn't go away to college, but I could've gone locally. I went for one semester, decided that it was a waste of time and money, and quit. I learned what I needed from online courses."

"Smart and frugal. I like it."

She gazed at him from under lowered lashes. "What would a rich guy like you know about being frugal?"

"A lot more than you think."

Cassandra

"A frugal billionaire. Well, I guess it's possible. I read that Warren Buffett lives in a modest house and drives an old pickup truck. How about you? Do you live in a mansion?"

"Nope. I live in a nice two-bedroom house, which I share with a roommate." He smiled. "Who's a guy, in case you are wondering whether I'm single."

"Are you?"

"Very."

"I find it hard to believe. You are a rich, handsome guy."

"I'm also very busy, and I don't get out much. We have that in common."

He probably used that line on all the hookups he collected. "Let me guess. You probably travel a lot as well."

That was another line that guys used to explain why they were not available. It was a perfect excuse for when they were testing the waters with someone else or just wanted to keep things casual.

"I travel for work, that's true, but lately not that much. Most of my days are spent in the office, either staring at a computer screen or in meetings. Occasionally, I meet with business associates on their turf, and once in a while, I attend events like this one." His hand on the small of her back caressed her gently through the sheer fabric. "Usually, I don't look forward to them, but I'm glad I came tonight." He drew her a fraction of an inch closer.

Onegus was about to say more, when Kevin got on the dance floor and headed their way.

"I just came to tell you that I'm going home." His eyes twinkled with mischief. "Obviously, you don't have to leave because I do. You can call a taxi, or perhaps Onegus could give you a lift." Kevin jerked his chin toward the photographers who were snapping pictures of her dancing with the dashing billionaire. "They love you."

Damn, she'd been so consumed by Onegus and his overwhelming presence that she hadn't noticed the photographers.

Kevin was practically salivating over the free publicity. Tomorrow, all the gossip magazines would post her picture in Onegus's arms and publish speculative articles about their non-existent fling.

"I'll take you home," Onegus said and then turned to her boss. "Good night, Kevin, and thank you for your generous contribution."

The nerve of the guy.

She cast him a saccharine smile. "Thank you for the offer, but I'd rather Kevin took me home."

Her boss paled. "And miss out on all that?" He pointed at the photographer with his chin again.

Smirking, Onegus leaned to whisper in her ear. "I promise to be a perfect gentleman."

She wasn't worried about him trying anything without her active encouragement. He wasn't the problem. The photographers and reporters were. If she left with him, they would make a story out of it even if all he did was to drive her home.

Kevin put his hand on her exposed shoulder. "Stay a little longer, Cassy, have some fun." His eyes were pleading with her to do as he asked. "It would be better if we didn't leave together if you know what I mean."

Damn him and his pleading eyes. "Same goes for me. I can stay, but I'll take a taxi home."

"Thank you." He leaned and kissed her cheek.

Was it her imagination or had Onegus growled quietly?

"Good night, Kevin." She kissed her boss's cheek back. When he left, she narrowed her eyes at Onegus. "Did you just growl at my boss?"

Assuming an innocent expression, he shrugged. "I had something in my throat." He reached for her hand. "Would you like a drink?"

"I would love one. I'm parched."

As they made their way to the bar, Onegus leaned to whisper in her ear, "We don't have to leave the hotel together. In fact, we don't need to leave at all. I have a suite upstairs, and we can sneak out one at a time. I can order coffee, and we can keep talking in private."

Right. Talking.

Well, at least he was trying to be polite.

It would be a lie if she claimed his proposition wasn't tempting. Onegus was the sexiest man she'd ever met or ever would, and to be with him, she might have considered bending her no hookups rule a little. But there was no way she was staying the night and then doing the walk of shame the next morning in her gala dress.

"I need to go home soon. My mom will be worried if I'm not back by midnight."

He arched a brow. "Can't you call her? You're thirty-four, not fourteen. You can tell your mother that you're having a good time and will come home later than usual."

"Do you mean the next morning?"

He smiled. "If I'm very lucky."

"Well, you are not."

"What's wrong with me?"

"Nothing." He was perfect, but his ego was inflated enough as it was.

"What would you like to drink?" he asked as they reached the bar.

"Vodka Cranberry."

He told the barman their choices, and when their drinks were ready, led her out onto the terrace, where several of the guests were smoking fat cigars.

"Is it allowed to smoke out here?" She leaned against the railing.

Onegus shrugged. "It's not my job to enforce the rules in this hotel."

It was an odd answer, but she shrugged it off and took a sip of her drink.

Leaning against the railing next to her, Onegus sipped on his whiskey for several long moments. "Are you involved with someone?"

"No."

"Don't you like me?"

She rolled her eyes. "What's not to like?"

"Then why not come up to my hotel room?"

"I don't do hookups, Onegus. And even if I did, I wouldn't do that here with photographers and reporters following us around. There is only so much that I'm willing to do to generate free publicity for Fifty Shades of Beauty."

"Is that why you danced with me?"

She wondered whether the vulnerable note she detected in his voice was genuine or an act.

"I enjoy your company, Onegus, and I like you, but if you are interested in more, you'll have to do it the old-fashioned way. Ask me on a date, come to my house and meet my mother, call me, ask me on another date, and so on. I'm not going to settle for less."

Onegus

On a gut level, Onegus had known that Cassandra wouldn't be an easy conquest, but it was rare that a woman her age adhered to such old-fashioned standards of dating. Most were more than happy to engage in casual hookups and had very few expectations from him, if any.

Maybe he was old-fashioned as well. He liked that Cassandra was demanding, that she was confident enough to believe that she deserved the investment of time and effort, and that sex was not a casual thing for her.

When she shivered, he wrapped his arm around her. "Do you want to go back in?"

"No, I like it out here. Especially since the photographers and reporters stayed inside."

His doing, but she had no way of knowing that. One signal to the guy in charge of security, and no reporter or photographer was allowed to go out on the terrace.

"Hold my drink." He handed her his glass and shrugged his jacket off. "Here you go." He wrapped it around her shoulders. "Better?"

Her eyes roaming over his white dress shirt, she licked her lips. "Much, thank you."

He chuckled. "If you wish, I can drive you home, come in, and introduce myself to your mother. That would take care of one item on your list. Then you can change into something more comfortable but leave the shoes on. They are sexy as hell."

Stifling a smile, she huddled inside his much too large jacket. "Thanks for the offer, but it's still a no."

"Can't blame a guy for trying." He sighed dramatically

"Invite me on several dates, and after a couple of months, you can try again."

He groaned. "You're killing me, Cassandra."

"You'll live."

Shaking his head, he reached into the jacket pocket and pulled out his phone. "Give me your number. I'm going to start tomorrow."

"I'd rather take yours."

He narrowed his eyes at her. "Nice try, but I know that you are not going to call. Give me your number, Cassandra."

"Why do you think that I'm not going to call?"

"A gut feeling. You probably think that I'm a spoiled rich guy who needs to conquer every woman he meets, and you refuse to be one of many. You want to be the one I fall for."

She shook her head. "I'm not thinking that far into the future, and love is not what I'm after. Not to start with, anyway. I just can't imagine being intimate with anyone who I didn't get to know first. Respect is non-negotiable. I need to know that you respect me, and I need to respect you."

"I respect the hell out of you, Cassandra." He took her hand and brought it to his lips. "You are a worthy woman, and I want to get to know you."

"But?"

"No buts. Just give me your phone number. If you don't, I'm going to call your boss and get it from him."

She narrowed her eyes at him. "I have a better idea. Let's decide on a time and place right now, and I'll meet you there."

"Tomorrow, eleven in the morning, Venice Beach. But I need your number in case I'm delayed."

She looked surprised. "Why the beach? And why so early?"

He leaned toward her and smiled. "So you don't suspect me of asking you out only to seduce you. If we want, we can spend the entire day getting to know each other."

"And then go to your place, right?"

"It will be entirely up to you, my lady."

She smirked. "I love it. But I'm afraid that I'll have to disappoint you."

His forehead furrowed. "What now? If you want to meet somewhere else, just tell me."

"The beach is perfect, but I won't be wearing these sexy shoes for a walk on the sand." She wiggled her stiletto-clad foot.

"Naturally, I'm also going to take you to a restaurant, but it's not a fancy place, and you can wear sneakers if you wish."

She cast him a sidelong glance. "I finally meet a guy tall enough for me to wear heels, and he wants to take me to the beach. A girl just can't catch a break."

"Choose someplace else, then."

"No, I like your idea of spending the day together. If everything goes well, you will just have to take me out on another date somewhere that justifies getting dressed up for."

"Deal." He shook the hand he was still holding on to.

"It was a pleasure doing business with you, Mr. Onegus McLean." She shook it back and then pushed away from the railing. "But if we are to meet tomorrow morning, I need to go home and get some sleep." She started to take his jacket off.

"Keep it. You can get it back to me tomorrow." He smiled. "That will obligate you to actually show up."

Pushing one leg forward, she looked at him down her pretty little nose. "I don't make promises that I don't intend to keep." She pulled her phone out of her evening purse. "What's your number?"

When he arched a brow, she smiled and patted his arm. "I need it so I can call you and so you'll have mine."

Eleanor

"Good morning, family." Eleanor walked into the dining room. "How is everyone feeling?"

Vivian cast her a curious look. "You seem in a good mood today."

Parker used the opportunity of his mother and Magnus's attention being diverted to slip Scarlett a slice of roast beef.

The dog snatched it from his fingers, swallowed it in one bite, and was looking at him with pleading puppy eyes, begging for more.

"I am in a great mood." Eleanor poured herself a cup of coffee and pulled out a chair. "And when you hear my announcement, you will be too. I'm moving in with Peter."

Leaning back, Magnus folded his arms over his chest and gave her the displeased father look. "That was fast. Since when did the two of you become an item?"

Stifling a chuckle, Eleanor shook her head. "Peter and I are not dating. Leon and Anastasia are coming to the village soon, and they will need a place of their own. Leon prefers to move into a new house, so there will be room in his old one, and Peter is okay with me as his new roommate. I also no longer need a keeper. Kian trusts me." She took a sip from her coffee. "To a certain extent."

Magnus didn't look happy, which was surprising. He should be glad to be rid of her. "Did you check with Kian or Onegus that you are allowed to move out?"

"Do I need to? I thought that my probation period was over. I'm allowed to come and go as I please, so I'm quite sure I'm allowed to choose where I live as well. I've imposed on your hospitality for long enough."

Vivian put her fork down. "Kian shouldn't mind. I think that Magnus just doesn't want you to leave."

Eleanor snorted. "You're too sweet. Magnus is going to throw a party when I'm gone, true?" She cast him an amused glance.

He shrugged. "I've gotten used to you. The house will feel empty without you."

"I'll miss you," Parker said.

"You can visit me anytime you want. It's not like I'm moving out of town. I'll be a ten-minute walk away."

"It's not the same." He patted the dog's head. "And Scarlett is going to miss you too."

"You can bring her along when you come to visit me."

The dog would probably be the only one who really missed her. Parker was busy with school, and the rest of the time he was hanging out with Lisa. The kid was head over heels in love with the girl, but she had no clue, thinking that they were just buddies.

Was she being as clueless as Lisa?

Moving in with Peter could be a mistake. He was an attractive guy, and she wasn't blind to his charms, but he wasn't her type, and she wasn't his. Still, cohabitation would bring them closer, and things might get dicey.

"When are you moving?" Vivian asked.

"I can move right away, but all of Leon's things are still at the house and I don't want to do the packing for him. I could wait until he and Anastasia come to the village and he takes his stuff to their new house, which will probably be in this section. On the other hand, I'd rather move sooner than later because of Greggory. There will be less of a chance of me bumping into him in the old village."

Magnus cast her a pitying look. "If you don't want to see him, I suggest that you stay away from the café. Now that he's single, he will be hanging out there a lot."

Vivian shook her head. "Eleanor can't avoid the café. Where is she going to meet males? She needs to find someone new."

"Don't worry about me. I meet plenty of people in the training center. The café is not the only hunting ground in the village."

"Gross," Parker murmured.

Magnus clapped him on the back. "Finding a mate is like a treasure hunt. If you don't look, you won't find her."

"Perhaps I already did." He pushed away from the table. "I'm taking Scarlett for a walk."

When he was gone, Vivian sighed. "Lisa is either blind or she's pretending not to see how in love with her Parker is."

"She probably doesn't want to hurt his feelings," Magnus said. "Besides, they are both just kids, and it's nothing more than infatuation."

He didn't sound convincing at all.

"How old were Romeo and Juliet?" Vivian asked. "The young feel everything more fiercely, and first love is the most powerful. Romeo and Juliet were willing to die for each other."

It was possible to fall deeply in love at fourteen, and just as quickly fall out of love. Teenagers saw the world in black and white, and they were either all in or all out.

"Romeo and Juliet weren't immortal," Magnus said. "We operate differently." He reached for Vivian's small hand and put it on his chest. "We are bound to each other for eternity."

Lucky bastards.

Was there someone out there for her? Or were the fickle Fates ignoring her as usual?

Remembering Emmett's intense dark eyes, a shiver ran down Eleanor's spine. She sincerely hoped that he wasn't the one the Fates had chosen for her. She wanted a nice, uncomplicated guy who would treat her well and have her back, and that wasn't Emmett.

Vlad

Vlad walked into the café expecting to find few if any people sitting at the tables, but it seemed that the pleasant spring weather had drawn many more customers than usual this Sunday morning.

There was no service on Sundays, but people could still buy coffees, sandwiches, and pastries from the vending machines that Jackson kept well-stocked, replenishing them with fresh supplies daily and sometimes twice a day.

Navigating between the tables, Vlad smiled and nodded to those he passed until he found a secluded one that was tucked against the wall of greenery.

He put his art bag down and pulled out a chair.

Coming out here to draw was just an excuse to get out of the house. Wendy had gone shopping with Sharon and Tessa, and Vlad wasn't in the mood to stay in the house or visit his mother and Richard.

He was still reeling from her revelation and hoping that she was wrong. Perhaps she'd gotten pregnant with him before meeting the Kra-ell male and had just assumed that he'd been the father.

After believing his entire life that his father was human, it was a difficult adjustment to accept that he was fathered by a member of another species of immortals.

He hadn't even told Wendy yet.

He hadn't asked Kian to allow him to see the captured Kra-ell either.

Maybe if he pretended that nothing had changed, nothing would. He was still the same guy, too tall, too skinny, and too strong. Had anything changed on the inside with the knowledge that he wasn't like other members of his clan?

He should find out more, ask the Kra-ell male to tell him all he knew about his kind, and figure out if any of it had shaped the man Vlad had become.

Perhaps he would do that after the business with Wendy's father was done. There was only so much that he could deal with at once.

Right now, he had a school assignment he hadn't even started, and it was due on Tuesday. Pulling out his drawing tablet, he moved his chair so the sun wasn't shining directly onto it. Vlad sketched a quick outline, saved it, and opened another layer on top of it for the more precise outlining. He was about to get started on that when he spotted Brundar's long blond ponytail next to the vending machines.

He still hadn't talked to the Guardian as Kian had suggested.

Leaving the tablet behind, he walked over to the coffee machine and swiped his card, pretending like that was what he'd come for.

"Good morning," he murmured to Brundar.

The Guardian only nodded.

"Do you have a moment?"

"For what?" Brundar unwrapped a pastry and took a bite.

"I need to ask you something."

"Ask."

The guy acted as if every word was precious, and he had to be frugal with them.

Vlad leaned closer to the Guardian and lowered his voice. "Kian said that you were once faced with the dilemma of knowingly breaking clan law to seek vengeance. I'm faced with the same dilemma, and I wondered if you can give me advice."

When Brundar just turned around and started walking, Vlad heaved out a sigh, but then the Guardian motioned for him to follow.

When they were out of the café's enclosure, Brundar cast him a sidelong glance. "Stop talking in riddles, and just spit it out."

"You are a Guardian. If I plan on doing something illegal, I shouldn't tell you about it."

A barely perceptible smile lifted one corner of Brundar's mouth. "Talking is not a crime. We will just treat it as hypothetical."

"Right." Vlad pushed his bangs out of his eyes. "Wendy's mother left her when she was a baby, and she's been missing ever since. Her father is a monster who abused his wife and daughter. I want to find out whether he killed Wendy's mother, and to do so, I need to thrall him to get him to talk. I know that thralling humans is allowed only under certain circumstances, and that's not one of them."

"What if you find out that he killed her?"

"I'll thrall him to walk into a police station and confess. Wendy doesn't want his blood on my hands. She wants to kill him herself."

Brundar's expression didn't change. "Would she still want to kill her father if he didn't kill the mother?"

"No."

"What are you going to do if he didn't?"

"I'll make him tell me all he knows about where she might be. If I can find the mother before our wedding and have her attend, it would be the best wedding present I can give Wendy."

Brundar nodded. "Both are worthy goals. My situation was a little different, though. I beat the shit out of Callie's murderous bastard of an ex-husband, forcing him to sign her divorce papers, and then I thralled him to forget me. I wanted her to be free of him. After I did that, I walked into Edna's office, confessed my transgression, and submitted to the punishment such an offense calls for, which is whipping."

Vlad winced. "Didn't Edna take into account the extenuating circumstances?"

"She did. Edna wanted to give me a reduced sentence of a few days of incarceration, but I preferred to be done with it as soon as possible and get back to Callie, so I chose the whipping. If you decide to go through with it, you can ask for the reduced sentence. Just try not to murder the human."

"Do you think I should do it?"

"Murder him?"

"I promised Wendy that I wouldn't, but what if I'm consumed by rage and Richard can't control me?"

"You plan on taking Richard with you?"

Vlad nodded. "He will have to bring a taser. He won't be able to restrain me otherwise."

"If you take him with you, he becomes an accomplice." Brundar turned his eyes heavenward. "Hypothetically speaking, if a civilian breaks the law, it's up to them if they wish to confess. If they are caught later, the punishment might be more severe, but they might also get away with it. And in this hypothetical case, if no bodily harm was done, it might count only as an infraction."

Cassandra

Cassandra stood in front of the mirror and grimaced at her reflection. The black shorts were sexy and beach-appropriate, but they were showing too much ass, and Onegus might get the wrong impression.

Or the right one.

Last night, she hadn't been able to fall asleep for hours. Every time she'd closed her eyes, Onegus's gorgeous blue eyes and charming smile had popped behind her lids. Remembering how his large hands had felt on her while they danced had sent sizzling currents through her body, and the only way to release all the pent-up tension had been to pleasure herself while pretending she was with him.

She'd exploded like a firecracker, barely able to stifle the loud moan that had torn out of her throat.

Even now, thinking about him made her nipples stand to attention and her core tingle.

His effect on her was unprecedented and also dangerous.

For the first time ever, the build-up was caused by sexual attraction instead of anger or frustration, but the result was the same. If she didn't release it, things would start to explode. But after her self-righteous speech about needing to get to know each other before getting intimate, she couldn't drag him into her bed and have her way with him.

Cassandra hated playing the age-old game of luring a guy into seducing her and then pretending that she was helpless to resist. She'd never been that girl. Her no was a hard no, and her yes was a definite yes. She didn't send mixed messages, and she didn't play games.

Then again, she was a good-looking, successful woman who'd been without male companionship for most of her life. So maybe she was missing something?

Perhaps all those games other women played were a vital part of the interplay between the sexes, and without them, she seemed uninterested? Unapproachable?

Or was it just her abrasive personality that scared men off?

It hadn't scared Onegus though, which was a big part of her intense attraction to him. He was worthy, his lion strong enough to tame her lioness.

Or not.

Her bizarre destructive power was unpredictable, and its sudden connection to Onegus might put him in danger.

Or not.

Obsessing about what-ifs was pointless.

The shorts would have to do. Paired with a pair of white Keds, a black tank top, and a cute little bomber jacket that was made from fake leather and lace inserts, she looked sexy and casual. The outfit also showcased her long legs and pert bottom.

Onegus was going to salivate.

As Cassandra walked into the living room, her mother lifted her head from the magazine she'd been flipping through and smiled. "You look beautiful, Cassy. Are you meeting with friends?"

She hadn't met with friends since quitting high school, but for her mother, it probably seemed like yesterday.

"Actually, I have a date. I'm meeting a guy, and we are going for a walk on the beach."

"That's lovely." Her mother frowned. "Just stay away from the water. The ocean is dangerous."

Geraldine was terrified of getting even her feet wet at the beach, but she loved sitting on the sand and watching the waves. She also loved swimming in their pool at home, which didn't make sense to Cassandra. Her mother claimed that the vastness of the ocean scared her, and knowing that there were fish and other creatures in the water grossed her out.

"I'm not even wearing a swimsuit." Cassandra parted her jacket to show her mom the tank top. "We are going to a restaurant overlooking Venice Beach, and after that, we are going on a walk."

"Who is the young man? Is he someone from work?"

"You could say so. I met him at the charity event I attended with Kevin."

"Is he handsome?"

"Devastatingly so."

"Oh, my." Her mother's lips lifted in a smile and her hand lifted to her chest. "Just don't let him devastate you."

"It's just an expression."

"Do you have a picture?"

There were probably dozens of them all over the gossip magazines, but Cassandra refused to look. God only knew what kind of trash they had written about her and Onegus.

"I don't have a picture, but he's tall, taller than me with heels on, and built like a tank. He also has a charming smile, blond curly hair that he tries to tame with hair products, blue eyes that twinkle with mischief, and a square, strong jaw." Cassandra chuckled. "He looks like one of the models on your billionaire romance novels."

"Oh, dear. You sound like you are half in love with the man already."

"I'm not." Cassandra leaned and kissed her mother's cheek. "I might be gone the whole day, so don't worry about me. And if you do, just call me or text me, and I'll call you back."

Her mother smiled. "I'm not going to bother you on your date, sweetheart. Besides, I'm not staying home. The book club is meeting for lunch at Danny's."

Geraldine's book club must be the most active one in the entire nation, but Cassandra had a feeling that not all of her mother's book club meetings were about books.

"That's great. Have fun, Mom."

Onegus

Onegus parked his car in Hotel Erwin's self-parking garage and headed to the rooftop bar to wait for Cassandra.

He was half an hour early for their date, plenty of time to relax with a glass of whiskey and ponder the idiocy of asking her on a date.

When she'd made her attitude about hookups clear, he should have let it go, but he just couldn't resist. It was like she'd bewitched him, and he'd had to see her again.

Onegus had no intentions of making it to the second or third date, though. Meeting Cassandra during the day made seduction even less likely, which was why he'd chosen the time and location. His main purpose was to find out more about the peculiar current that had arced between them when they touched.

She'd explained it as static electricity, and he might have accepted that if not for the guilty look that had passed over her eyes. She'd known what had caused it and had tried to cover it up.

A good excuse, but who was he trying to convince?

Onegus was curious about much more than that zap. Cassandra intrigued him, challenged him, and staying away from her required willpower that he was apparently short on. Eventually he would flex that muscle, but today, he would enjoy her company and not think about why letting her go was the decent thing to do.

Sitting with his back to the bar, he watched the roof access as more humans arrived to enjoy the beautiful spring day and the views of Venice Beach below. Couples young and old, holding hands, friends meeting to hang out together, their carefree laughter enviable.

For at least a few hours of the glorious Sunday morning, they were able to forget their daily struggles, their troubles, and just enjoy being.

Onegus wished he could be like them, but despite his easy smiles and seemingly mellow nature, his mind was never at ease. Being in charge of the Guardian force and the clan's security was a huge responsibility, and his occasional sojourns as Kian's stand-in were a welcome break.

Motioning to the barman with the empty glass, he asked for a refill.

It was a little early in the day for another shot of whiskey, but with his immortal metabolism, it would take much more for him to feel even a slight buzz.

When the barman handed him a fresh one, Onegus turned around and nearly dropped the glass.

Cassandra was even more beautiful in casual attire and minimal makeup than she had been when all decked out in her evening gown.

She smiled as she waved at him, sauntering over in her tiny black shorts and white sneakers. Her legs went on forever, the skin on them so smooth that it gleamed in the sun. Had she smeared suntan oil all over her legs? Or did her skin shine naturally?

"Good morning." He rose to his feet and leaned to kiss her cheek.

"Good morning to you too." She took a step back. "Are you sure that you are not a vampire?"

Onegus tensed. Were his fangs showing?

Usually, he had excellent control over every part of his body, including the scents that could reveal his emotions to other immortals. That was one of the things that made him such a good chief and negotiator for Kian. But it had been centuries since a female had elicited such a strong response from him.

"What do you mean?" He put his hand on the small of her back and led her to the table he'd reserved.

As they passed by the other guests, there was no male who didn't devour her with his eyes, and Onegus had to stifle the urge to growl a warning that would have them cowering beneath the tables.

"I didn't notice it last night, but you look like you haven't been out in the sun in years. You are so white that it's blinding." She pretended to shield her eyes from the glare. "I hope that you put sunscreen on before leaving your lair or you will turn red like a cooked shrimp."

Onegus couldn't get a tan even if he wanted to. His body's self-healing would take care of that. "I have to admit that I didn't." He pulled out a chair for her. "But I probably should have." He waited until she sat down before taking the seat next to her.

Lifting her large purse, Cassandra sifted through the contents and pulled out a small tube. "You're lucky that I always carry sunscreen with me. If there is one thing you can do to slow down aging, it's to put it on every morning even if you don't plan on being out in the sun. Especially with fair skin like yours, wrinkles and dark spots are not the only things to worry about."

She handed it to him. "At least cover your face, and don't forget your ears, your nose, and the back of your neck."

Cassandra

"Yes, ma'am." Onegus popped the cover and squeezed out a small dollop into the palm of his hand.

Thankfully, he was still smiling after her idiotic tirade about his paleness and sunscreen. Had she put her foot in it again by bringing up a taboo subject?

And then she'd made things worse by lecturing him about it.

Cassandra was socially inept on most days, but the impact of seeing Onegus with those powerful muscles of his on display had scrambled her brain, making it much worse.

He'd looked amazing in a tux, and when he'd taken his jacket off, she'd seen the outline of those biceps through his dress shirt. But the white short-sleeved button-down that was open at the throat was much more revealing. He looked good enough to eat in it, not to mention the jeans, which were lovingly hugging his muscular thighs.

Distracted by her thoughts, she hadn't noticed the strange way he was going about smearing the sunscreen on his face until he asked, "Am I doing it right?"

He had a big white spot on his nose and two more on his cheeks. The rest of the sunscreen was still on the palm of his hand, and he was using it by dipping a finger in it and dabbing it on his face.

She chuckled. "Do you mind if I do that?"

"Not at all."

Leaning over the table, she gently spread the sunscreen all over his face, including behind his ears. The guy didn't have any wrinkles or dark spots, and his skin was smooth and soft, as if he got daily facials.

"How do you manage to have such great skin when you don't even know how to put sunscreen on?"

"I spend most of my days in a windowless office." He smiled, and her core clenched. "I guess I live like a vampire. Usually, when I leave the office, it's already dark outside."

She arched a brow. "A billionaire working in an office with no windows? How come? Are you afraid of someone spying on you through the glass?"

As his smile faltered, Cassandra wondered whether she'd committed another faux pas. She was so bad at simple social interactions that it was pathetic.

Perhaps she should hire a coach.

He leaned over the table. "I'll let you in on a secret. I'm just an employee, and I don't own the family business empire. Are you disappointed?"

Actually, it was a huge relief. If he was just a regular guy, working for his family's business, there was a chance that they could have a normal relationship. Provided that she didn't blow it up, that is, figuratively speaking or literally.

"I'm terribly disappointed." She leaned back and crossed her arms over her chest, pretending to be mad. "I finally meet a billionaire who looks like the ones on the covers of romance novels, and he turns out to be just a poor schmo, whose office is in the basement."

Onegus's left brow lifted. "I didn't say that I was poor. I'm not a billionaire, but I'm quite wealthy. And as for my office, I choose to work underground for various reasons."

Bummer.

Uncrossing her arms, Cassandra let out a sigh. "That's a shame. I was hoping that you were an ordinary person like me."

"There is nothing ordinary about you." He reached for her hand and clasped it in his much larger one. "You are radiating with inner power, and I find it sexy as hell."

Yeah, sexy, until things started exploding.

So far she'd been lucky, but if he kept looking at her like that, she wouldn't be able to contain that energy for much longer.

Perhaps a quick trip to the ladies' room was in order?

Gross.

Besides, how did he know?

The most anyone ever suspected her of was being a jinx. Kevin often joked about the office gremlins who caused pottery to crack, or the phones to malfunction, and all the other small damages that her temper had been responsible for.

"What's that grimace for?" Onegus asked.

"What did you mean by power?"

"I can sense it. It's like your body is humming with an electric current. Can't you feel it?"

"I don't know what you're talking about."

"Liar." He smiled and lifted her hand to his lips. "Remember what happened when our hands touched last night?"

She shrugged. "It was static electricity. It's not happening now, is it?"

He eyed her from under his dense, blond lashes. "I can still feel it, and it turns me on."

Cassandra scrambled for a quick change of topic.

"By the way, I didn't forget your jacket. I have it in my car. Remind me to give it back to you before we leave."

"There is no rush." He lifted his hand and motioned for the waiter to come to their table. "You are mine for the entire day."

She pulled her hand out of his. "What if I have other plans?"

"Do you?"

"No, but you shouldn't assume."

He dipped his head. "My apologies. It has been a very long time since I last dated, and I'm out of practice."

With his admission, a warm feeling washed over Cassandra, which was very strange since she could think of only one reason a gorgeous man like him hadn't been dating. He must have been married, and it had ended recently. But she was comforted by the fact that he was also unsure and fumbled with social rules.

"Apology accepted. God knows that I have no right to preach about etiquette."

Onegus

Onegus was enjoying himself way more than he should.

After a couple of drinks, Cassandra had loosened up, her smiles were coming in more easily, and she'd become less guarded.

Other than getting upset over the slow service and the waiter's dismissive attitude, Cassandra seemed to be enjoying his company as much as he was enjoying hers, but she was still far from trusting him.

So far, she'd refused to acknowledge the swirling energy he sensed in her, flat out denying that it even existed. One explanation could be that she wasn't aware of it, the other that she was afraid to admit it, which raised the question of why.

It had intensified when she'd gotten angry, leading him to believe that it was connected to her emotions.

As the waiter dropped their bill on the table and left, Onegus pulled a couple of hundreds out of his wallet and put them inside the folder.

"Are you ready for a walk on the beach?" He rose to his feet.

She was still eyeing the money he'd left. "We need to wait for the waiter to bring you the change."

"That's okay. He can keep the rest."

She shook her head. "That's a very generous tip, and it wasn't earned. The guy did a lousy job serving us, and he was cranky."

"True, but it wasn't his fault. He was the only waiter up here, serving all the tables by himself." He offered her a hand up.

"I don't think it's right to reward a subpar performance." She took his hand reluctantly, and just like the day before, the current arced between them.

"Did you feel that?"

She waved her other hand in dismissal. "Static electricity again. We must have opposite charges or something." She glanced in the waiter's direction. "He didn't even ask if we needed anything else before dropping the bill on the table, and you left him an eighty-dollar tip."

"How do you know that? You didn't see the bill."

"I didn't have to. I estimated how much our lunch and drinks cost given the prices on the menu."

He chuckled. "Let it go, Cassandra. It's not worth getting upset over."

"Yeah, you're right." She sent another baleful look at the waiter before lifting her bag and slinging the strap across her body.

As they started to walk away, someone dropped a glass, cursing as shards and liquids spread over the floor.

Onegus slowed his steps, but Cassandra ignored the incident as if nothing had happened and tugged on his hand, pulling him behind her.

"I want to see if anyone got hurt."

"It was just a glass. Nothing major." She kept walking.

For some reason, he had a feeling there was a connection between the drop of energy he sensed from her and the shattered glass.

Telekinesis?

He'd never met anyone who actually possessed the talent, and those he'd heard about sounded like charlatans. That didn't mean that the talent didn't exist, though.

Could Cassandra have somehow caused the glass to fall?

Only that didn't make much sense. If she wanted to get back at the waiter, she would have directed her power at a glass he was holding and not at some random customer. Then again, her intention might have been to create more work for him.

After all, the waiter would have to clean up the mess.

In all likelihood, she'd had nothing to do with it, and it was just his wishful thinking. A paranormal talent was a possible indicator of dormancy, and Onegus would have loved Cassandra to be one.

If she was a potential Dormant, he would be justified in seeking another date with her, seducing her, making love to her.

Fates, how he wanted to strip the hellcat naked, grab her succulent ass in his hands, and have his way with her. He had no doubt that she would be magnificent.

As they left the boardwalk and neared the waterline, Cassandra pulled the tube of sunscreen out of her purse. "You should reapply the sunscreen. It has been more than two hours since you applied it last."

Remembering how it felt to have her gentle fingers smearing the lotion on his face, he nodded. "Sure, why not?"

When she offered him the tube, he shook his head. "You'd better put it on me. You've seen how bad I am with that."

"Okay." She flipped the cap and squeezed a dollop into the palm of her hand.

Cassandra was tall, but without the stilettos she was still half a head shorter than Onegus, and as she looked up at him, her eyes zeroed in on his lips.

Did she want him to kiss her?

Cassandra

Damn, the guy had the most kissable lips. And those aquamarine eyes of his beheld her with such stark need that Cassandra found herself tilting toward him and parting her lips.

"You keep looking at me like that, and I'm going to kiss you regardless of who's watching."

Yes, she wanted to say. *Do it*. But that was such a bad idea.

After what had happened at the rooftop bar, some of the excess energy built up had been released, allowing her to breathe freely, and she would be a fool to let it accumulate again.

Except, they were on the beach, with nothing that could fall or explode in their vicinity.

Eh, what the hell. She only lived once.

Lifting on her toes, Cassandra quickly closed the distance between them and brushed her lips over his.

Sparks exploded, and she took a step back, quickly glancing around to check if anything had happened.

"That's it?" Onegus reached for her waist and pulled her against his rock-hard body. "That wasn't a kiss," he murmured against her lips. "That was a tease."

His mouth slammed over hers, and as her arms wrapped around his neck, she stifled a moan. Unapologetic, his tongue pushed past her lips, and she allowed it, leaning into his firm body and opening for him with a ravenous hunger that had roared to life once she released the leash.

Long minutes passed, and still he kissed her, and she didn't make a move to pull away or stop him, not until she was out of breath and it was either let go or pass out from lack of oxygen.

Someone behind them clapped, then whistled and made a lewd comment, but for once, Cassandra ignored the taunting, her eyes holding Onegus's gaze.

He smirked. "Now, that's what I call a kiss."

She lifted her sunscreen-covered palm. "I smeared it all over your neck."

He laughed. "I won't get sunburned there for sure." He took her hand. "Let's keep moving, or I'll go for another one. That kiss just whetted my appetite for more."

Hers too.

Cassandra had never been kissed like that, with such passion, such raw need, and she'd responded in kind.

She was tempted to drag Onegus back to that hotel and rent a room, tossing her rule about no hookups and caution to the wind.

"I should put some sunscreen on your face," she murmured.

"I don't think it's safe." He didn't look at her, keeping his eyes on the shore meandering before them. "Tell me more about yourself. Distract me."

Cassandra had a feeling that she needed distracting more than he did. Besides, she wanted to find out more about him, not the other way around. She still didn't know much about him other than his family owned the conglomerate he'd represented in the charity gala, and that he was just one of many owners. The quick internet search she'd done this morning hadn't revealed anything more than she'd already known, and curiously, there had been no stories about him dating heiresses or movie stars or hobnobbing with politicians. It seemed like he emerged once a year to attend the charity gala and then disappeared again.

"You know more about me than I know about you. Tell me something about yourself that you haven't told me yet."

He cast her a sidelong glance. "Only if you tell me something that no one else knows about you."

She laughed. "There are many things no one knows about me, and for good reason."

"Tell me one."

"I have a temper."

He chuckled. "I bet that's not a secret."

"It gets worse if I keep it bottled up. That's why people sometimes think that I'm rude." She looked up at him. "Your turn."

"I've never been in love. Have you?"

She nodded. "Twice."

"What happened?"

"I got disappointed. My mom thinks that my expectations are too high and that I'm picky, but that's not true. I have had requirements that I wasn't willing to compromise on, and when they were not met, I preferred to end things and move on. It kind of soured me on the whole dating thing. Besides, I don't have time to go out and meet people. I often work sixteen-hour days."

"What about the people you work with?"

She rolled her eyes. "Most of them are snowflakes a decade younger than me, and I have nothing in common with them." She sighed. "Frankly, I don't feel like I have a lot in common with anyone other than Kevin and Josie. Both of them are ambitious, hard-working, and nothing has been handed to them on a silver platter. They worked hard to get to where they are today, and they sacrificed a lot. More than I did."

"What do you mean?"

"They gave up on having kids. They are both in their late forties, so I assume it's no longer an option."

"Do you want children?"

"Very much so. How about you?"

He nodded. "With the right mate, of course."

She arched a brow. "A mate?"

"Significant other, wife, life-long partner. I'm tired of being alone." He smiled sadly. "I live with a roommate, even though I don't have to. I'm damn grateful to have a good friend who welcomes me home and asks about my day, but that's not the same as having a mate."

Onegus sounded even lonelier than she was. How was it possible? The guy was gorgeous, successful, and rich. Did he have some heinous hidden flaw she wasn't aware of?

"You must have women throwing themselves at you left and right. Why are you alone?"

"I could ask you the same question."

"In my case, that's kind of obvious. I'm opinionated, uncompromising, demanding, and I scare men away. I'm also all work and no play, and I live with my mother."

He laughed. "For someone with a natural knack for marketing, you are not doing a great job at selling yourself."

"I don't want to sell myself. You either like the package, the good and the bad, or not. I don't believe in false advertising."

Onegus lifted her hand and kissed her fingers. "I like the entire package very much. What are you doing tomorrow?"

"Working."

"I want to see you again."

"I want that too. What do you have in mind?"

He smirked. "I can come to your house, introduce myself to your mother, and then take you out on a date."

"Are you trying to knock out the items on my list of demands as quickly as possible?"

"Busted." He let go of her hand and wrapped his arm around her. "You are the boss, Cassandra. You decide the when and where. I decide the how. Just don't torture me for too long."

What did he mean by *I decide the how?* And why had his words excited her, making every female part of her tingle?

Vlad

"Hi, everyone." Wendy walked into Stella and Richard's home with two large bags in each hand. "I had a great time with Sharon and Tessa." She lifted the bags. "There was a huge sale at the outlet, and I went a little wild."

"The important thing is that you had fun." Vlad kissed her cheek and took the bags from her.

"What did you get?" Stella asked.

"I got three pairs of jeans, size four, five T-shirts, size small, and two dresses, also size small."

Vlad wanted to say that she was losing too much weight, but they'd had that discussion so many times that he'd gotten tired of bringing it up.

Perhaps he should ask Vanessa to intervene.

"I also got two pairs of shoes and a gorgeous pair of boots." Wendy lifted one of the bags. "Do you want to see?"

"Of course."

As the two grabbed the rest of the bags and ducked into the master bedroom, Vlad sat down on the couch next to Richard. "I talked with Brundar earlier."

"About?"

"Our plans. He basically told me that it's not a big deal if a civilian uses thralling as long as no one gets hurt. A few days in a dungeon is probably all we will get for thralling the information out of the bastard."

Richard put down his newspaper on the coffee table. "I heard that Brundar got a whipping for something similar. And if that's in the cards, I can tell you right now that I'm not on board for that."

"Brundar chose to get whipped because he didn't want to waste time in the dungeon. Edna gave him the option, and he turned it down. He'd also beaten up the guy, so more than thralling was involved. Besides, Brundar hinted that we don't have to confess. We just need to be careful not to get caught."

Richard shook his head. "I don't want to break any clan laws. I'm a new member, and I've just gotten my freedom back and can come and go as I please. I don't want to lose my privileges over this. If we do it, we will have to confess." He took a deep breath. "Even if all we get as punishment are a few days in the dungeon, I might lose my job over it. I'll have to tell Kalugal and ask whether he's okay with me missing several days of work."

"If we get caught, I'll take the blame and say that you tried to stop me."

"I still need to ask Kalugal for a few days off to go with you. How am I going to excuse it?"

"You can tell him the truth or just say that you need to keep an eye on me, so I don't do something stupid. I don't think Kalugal is going to spill the beans to Edna. Then again, he could blurt something to Rufsur, and the guy could tell his mate. You'll have to ask him to keep it confidential."

"Good point." Richard turned his head to glance at the hallway. "Did you tell Wendy?"

"About my father?"

"That too. But I meant about what you want to do to hers."

"No to the first, and yes to the second. She's okay with me thralling him to get the information, but she doesn't want his blood on my hands. I promised her that I won't kill him."

Richard nodded. "Then you definitely need me with you. I'll ask Kalugal first thing tomorrow morning, and if he doesn't mind losing me for a few days, I'll book us a flight for Wednesday. We've been pussyfooting about this for long enough."

"I agree."

"When are you going to tell Wendy about your father? And why didn't you yet?"

Vlad shrugged. "There is nothing to tell because I don't know anything about the Kra-ell."

"You know where you got your strength from, and your eyes."

"That's unimportant. I need to find out what kind of people they are, and what I heard so far doesn't inspire confidence. I was much happier believing that my father was some random human."

Richard chuckled. "When your mother acted all mysterious about who your father was, I thought that he might have been a criminal, and that was why she'd kept his identity a secret. A human father is not necessarily better than a Kra-ell. Emmett isn't evil. He's smart, cunning, and self-serving, but he didn't kill or harm Eleanor, although he could have. So even though he's a bloodsucker, he's not a murderous bastard."

"Yeah, I guess. But he is a bloodsucker, and that's disturbing."

Richard regarded him with a smile tugging at his lips. "I assume that you never had a craving for blood."

"Gross. I get nauseous just thinking about it."

Richard shrugged. "I don't know why. You bite during sex, and there is always a little blood that you need to lick. Does that gross you out?"

"Of course not. It's Wendy's blood, and it's just a few drops."

"Did it taste good?"

It didn't taste bad, but he didn't crave it.

"It does, but I never felt the need to take more."

"But you don't get nauseous from licking her blood, so the rest is probably all in your head. If you didn't think of bloodsucking as gross, you might have enjoyed it, at least a little bit."

"Why? Do you think you would have liked it?"

"I'm the type of guy who's willing to try almost anything at least once before I knock it down."

Vlad grimaced. "I really don't want to hear about your sexual preferences. You are mated to my mother."

"You asked, and I answered."

Margaret

"Are you excited?" Ana lifted another section of Margaret's hair and wrapped it around the curling iron.

"I don't know what to think. Why is Bowen taking me out on a date?"

Ever since Ana and Leon had returned to the cabin, Bowen had been acting strange. He was as courteous and as helpful as before, but Margaret sensed a distance between them as if he was uncomfortable being around her.

At first, she'd thought that he'd figured out she was attracted to him and wanted to let her down gently, but then, out of the blue, he asked her out.

"Isn't it obvious?" Letting the curl she'd made cascade down Margaret's front, Ana separated another section to curl. "He likes you, and he wants to take your friendship to the next stage."

"What next stage? He hasn't given me any indications that he was interested. And why would he?" She waved her hand at the mirror she was sitting in front of. "Just look at me."

Ana released the curl and leaned over Margaret's head, looking at her in the mirror. "You are beautiful. You just haven't done anything to accentuate your beauty in ages. Once I'm done with you, you will look like a new woman." She sighed. "I wish I had told Leon to get some hair color when he and Bowen went shopping. Blond highlights would have brightened your face." She separated another section and wound it around the curling iron. "Except, God knows what he would have brought back. You can't send a guy to buy stuff like that."

Looking at the dark circles under her eyes and her hollow cheeks, Margaret doubted Ana would be able to pull off a miracle and transform her into a beauty with a curling iron and some makeup.

Even after more than a week of rest and being fed and pampered by Bowen, she still looked haggard. She wasn't attractive, not on the outside, and not on the inside. He just didn't know enough about her to realize that her lack of beauty was more than skin deep.

"Stop looking like you are getting ready for a funeral." Ana waved the iron around. "You are going to a nice restaurant with a handsome guy. Smile!"

When Margaret's smile turned out to look more like a grimace, Ana shook her head. "Close your eyes."

"Why?"

"Because I don't want to stare at your sad face when I'm trying to make you beautiful. Imagine happy things and try to relax. I'll tell you when I'm done."

"Yes, ma'am."

Margaret closed her eyes and imagined herself back at Safe Haven, teaching the workshop she'd started putting together in the cabin.

It was about making chocolates and truffles as an expression of love. What could be more satisfying than combining her favorite treat with craftsmanship and art? She doubted there would be even one community member who wouldn't want to participate.

The internet was a fabulous source of information, providing her with everything she ever needed to know about making chocolates. She'd watched YouTube videos, copied recipes and pictures, and neatly organized everything in the application Bowen had downloaded for her.

Perhaps now that Emmett was gone, she could convince Riley to allow community members to have computers and cell phones.

As time away from Safe Haven passed, Margaret's blind worship of Emmett and everything he'd preached was starting to fade. It made her sad to admit that Emmett hadn't been right about limiting the community's access to the internet. It was true that it was easy to get lost in it and get distracted away from productive endeavors, but there was so much information out there. So much to be learned. It was as if all of humanity's accumulated knowledge was accessible to everyone on the globe.

It was a revolution that had completely passed her by. But she was part of it now, and she wasn't willing to let it go. If Riley resisted, Margaret was going to fight her hard and put the issue to a community vote. With Emmett gone, they could become a real commune, where everyone had a voice.

At some point during her musings, Ana switched from doing her hair to applying makeup. It was like getting a massage or a facial. It was relaxing, and Margaret wasn't even curious to see the transformation. Given the canvas Ana had to work with, there was only so much she could do.

"You can open your eyes." Ana patted her shoulder.

"I don't want to."

"Why not?"

"Until I see myself, I can imagine that you've managed a miracle. When I open my eyes, I'll have to face reality."

"I think you'll be pleasantly surprised." Ana gently squeezed her shoulder. "Come on, Margaret. On the count of three. One, two, three!"

Cracking one eye open experimentally, Margaret looked at the mirror, but it was hard to see with just one eye and she opened both.

"Oh, wow." She leaned closer. "You're good."

Her hair was no longer dull and hanging limply around her shoulders. Instead, soft, shiny waves framed her face. The dark circles were gone, and her big brown eyes were framed with a delicate dark brown line and black eyelashes. Coral tone lipstick added a splash of color to her face, which no longer looked grayish.

She actually looked pretty.

"Thank you."

Ana beamed at her through the mirror. "Now, let's get you dressed."

"My options are very limited."

Ana walked over to the closet and pulled out one of the three dresses Bowen had gotten for her. "Don't worry. We will make it work."

Bowen

Bowen was as nervous as a teenage boy going on his first date. He hadn't even told Margaret how beautiful she looked because he'd been too stunned by the transformation to say anything.

She'd expected him to say something, he'd seen it in her eyes, and yet the only words that had left his mouth had been, "Let's go. Our reservations are for eight."

Suave. It was a miracle he'd managed as many hookups as he had.

But what could he have said? That she looked beautiful because her hair was done and her makeup hid the dark shadows under her eyes? Nothing about her had changed intrinsically, and to compliment the superficial seemed wrong on some level.

Sitting next to him in the car, Margaret fidgeted with the clasp of her purse. "It was nice of you to think of a way to give Ana and Leon some privacy. Given the long drive, we will be gone for more than four hours. I'm sure they appreciate it."

Bowen wanted to bang his head against the wheel. Of course, Margaret would think that. He hadn't given her any reason to think that he wanted to spend time with her, to woo her.

"That's not why I asked you out."

She chuckled nervously. "That's okay. You won't hurt my feelings by admitting the truth. I'm happy to do this for them, and I will enjoy an evening out with you even if it's not a real date."

The woman was too selfless and unassuming for her own good.

"Is it so hard to believe that I asked you out because of you and no one else?"

Smiling, she turned to him. "We spend all of our days together. You don't need to ask me out to get to know me. I think that by now, you know me better than most of my friends in Safe Haven."

If that was true, then she didn't have any real friends. He knew practically nothing about her, aside from the things he'd guessed, and those were just speculation. The only glimpses she'd allowed him into her life before Safe Haven had been her admission to an opioid problem she'd overcome and her cryptic remark about having seen evil.

Bowen wanted to know more, but as long as he was just a friend, she had no reason to confide in him. He hadn't told her much about himself either.

But if they were to become more than friends, someone had to make the first move, and that someone had to be him.

"What if I want to be more than your friend?"

She laughed. "Oh, Bowen. Did Leon put you up to this?"

In a way he had, but she couldn't have known that, and it was irrelevant. Leon had just given him a push in the right direction.

"He has nothing to do with it."

It took Margaret a long time to respond. "Why would a guy like you be interested in me?"

"Why not? You are smart, compassionate, and pretty."

"I'm nothing special. I have very little going for me, and I live in a community that you consider a cult. I really don't understand what's your game, Bowen. I have nothing you need or want." She turned her face to look out the window.

If Margaret was a Dormant, she had everything he needed, but he couldn't tell her that.

"I feel a pull toward you, and I know that you feel it too. All I want is a chance to explore it, and I'd rather have a nice talk away from the cabin over dinner in a restaurant." He turned toward her and smiled. "Besides, you've been cooped up in that cabin for days on end. I figured you would enjoy a night out."

"It was very nice of you to take me out to dinner." Margaret let out a breath. "It's just that you are doing so much for me, and I don't understand why. No one is that selfless."

He shrugged. "I told you my motives. I needed a vacation, and you provided me with a perfect excuse to take one."

She cast him a sidelong glance. "We both know that was just an excuse. You did it for Leon and Ana."

"In part." He took a deep breath. "So, here's the truth. Something about you called to me, and I couldn't bring myself to let go of you. In fact, every time I think about you returning to Safe Haven, I feel an ache right here." He rubbed a hand over his chest.

"I feel the same," she murmured. "It makes sense why I feel that way, but it doesn't for you."

"We are about to figure it out." He cast her an amused smile. "Relax, Margaret. We are only going to a restaurant, not eloping to Vegas."

Margaret

For the rest of the drive, Margaret tried to keep things from getting too serious.

Bowen was right. It was just a date, and neither of them was committing to anything other than enjoying each other's company. So she talked about her workshop, and how she was planning to convince Riley to allow computers and cellphones for each one of the community members.

Bowen nodded. "The retreats generate enough money to allow for much more luxury than the community members enjoy. The question is whether people will keep coming without Emmett's charismatic presence adding to the mystic allure of Safe Haven."

She hadn't thought of that. "Perhaps we can keep pretending that he's still there."

Bowen chuckled. "Doing what? Meditating in his secret chapel?"

"Why not?" She lifted her arms. "We can claim that by meditating, Emmett is projecting his awesomeness to every guest of the retreat."

It was so much easier to talk with Bowen about anything other than their so-called relationship.

As long as he hadn't shown interest in her, Margaret had successfully stifled her attraction to him, and she would have preferred to keep it that way. Having him as a friend was better than losing him entirely because she desired a man she shouldn't. But now that Bowen was hinting at his interest, her subdued urges were bubbling to the surface.

"Unfortunately, they don't have a valet service at this place," Bowen said as he turned into the restaurant's parking lot. "It's not as fancy as I would have liked it to be." He cast her an apologetic smile. "But a place like that would have taken another forty-five-minute drive."

"I don't want anything fancy, and I can hobble to the entrance."

"I have the wheelchair in the trunk. Do you prefer that to the crutches?"

"Actually, I do. It will be easier for everyone if you just wheel me in instead of me hobbling on one foot. There'll be less staring."

He let out a breath. "I love how reasonable you are. If it were Anastasia, she would have insisted on walking."

He was probably right. Ana was prideful, while Margaret's pride had been stripped away a long time ago. When she insisted on fending for herself, it was because she didn't want to be a burden, not because she was embarrassed to accept assistance.

Help wasn't offered often or freely, and when it was, she'd learned to take it and say thank you.

Life was difficult enough as it was.

Bowen took the wheelchair out of the trunk, unfolded it, and then pushed it to her side of the car. When he opened the door and reached for her, Margaret didn't argue even though she could have gotten into the chair on her own.

She probably should have, though.

Being carried in his strong arms, inhaling his masculine scent, it was impossible to suppress her raw attraction to him.

He lowered her gently into the chair and then draped the coat Ana had loaned her over her knees. "Ready?"

"Yes, sir."

When they entered the restaurant, the hostess smiled at her. "Skiing accident?"

"I wish. Unfortunately, it was just a bad fall."

"I hope you get better soon," she said and turned her attention to Bowen. "This way, please." She sauntered in front of them, sashaying her shapely hips and butt for Bowen's benefit.

To his credit, his eyes hadn't shifted to her ass even once.

When they were seated, the hostess handed them the menus, flashed Bowen an inviting smile, and sashayed away.

"She couldn't have been more obvious if she tried," Margaret murmured from behind the open menu.

"She's just a kid."

Margaret lowered the folder. "She's no more than a couple of years younger than you."

"I'm not as young as I look."

She'd never asked him how old he was, but he couldn't be more than thirty. Should she ask?

"How old are you?"

He smiled. "Guess."

"Twenty-nine?"

"Guess again."

"Thirty?"

He shook his head.

"Twenty-seven?"

"You're getting colder."

"Just tell me."

"You have to guess."

The waiter's arrival stopped the guessing game, but after they ordered, it was on again.

"Thirty-one."

When he shook his head, Margaret kept going until she reached her own age. "No way." She crossed her arms over her chest. "You can't be thirty-eight."

He smirked. "I didn't say that I was."

"Thirty-nine?"

Bowen shrugged.

"Show me your driver's license."

"Why? Don't you believe me?"

"I don't. You just want me to feel more comfortable with you."

"I give you my word that I'm older than you."

"You don't know how old I am."

"Yes, I do. Did you forget that I was in the hospital with you when you were admitted? You filled out the questionnaire right next to me."

"You must tell me your secret then. How do you manage to look so young?"

He winked. "I work out a lot."

Other than lifting her and carrying her around, Margaret hadn't seen Bowen exercise even once in all the time they'd been together in the cabin. But then he usually woke up hours before her, so he might have finished his workout routine by the time she got up.

"That's it." She tapped the table. "Once this damn cast is off, I'm starting to lift weights every day. Apparently, my walks on the beach are not doing the trick."

"To build muscle, you need to eat protein, and you don't eat enough of it or anything else for that matter. Chocolate doesn't count."

"You are right. I should have ordered the steak in addition to the fish." She lifted her hand, pretending to summon the waiter.

"Don't forget a side of spinach." He flexed both arms without even lifting them.

The bulges were impressive enough to draw the attention of other diners.

How could he be older than her? He'd given her his word that he was, and Bowen wasn't the type of guy who would do that and lie.

Perhaps he was just blessed with incredible genes.

Bowen

"Did you enjoy yourself?" Bowen asked as he pulled out of the restaurant's parking lot.

"I did. Thank you." Margaret readjusted her dress. "In fact, I don't remember ever enjoying myself as much."

It had been a very pleasant evening, especially after he'd convinced Margaret that he was older than her. Bowen had employed Leon's tactics, and they had worked remarkably well. All he'd said was that he was older and let her assume the rest. She'd stopped guessing at thirty-nine.

Still, if that was the most Margaret had ever enjoyed herself, her life must have been pretty dull. It wasn't surprising given how long she'd lived in Safe Haven, basically working herself to the bone.

"I'm glad." He reached over the center console and gripped her slim hand. "We should do it again tomorrow."

She didn't pull her hand out of his. "You're spoiling me, Bowen." She looked at their conjoined hands. "But the truth is that I'm well enough to return to Safe Haven, and I shouldn't keep you away from your work any longer."

"You still need help."

"Not really. I can shower by myself, and I can get dressed without help. I also suspect that Leon and Ana are staying in the cabin for my sake. We all need to get back to our lives."

"Not yet." He lifted her hand and brushed his lips over her knuckles. "Stay at least until next Monday."

"That's an entire week."

"It will give you time to get stronger. Besides, my goal of fattening you up hasn't been achieved yet. I want you to gain at least five pounds before you return to Safe Haven."

She chuckled. "There are no scales in the cabin. How would you know if I gained anything?"

"Easy. My arms will be the scales, and I'll weigh you every morning."

Given the soft curve of her lips, she liked the idea. "Frankly, I'm not in a rush to go back. I just don't want to keep the three of you from getting on with your lives."

He cast her a sidelong glance. "If you want to get rid of Leon and Anastasia, just say the word. I wouldn't mind having you all to myself."

She swallowed. "I don't think that's a good idea."

"Are you scared of being alone with me?"

"What? No! Of course not. You are the only man other than Emmett who I feel safe with." She looked at her cast. "I'm no good for you, Bowen."

"Because of that? That's temporary."

"It's still going to be there by next Monday. But that's not the only thing that's broken about me." She let out a sigh. "Do you really want to get involved with a former junkie?"

"As long as it is former and not current, it doesn't bother me. You've hinted at it enough times, so it's not like I didn't know. Getting over addiction and keeping clean is a monumental achievement. You should be proud of it rather than ashamed."

"There is nothing to be proud of. I was young, weak, and stupid, and I got addicted to painkillers. I wasn't able to stop, and I only sank deeper and deeper." She lowered her head. "It got so bad that I was willing to do anything for my next fix."

His heart broke for her.

Had she sold her body for drugs?

"It's not what you think," she whispered. "I didn't prostitute myself, but I deliberately sought injury to get hospitalized and prescribed more painkillers."

He didn't want to think about how she'd done that, but he had a good idea.

"How did you get out of it?"

"I was forced into rehab. While I was there, I met a woman who told me about Safe Haven. At the time, it seemed like my only option. I had nowhere to go and no money, and I was afraid for my life."

"Why were you afraid?" He had a good idea, but he needed to hear it from her.

Margaret shook her head. "That's a story for another time, or maybe never."

Bowen didn't want to press her. She was opening to him, telling him things she hadn't before, and if he insisted, she might clam up again.

"How did you get to Safe Haven?"

She smiled. "I hitchhiked. Even though I was a recovering junkie, I was still pretty back then. It took me nearly a week to get to Safe Haven, and when I did, I looked like a dirty, starved rat. Emmett took me in, no questions asked. Later, I told him everything, and he still gave me a home and a job. With Emmett's help, I was reborn in Safe Haven, becoming a completely different person."

"He did a good deed, but that doesn't compensate for what he did to you and the other females in your community. I'm surprised that you never suspected him of drugging you."

"Do you know what kind of drugs he used? Maybe they were just mild relaxants?"

"I have no idea. We should have searched his place, but there was no time."

Margaret nodded. "I don't know what he has done to your people directly, but if they ever catch him, tell them to be kind to him. I'm not mad at Emmett for what he has allegedly done to me, and I bet the others aren't either. In my opinion, Emmett's good deeds outweigh the bad."

Bowen wasn't sure of that. He hadn't heard the latest updates from the interrogation. He should call Peter and ask him what else had been uncovered. Most likely, it was nothing good.

Eleanor

It was early in the morning when Eleanor made her way to the office building, the cold air cooling her heated face. When she'd sent Kian a text message asking to speak with him, she hadn't expected him to invite her to come to his office right away.

What she needed to talk to him about wasn't urgent, and her text hadn't implied that it was.

The café was still closed, but a few people were already sitting at the tables, enjoying coffee and pastries from the vending machines. A couple of males even smiled her way, which was new.

It could be because they had heard of her breakup with Greggory, or perhaps people were starting to view her more favorably now that she'd proven her loyalty to the clan.

The office building's front door was open, but she didn't encounter anyone as she climbed to the second floor. The place was completely quiet, which meant that no one other than Kian started their workday that early.

As she reached his door, Eleanor took a deep breath and knocked.

"Come in." His gruff voice didn't sound welcoming.

Perhaps he was pissed about something else. The guy had a thousand balls in the air at all times, and she was just the thousand and one.

Depressing the handle, Eleanor pushed the door open and walked in. "Thanks for agreeing to see me." She closed it behind her.

"Take a seat." The gruff tone didn't soften, but he motioned to the chairs in front of his desk.

"Thank you." She pulled one out and sat down.

"How can I help you, Eleanor?"

She smiled nervously. "Perhaps the better question is how can I help you." She straightened her back and forced herself to look into his intense eyes. "Since I am immune to compulsion, I think that I should be part of the team guarding Emmett."

"Annani compelled Emmett not to use his compulsion on clan members, so that's no longer an issue. Besides, you are not a Guardian yet."

"I'm training."

"You won't be ready for many years, and don't think I'm saying that because I don't trust you, it just takes that long to go through the training."

"Physically, I might not be anywhere near the Guardians' level of ability, but I have the kind of experience that's precisely what's needed in this case, and I believe that I can do a better job with Emmett than they can. Especially given my immunity and my other assets."

"Annani also compelled Emmett to tell her everything he knows about his people."

Eleanor smiled. "Compulsion is good for many things, but not for getting information unless you know exactly what to ask. If you don't believe me, ask Peter. He managed to avoid answering many of Emmett's questions."

"I hadn't considered that, but you are right." Leaning back, Kian regarded her for a long moment. "Perhaps you can be part of a team. I'll have to discuss this with Onegus."

"So, is it a yes or a maybe?"

"It's a maybe."

"When will you have an answer for me?"

He leaned forward. "First, tell me why you want to guard Emmett. Do you want to get back at him for what he did to you?"

"I'm madder about what Emmett did to Peter than what he did to me, but revenge is not my motive."

"Then what is? I know that you are not doing it out of the goodness of your heart or because you believe that you are the best woman for the job."

Damn. She didn't mind telling Peter or even Magnus why she needed to do this, but admitting her real motives to Kian would be awkward in the extreme.

"Well?" He arched a brow.

"Actually, I do believe that I'm the best woman for the job. Emmett is attracted to me." She pushed her chest out. "When Kri suggested I volunteer for the job, she put it quite crudely. She said that boobs make men stupid, meaning that as a female, I have a better chance of getting Emmett to reveal information that he would never have shared with the male Guardians."

Kian looked surprised. "Do you plan on seducing him?"

Eleanor shrugged. "I'm single again, so why not? I can scratch an itch and help the clan at the same time. It's a win-win."

He nodded. "I'm sorry that things didn't work out between you and Greggory."

"Yeah, well. Me too. But it is what it is, and I'm ready to move on."

"To Emmett?"

"Maybe." She chuckled. "It's so like me to go for the worst possible candidate. First, I choose a former Doomer, and then I move on to a member of another potentially hostile immortal species, who is locked up in a cell indefinitely. I need a third option. A nice clan member who doesn't think that I'm a shrew."

Kian cracked a smile. "I'm sure there are plenty of those. But in case you develop feelings for Emmett, you won't be falling for a lifer. I promised him a place in the village provided that the information he gave me about the last location of his people is true."

"What if they moved to a different location and didn't leave any traces behind?"

"Then the deal is off. Emmett will have to earn his freedom some other way."

Kian

"Good morning, boss." Onegus strode into Kian's office and pulled out a chair. "How is your day going so far?" He spread his long legs in front of him.

"You seem in a good mood. I assume that the gala was successful?"

"Very much so. Brandon says that the contributions were even larger than the year before." Onegus flashed him his signature smile. "I would like to think that it was my speech that made the difference."

"Bridget said that you dismissed most of her suggestions."

Onegus shrugged. "I only took out the tearjerkers. I left everything else in. People come to events like that to enjoy themselves, to hobnob, to mingle, to be seen. You can't douse them with depressing stuff and expect them to be in a charitable mood. The best way to encourage them to donate is to show them how much good their money will do, insert a little humor and humility, and sprinkle it with some individual success stories to bring it home."

Kian hadn't seen Onegus this upbeat in a long time, and he doubted the generous pledges were solely responsible for it.

"Did you enjoy yourself?"

The grin splitting Onegus's face was infectious. "More than I expected."

He had probably met someone whose company he'd enjoyed, but Kian wasn't interested in the details.

"Eleanor came to see me earlier. She wants to be part of the team that guards Emmett."

"Why? Does she want revenge?"

"That was my reaction as well, but that's not what she's after. Kri convinced Eleanor that she has a better chance of getting Emmett to open up than any of us, and she might be onto something."

Onegus shook his head. "Once was not enough for her? Eleanor already played that part with Emmett in Safe Haven, and it didn't end well for her."

"Indeed." Kian nodded. "She also lost Greggory because of it. Apparently, he couldn't handle what happened between her and Emmett, which would give the revenge hypothesis more credence, especially given Eleanor's personality. She's not the forgive and forget type. On the other hand, she admitted to feeling a strange attraction to Emmett, so it might be about her need to explore that."

Onegus rubbed a finger over the cleft in his chin. "That complicates things. It's one thing for her to go into it with a cold heart and manipulate Emmett to open up to her. It's another thing altogether if she falls for the bloodsucker."

Kian crossed his arms over his chest. "I don't see a problem with that. Carol fell for Lokan, but she never betrayed our trust even once. The clan came before her feelings for him, and him falling for her played a big part in his willingness to cooperate with us and reveal the location of the Doomers' island."

"Eleanor is not Carol. But we can mitigate the risk by assigning Peter to the case as well. He knows her, and he can keep an eye on her."

"I like your idea with one caveat. Peter also has a grudge against Emmett, even worse than Eleanor, and if I put him in charge, things could get ugly."

"Peter wouldn't do anything that wasn't sanctioned by you or me. And having him in charge might be another way to encourage Emmett's cooperation."

Uncrossing his arms, Kian leaned forward. "Are you comfortable with promoting Peter? It would be the first time he'd be in charge."

"He's experienced enough, and this is a low-risk assignment. I'm not worried."

Peter had failed his Safe Haven mission, but it hadn't been his fault. Kian, Onegus, and Turner were as much to blame as he was. The problem was that none of them had taken Eleanor's suspicion seriously. It had been a curiosity that Kian had wanted to investigate, and they hadn't put in place contingencies in the event that her suspicions were correct. They had also relied too much on Eleanor's immunity to compulsion. None of them could have suspected that Emmett was a different breed of immortal who was incredibly strong physically, on top of being a powerful compeller.

"Put Peter in charge, but have him report to Magnus or directly to you, and keep an eye on him."

"Done. When do you want him to start?"

"As soon as possible. I want to send Arwel to China, and Peter will need a few days to learn the routine."

"What about Eleanor? Do you want them to start at the same time?"

"First, let's summon them both and see if they are willing to work together."

"I don't see why not." Onegus pulled out his phone. "I assume that you want to see them right away?"

"Indeed." Kian opened the drawer and pulled out his cigarillo box. "I'm going to take a break on the roof. Text me when they get here."

Eleanor

One advantage of working for Kian, Eleanor realized, was how fast he made and implemented his decisions. He'd promised her an answer right after he spoke with Onegus, and since they were meeting right now, she expected him to call her back soon.

It didn't make sense to go back home, and she decided to go for a walk around the old village instead. She could use the quiet time to sharpen her arguments in case the answer was no.

Eleanor needed this assignment, and not just so she could be close to Emmett and figure out what had caused her attraction to him.

The simple truth was that she needed a job, and being Kri's assistant in self-defense classes wasn't it.

She had plenty of money saved up, and now that she was free to leave the village, she had access to it, but having a job wasn't just about earning an income. She needed to be busy, and she needed to be challenged. Working out for hours a day had made her into a lean, mean fighting machine, but if she couldn't use it, then what was the point?

When the text from Kian came, Eleanor turned around and jogged back to the office building. After taking the stairs two at a time, she forced herself to slow down as she walked down the corridor and then knocked on Kian's door.

"Come in!"

When she walked into the office, Onegus flashed her his toothy smile. "How did you get here so fast? Were you waiting in the café?"

"I took a walk." She pulled out a chair and sat next to him at the oblong conference table.

"We need to wait for Peter." The chief leaned back and crossed his arms over his chest.

"What does Peter have to do with my assignment?"

"Since the two of you seem to work so well together, Kian and I decided to have you both stationed in the keep."

"What about Arwel? With all due respect to Emmett and his powers, he doesn't need so many people to guard him."

Kian lifted a hand. "Let's wait for Peter to get here. I don't want to answer every question twice."

"Makes sense." The problem was that now she would have to engage in small talk, and she sucked at it. "How did the gala go?" she asked Onegus.

His smile was so broad that he was all teeth. "Excellent. We collected so much money that we have enough to open another halfway house."

"Do we need more than one?"

"If we have more room, we can let the residents stay longer. Julian and Vanessa are complaining that they need to nudge them to move on before they are ready."

Eleanor shrugged. "Nudging is good. It forces them to become independent sooner, and once they are, they feel better about themselves. Dependency might feel safe, but it doesn't feel good."

"Not everyone is as tough as you, Eleanor," Kian said.

"Thank you. That's the best compliment you've ever given me."

Kian looked as if he was about to retort when a knock sounded on the door, and Peter walked in. "Apologies for the late arrival." He looked at Onegus. "I was under the impression that I was still on a leave of absence, and your text found me in bed." He pulled out a chair on the chief's other side. "Do you have a new assignment for me?"

"I might." Onegus turned toward Peter. "But first, I need you to tell me how you feel about Emmett. Specifically, do you have the urge to tear his throat out when you see him?"

"Not at all. I'm not one to hold a grudge. Besides, if I were in the guy's position, I would have done the same thing. The survival of my people trumps any other considerations."

"Good." Onegus clapped him on the back. "I'm putting you in charge of the team guarding him. Congratulations."

Great. Peter hadn't even asked for it, and they were putting him in charge as if he had done such a great job in Safe Haven. Then again, she'd messed up as well.

Eleanor crossed her arms over her chest. "What about Arwel? Isn't he in charge?"

"He will be in charge of checking the information Emmett gave us." Kian turned to Peter. "Are you okay with the assignment?"

"Sure. I just got promoted. Does that mean a raise?"

Onegus chuckled. "Let's see first how well you do."

"What about me?" Eleanor asked. "What's my status?"

Onegus looked at Kian. "Do we officially make Eleanor a Guardian in training?"

Kian nodded and turned to her. "Guardians in training are paid a salary. It's much less than full-fledged Guardians are paid, but it's enough to live on, and it makes your status official."

Onegus extended his hand to her. "Welcome to the force."

"Thank you." She shook it. "I'm truly honored."

In fact, it was quite unbelievable. From a prisoner to a Guardian in training in a matter of months instead of years. She'd thought it would take forever before people stopped giving her the evil eye.

"When do we start?" Peter asked.

"You can start tomorrow," Onegus said. "Arwel will show you the routine, and you'll work under his supervision until he's comfortable leaving Emmett's guardianship in your hands."

Eleanor's stomach clenched. She hadn't expected it to happen so fast, but she was glad that it had. Waiting and thinking and speculating would have driven her nuts.

"It's a pleasure working with you." She smiled at him and then turned to Kian. "Things go from concept to execution in a matter of hours or days. When I still worked for the government, everything took forever."

"That's the advantage of a small organization," Onegus said. "There's no bureaucracy to deal with."

Arwel

"Are you sure about that?" Arwel rose to his feet and started pacing the length of the small living room.

He didn't like Kian's plan to put Eleanor and Peter in charge of guarding Emmett. The three had a history together, and it was never a good idea to have the prisoner and his jailers emotionally involved, either in a positive or negative way.

"Eleanor offered to use her feminine wiles on Emmett. I talked it over with Onegus, and he doesn't have a problem with that."

Arwel chuckled. "What feminine wiles? She is not a bad-looking woman, but she's not a seductress. Let's face it, Eleanor is not Carol."

"No one is like Carol, but as the saying goes, there is a lid for every pot, or is it the other way around? Anyway, Emmett might find Eleanor's assertiveness enticing since she's more like the females in his original community."

"Good point. I hadn't considered that. But since Annani compelled him to tell her everything about his people, what else can Eleanor learn?"

"Compulsion is not very effective for retrieving information. Unless you know exactly what to ask and how to phrase it, there are ways to work around it. That's how Peter managed to avoid telling Emmett our location or anything else that he could have used against us. Peter's experience taught us that compulsion is more effective at the physical level because the commands can be precise."

"You have a point. How do you want the transition to work?"

"Peter and Eleanor will be there sometime this afternoon, so you can give them an overview of what they are required to do. Perhaps it would be a good idea to have a talk with Emmett and tell him about the guard switch. They will start tomorrow morning, and you will need to stay for a few days to supervise. I want you to leave for China as soon as possible."

"We don't have a plan ready, and Jin hasn't given me her final answer yet."

"We will have to wing it. I don't want to waste time, and we need to collect information before Turner can devise a plan. He can do that while you are there."

"I can't argue with your logic. I'll talk with Jin when she comes over this afternoon."

Kian sighed. "I want to make myself clear. You are going with her or without her. I need you there at least for the initial investigation."

"She knows that."

"Good. Then we are all on the same page."

After Kian ended the call, Arwel kept pacing for several moments. It would be difficult to be apart from Jin, but he had a job to do, and he couldn't pick and choose his assignments based on her preferences.

Kian and Onegus accommodated the mated Guardians as much as they could, but Arwel had to agree that he was the best choice for this investigation. Well, if he had a mastery of Mandarin, that would have been better, but so far he hadn't made much progress with the Rosetta Stone. For immortals, learning a new language while being immersed in it was easier. Morris was fluent, though, and the pilot could be part of their team.

Arwel was still pacing when Jin walked into the suite an hour later. "Is this your new form of exercise?" She threw her purse on the couch and wrapped her arms around his neck.

He cupped her bottom and squeezed. "I much prefer a different form of physical activity."

She kissed him lightly on the lips. "Close the door, and it can be arranged."

"We need to talk."

Jin frowned. "About what?"

"China." He wrapped his arm around her waist and led her to the couch. "Kian is putting Eleanor and Peter in charge of Emmett, and as soon as I'm comfortable that they got the routine down, he wants me to head out there."

"I'm happy that you're getting out of the dungeon, but why Eleanor? She's not a Guardian, and frankly, I don't trust her."

"She's immune, and as Kian pointed out, she might be just the kind of woman Emmett would find irresistible. She would remind him of the females in his community."

"I don't know about that. Eleanor is full of bluster, but she's emotionally vulnerable, especially now that Greggory dumped her. Combine that with her intrinsic lack of moral compass, and the result could be the exact opposite of what Kian wants to achieve. Emmett might use her to either learn more about us or to get free."

"That's why they are putting Peter in charge." He clasped her hand. "If you don't want to come, that's okay. I won't be gone for more than a couple of weeks."

Jin shook her head. "I'm coming with you, but don't expect me to speak Mandarin anytime soon. I think that I'm linguistically challenged. I don't understand why it's so difficult for me. I'm already bilingual, but then I learned both English and Hebrew as a child." She sighed. "My adult brain is refusing to cooperate."

"It's difficult for me as well. I think immortals learn languages better by getting immersed in them. Perhaps our mental abilities let us absorb it from the humans we interact with."

"Like mental osmosis?"

"That's the idea. But that's just my hypothesis. I need to run it by Vanessa."

Jin shrugged. "She has enough on her plate. I guess we will find out when we get to China."

"I'm so glad that you decided to come with me. I don't know how I would've survived without you." Wrapping his arms around his mate, Arwel kissed her softly.

Margaret

"We are off on a walk." Ana waved goodbye. "We won't be back before dinner."

Margaret lifted her head and smiled. "Have fun."

"Plan to be back by six," Bowen said. "I'm firing up the grill at five forty-five. If you're late, you'll eat it cold."

"No problem," Leon said before closing the door.

Bending to look at her phone, Margaret pretended to return to her internet research.

Things had been a little awkward between her and Bowen. After admitting that he wanted more than friendship with her, he hadn't done anything differently from what he'd done before. He was still friendly and eager to help in any way he could. He gave her space and didn't try to talk to her while she was reading articles or collecting recipes for her workshop.

Did he expect her to make the first move?

If so, he would be waiting for a long time. Not because she didn't want to, but because she didn't have the nerve.

Margaret had never actually initiated the few interludes she'd had with community members. And the only reason she'd responded to their flirting was to avoid being shunned for selfishness. The truth was that she hadn't been interested, and since she'd always seemed rushed, only a handful had bothered to flirt with her.

Those who had persisted had been disappointed with her performance and hadn't returned for seconds, which had been perfectly fine with her. The only one she'd enjoyed being with had been Emmett, and apparently even that had been chemically induced.

Bottom line, she was an unenthusiastic and less than mediocre sex partner, who treated it more as an obligation and a chore to be suffered through than something to relish and enjoy.

"Do you mind if I watch a movie?" Bowen sat next to her on the couch. "I can put headphones on if you wish."

Always so considerate and polite. How did he expect anything to happen between them when he kept acting so formal and proper?

Her own experience of being part of a couple shouldn't be the guideline for any sane person, but watching Ana and Leon together, Margaret had figured that the teasing and bickering meant that they felt safe enough with each other not to watch every word, and it made them closer.

All that politeness shored up the invisible wall between her and Bowen, keeping them in the friend zone.

She put her phone down. "Perhaps I'll take a break and watch a movie with you. What do you have in mind?"

"Something light." He smiled sheepishly. "You'd laugh, but romcoms are my favorite."

"What are romcoms?"

"Romantic comedies."

"That's really surprising since you like reading Stephen King."

"I don't like watching the movie adaptations of his books."

"Well, in that case, let's watch a romcom."

"Any in particular?"

Margaret smiled sadly. "Since I don't know any that are less than twenty years old, any would do."

"I have one." He clicked the television on and started scrolling through the selection. "It hasn't been released yet, but one of my cousins is the producer, so we have it on our servers."

Bowen and Leon used the term cousin loosely. It encompassed most of their extended family members, or the clan, as they referred to them, and Margaret suspected that it didn't imply any real family connection. It was nice, though. Even if the cousins weren't blood relatives, referring to them as such made them feel like family, and that was good.

"What's the movie's title?"

"*Shoeless Sally*. It's a humorous take on the classic Cinderella story."

"Sounds lovely."

"You'll laugh your pants off." He cast her a sheepish sidelong look. "If you were wearing pants, that is."

Margaret wished she had a teasing answer, or at least something funny to say, but nothing came to mind, so she adjusted her skirt and smiled instead.

"Found it." He clicked on the title and leaned back.

As the opening credits started rolling, Bowen wrapped his arm around her shoulders, and her first response was to stiffen, but then she forced herself to relax and leaned her head on his bicep.

After all, that was precisely what she craved—the closeness, the lightheartedness, the lack of formality. She wanted Bowen to tease her, maybe even make some suggestive remarks like Leon was constantly doing to get a rise out of Ana.

"Would you like me to make some tea?" Bowen asked. "I've already seen the movie, so I can miss the opening scenes."

Margaret would have loved a cup, but that would mean losing his arm around her and she didn't want to chance him not returning to the same position. "Maybe later." She cuddled even closer, signaling in the only way she could that she was enjoying the closeness and didn't want it to end.

His hand on her arm moved down and then up, gently caressing and raising goosebumps all over it.

Except, calling what she felt goosebumps was a gross understatement. It was more like the pins and needles she'd used to get after sitting with her leg folded under her for too long.

This time though, it wasn't just a numb limb awakening, it was her entire body.

Bowen

As Margaret snuggled closer, Bowen forced himself not to stiffen. Appearing relaxed became nearly impossible to do, especially after the faint scent of her arousal hit him.

He wasn't paying much attention to the movie, but maybe he should in order to take his mind off the woman pressed so trustingly against him. In her shy way she was signaling her interest, but he didn't know how to take it from there.

The damn cast was acting as a better chaperone than the strictest of matrons, and Margaret's fragility wasn't helping either. Whenever carnal thoughts filtered through his shield, Bowen felt ashamed. How could he imagine himself holding this highly breakable woman pinned against the wall and thrusting into her?

That was what the internet article had suggested as a suitable position for sex with a cast, and when he'd read it, for a brief moment Bowen's stifled libido had roared to life with need. Except, when he'd imagined himself with Margaret like that, the cast was gone, and she had her legs wrapped around his waist.

He needed her to be healthy and whole before he made love to her, but he couldn't wait that long. By then, she would be back to Safe Haven and out of his life, and he would never know whether she'd been his one.

Was making love really necessary to establish that she was the one for him? Wouldn't he know that even without it?

He might, but the only way to induce her transition, providing that she was a Dormant, would be to have sex with her. There was no way around it, and he couldn't wait five more weeks for the cast to come off.

But even if he seduced her tonight, he would only have one week to induce her and that was not enough. Unless he managed to convince Margaret to stay longer, she was scheduled to leave Sunday afternoon.

Maybe he could ask for an extended vacation and join the damn cult until Margaret was good to go? But what about that free-love philosophy they had? He wouldn't let anyone near her. Then again, until the cast came off, she probably wouldn't invite anyone, and the bastards had to wait for an invitation. They were not allowed to pester the females, which he had to grudgingly give Emmett kudos for.

But what if he got invited? He would just refuse, maybe making up a story about some trauma he was working through. According to Anastasia, new members were allowed some leeway, which was how she'd managed to avoid inviting anyone to her bed until Leon had shown up.

Onegus wouldn't be happy about the long leave of absence. He'd already informed Leon that he needed him back by Thursday.

With the influx of clan members arriving for the wedding and Kian's birthday, Guardians had been allocated to their security, and the force would be stretched thinner than ever. Already some of the rescue missions had been canceled, and Onegus was calling in every available Guardian back to work. Vacations were officially suspended until after the celebrations.

Bowen was the exception only because Margaret might be a potential Dormant, and Dormants took precedence over almost everything. The question was whether Onegus would approve an even longer leave of absence.

After the celebrations were over, the plan was to increase the number of weekly rescue missions to compensate for the cancellations until they were all caught up.

Next to him Margaret laughed, jerking Bowen out of his thoughts.

He glanced at the screen, trying to figure out what she'd found funny, in case she commented on it and expected him to answer coherently. The truth was that he didn't remember much of the lighthearted romantic comedy, and the details were fuzzy.

"Here she goes again." Margaret waved her hand at the screen. "Trying to walk in her boss's large shoes."

He remembered it now. Instead of glass slippers, the story started with a pair of ill-fitting shoes. The prince was the grouchy owner of the company, and the big ball was a party at Sally's boss's penthouse. Sally borrowed a nice dress from her roommate, but she didn't have money to buy fancy shoes to match. When she got to the party, she snuck into the boss's closet and borrowed a pair from her, but they were too big. The actress had done a fantastic comedic job with Sally wobbling on the too-tall, too-big shoes, grabbing people on her way and apologizing profusely. Eventually she got the owner, causing him to spill his drink, and that's how their love story started.

"You're not watching." Margaret finally noticed.

"I was thinking."

"About what?"

"Going to Safe Haven with you. If you put in a good word for me, do you think the new management will accept me as a member?"

Margaret quirked a brow. "You're joking, right?"

"No. I'm serious. I know that you want to go back, but I'm not ready to be apart from you. I'll ask my boss for a leave of absence."

"Oh, Bowen." She cupped his cheek. "You are serious."

"Did you think I was making it up?"

"You are always so formal with me," she whispered. "I didn't know what to think."

Her lips were so close, and there was nothing broken or fragile about them. They were full and plump, and he knew he could taste them without fear or guilt. The problem was what would happen after that, but he would just have to figure it out.

If he hesitated, if he refused the invitation he saw in her eyes, she might never get the courage to issue it again.

Dipping his head, Bowen gently pressed his lips to Margaret's, and when she eagerly parted them for him, he swept in with his tongue. To finally hold her close, pressed against him, and to kiss her was like an electrical shock to his system, but he never loosened the tight control he had over his fangs and his eyes.

As she moaned and tilted her head to give him better access, some of his self-control slipped. Holding her with one hand on the small of her back and the other on her hip, he deepened the kiss, devouring her as if he was a starved man, which he was.

After a long moment she pushed on his chest, and he realized that she needed to breathe and released her mouth.

"I'm sorry."

"I'm not." Margaret brought a trembling finger to touch her lips. "I wish I didn't have to take a breath."

"Have you taken enough?"

"I have."

"Then, kiss me back."

She tilted her head up and did precisely as he'd commanded.

Cassandra

Onegus hadn't called yet.

It was after six o'clock, the staff were already gone, and the only ones left in the office were Cassandra and her boss.

She couldn't remember the last time she'd checked her phone every five minutes to make sure that she hadn't missed a call from a guy. But that was what she'd been doing throughout the day. Onegus had said that he would call as soon as he knew what time he would be done with work, and that should have been a while ago.

What if he didn't call?

He'd seemed interested enough, but what if he'd changed his mind?

Normally she didn't suffer from insecurities, but Cassandra was a realist, and Onegus was a much bigger catch than she was.

Even if he wasn't a billionaire, he was still rich, and he looked like a movie star. Scratch that, he looked like a god. If he could have any woman on the face of the planet, why would he bother with an obstinate, opinionated, and demanding one like her?

Not to mention her short temper and its destructive power, but he didn't know about that yet.

So yeah, she had a great body and a pretty face, and she had a well-paying job, but she wasn't young, lived with her mother, and she'd told him that she didn't do hookups. And to top it off, she'd also told him that he would have to come to her house and introduce himself to her mother.

What the hell had possessed her to do that?

Meeting her loony mother was a sure way to scare the guy away, and that was the last thing she wanted.

It had been a test, one of many she'd thrown at him to make sure that he deserved her time and attention, and she'd expected him to fail. But so far, Onegus had passed each one she'd challenged him with. The question was whether he would pass them all.

Cassandra huffed out a breath.

Subconsciously, or maybe consciously, she'd created an obstacle course designed to weed out the half-hearted contenders and the flakes. The prize for the one who reached the finish line would be her love and devotion.

Except, she was no princess, and there was a serious dearth of worthy knights. Chances were that no one would be willing to work so hard to win her heart, and she would end up a spinster.

When her phone finally rang at 6:37 and Onegus's name appeared on the screen, she sagged in relief. Not to appear overly anxious, Cassandra let it ring three times before accepting the call.

"Hello?" She pretended as if she didn't recognize the number.

"It's Onegus."

She switched the phone to her other ear and leaned back in her chair. "Oh, hi. How are you doing?"

"Great. How about yourself?"

"I'm good."

"Are you still in the office?"

"Yes. I'm just finishing a few things." She could leave right away, but again, she didn't want to sound overly eager.

"When can you leave?"

"I have about half an hour's worth of work left."

"Are you heading straight home?"

Cassandra slumped in her chair. He hadn't called to ask her out after all. "I am. Why?"

"When are you going to get there?"

Maybe he wanted to pick her up at home? That was nice of him.

"Seven-thirty or eight."

"If you give me the address, I can come to pick you up at eight, and you can introduce me to your mother."

She chuckled. "I won't subject you to that. Let's meet somewhere in town."

"That's not what we agreed on yesterday. I'm picking you up at home and saying hello to your mother. You don't need to invite me for tea, but I want to introduce myself."

Perhaps she could make it quick and warn her mother not to say anything strange or embarrassing. If she kept refusing, Onegus would think that she was embarrassed about her home or about her mother.

She wasn't about either.

The house she'd bought wasn't a mansion, but it was in a new gated community, and she had it beautifully furnished. As for her mother, there was nothing wrong with Geraldine except the memory lapses and the crazy stories that she sometimes spouted. Her mother was a beautiful woman with impeccable manners.

"I don't know if she's even going to be home. My mother has a busy social life. But you can come over at eight, and if she's there, I'll introduce you."

"Fair enough."

"I'll text you the address. It's a gated community, so when you stop at the gate, tell the guard that you are visiting the Beaumonts."

"I remember your last name, Cassandra."

"Cassy. That's what my friends call me."

"I'm glad that you consider me a friend, but I love your full name. Cassandra," he purred.

She chuckled. "Of course, I consider you a friend. I don't let strangers or mere acquaintances kiss me."

Just thinking about that had her nipples tighten into two hard knobs. No man had ever rocked her world with just one kiss, and if Onegus made love the way he kissed, she was in for the experience of a lifetime.

"I'm also glad for that. I'll see you at eight."

"Wait. Where are we going? I need to know how to dress."

"Wear whatever makes you feel sexy, and we will take it from there."

"That's kind of vague. I felt sexy wearing those shorts, but that's not what I would wear to a dinner date."

He was quiet for a moment. "Dinner it is, then. Have you ever heard of a place called By Invitation Only?"

"I have, but I've never been there. Have you?"

"No, but I can get us in. My boss has a membership."

That was impressive as hell, but if he hadn't made reservations, there was no way he could get them a spot in a place like that.

"I doubt they will have a table available. Besides, it's too fancy for a weekday evening, second date."

"Nothing is too fancy for you, my beautiful Cassandra. I'll see what I can do, but even if I can't get us reservations at By Invitation Only, I'm taking you somewhere fancy. Dress accordingly."

Onegus

Being the chief of Guardians had its advantages.

Gerard had tried to argue that he couldn't possibly find a table for Onegus and his date on such short notice, but it hadn't taken Onegus long to convince the prick that it was in his best interest to find them a table.

He didn't care if his cousin had to squeeze an additional table in or put it in the restaurant's covered patio in the back. One way or another, he and Cassandra were dining at By Invitation Only tonight.

The reservation was for nine-fifteen, and it was five minutes to eight when Onegus parked in front of Cassandra's manicured front lawn. The restaurant was only a twenty-minute drive away, which gave him plenty of time to chat with the mother and get that obstacle checked off.

Grabbing the bouquets of flowers he'd bought on the way, he got out of his car and walked up to the front door.

It opened before he had a chance to knock.

"Flowers? How gallant." Cassandra reached for the bouquets. "For my mother and me?"

"The tulips are for your mother. The orchids are for you."

"Thank you. Both are lovely."

She looked resplendent in a figure-hugging silver-hued dress that reached a little above her knees. The slightly shiny fabric accentuated her warm caramel-colored skin, and the sophisticated cut complemented her tall frame and long limbs. Spiky-heeled silver sandals adorned her slender feet, held only by narrow straps. Long silver earrings dangled from her dainty ears, and a chunky matching necklace gleamed around her long neck.

He didn't know much about makeup, but he'd seen her yesterday with barely anything on her face, so he knew she had it expertly applied now. Cassandra was a natural beauty, but all decked out, she was magazine-cover perfect.

"You look ready for the runway." He followed her inside. "Silver looks good on you."

She gave him a crooked smile, followed by a hooded eyed once-over. "You clean up nicely yourself."

He waved a hand over his charcoal suit. "This old thing?"

Cassandra laughed. "You stole my line."

"Is your mother home?"

"Let me first find vases for these, and then I'll call her."

"No rush. Our reservation is for nine-fifteen."

Looking at him over her shoulder, she arched a perfectly shaped brow. "Did you manage to get us a reservation for By Invitation Only?"

"Of course." He stuffed his left hand in the pocket of his slacks and looked around the beautifully decorated living area.

It wasn't professionally done like Ingrid's interiors, and not everything matched or was even in the same style, but it was still elegant and yet warm and inviting. Cassandra had impeccable taste, which explained her success as the creative director of Fifty Shades of Beauty.

"I'm duly impressed." She put the flowers on the counter and pulled two vases down from one of the shelves. "Who did you have to bribe?"

He chuckled. "My cousin is the owner. But it took threats of bodily harm to convince him to secure a table for us."

Her brows dipped. "I hope he doesn't spit in our food out of spite."

"Gerard is obsessed with providing his super-important guests with an incomparable culinary experience. He would never do something like that."

She cast him an appreciative glance. "You are well connected, but then I shouldn't be surprised. Your family owns a multinational conglomerate."

She didn't know the half of it, but that was how the clan needed it to be.

As Cassandra filled the vases with water and unwrapped the flowers, Onegus examined the artwork. Noticing her name scribbled at the bottom of one, he checked the other paintings and charcoal drawings, and sure enough, her name was on each one of them.

"You are a very talented lady, Cassandra."

She lifted her eyes and smiled. "Thank you."

When a door opened somewhere on the second floor, and a moment later light footsteps sounded going down the stairs, Onegus turned and prepared to flash a charming smile that would disarm the most protective of mothers.

The woman who entered the living room was nothing like what he'd expected, and for a moment he wondered whether she was a visitor, perhaps a friend whom Cassandra had forgotten to mention.

Dark hair cascading around slim shoulders framed a pale, unlined face that was much too young to belong to Cassandra's mother. Big blue eyes eyed him with curiosity, and her red-colored lips curved in a mysterious smile.

"You must be Onegus." She offered him her hand.

"Indeed." He shook it. "And you are?"

She laughed. "I'm Geraldine. Cassy's mother."

"Impossible. You can't be. A sister, maybe. But her mother? No way."

"Oh, dear. You are a charmer, aren't you? And so handsome. I thought that Cassy was exaggerating when she told me you were a god among men. But every word was true."

"Mother." Cassandra walked over to the much shorter woman and wrapped her arm around her shoulders. "You are embarrassing me."

"I'm sorry." Geraldine lifted her face to look up at her daughter. "You two look perfect together." She giggled. "Like Ken and Barbie. You are both so tall and beautiful."

"The tulips are for you." Cassandra kissed her mother's cheek and then grabbed a small purse off the counter. "Let's go before my mom decides to show you my naked baby pictures to prove that she's indeed my mother." She walked over to Onegus and threaded her arm through his.

"It was a pleasure to meet you, Mrs. Beaumont." Onegus smiled at the woman.

"Just Geraldine." She walked over and patted his arm. "Thank you for the flowers. It was my pleasure to make your acquaintance as well. Enjoy your evening."

"Thank you."

Cassandra

Cassandra had been to fancy restaurants before, where a couple could easily spend over three hundred dollars without even overindulging in exotic drinks or delicacies, but By Invitation Only was by far the most exclusive gig in town, perhaps even in the entire country.

It was a well-hidden gem that wasn't marked by a sign, and the only indication that there was anything happening beyond its sprawling gardens was the valet service, but even that was done so discreetly that only those in the know could find the place.

It was also run more efficiently than any of the other high-end restaurants she'd ever been to.

As soon as Onegus had given his name, they were quickly led by the hostess to one of the secluded enclaves. Candles burned on the tables they passed on the way, their light too faint to illuminate the patrons' faces.

She had no doubt that it was intentional, providing privacy to the movers and shakers who owned a membership.

As soon as they were seated, the hostess took their drink orders so they could sip on them while going over the menu. Looking at the offerings, Cassandra was glad of having taken French as a second language in high school. Otherwise, she would have been forced to guess what she was ordering. It also bothered her that the prices were not listed.

It probably didn't matter. Everything was no doubt so costly that her choice of entree wouldn't make a difference in the bill Onegus got.

She glanced at him over her menu. "Do you get a discount because your cousin owns the place?"

He chuckled. "No, but don't worry about it."

"I'm not worried. I'm just curious. There are no prices on the menu. Does he charge a lump sum no matter what we order? Or is the cost included in the membership? How does it work?"

Onegus leaned forward. "Frankly, I have no clue. It's my first time here."

That was surprising. "I know that this place is not new. Why only now?"

He flashed her one of his panty-melting smiles. "I've never met a woman whom I wanted to impress as much as I want to impress you."

"I see." Leaning back, she stifled the urge to fold her arms over her chest.

Should she feel flattered that the guy was so desperate to shorten the wait until he had sex with her?

"What does that mean?" Onegus asked. "What do you see?"

"A guy who, for some reason, can't wait to get into my panties."

"I don't think your panties will fit me."

She rolled her eyes. "You know what I mean."

"That's not why I brought you here."

"Oh, yeah? You admitted that you wanted to meet my mother as soon as possible just so you could cross off that item on my list of prerequisites."

"I don't deny that. But I didn't bring you here expecting to wow you into dropping your panties for me." Smirking, he leaned closer. "You will drop them, but only because you find me irresistible."

"Overconfident much?"

"No. Just confident."

Damn. Why did she find his cocky attitude so sexy?

Usually, that sort of response would have annoyed her because it would have been empty boasting. In Onegus's case, though, it was just a statement of fact.

The way her body was fighting her resolve to wait, she might only hold off until the end of dinner and then drag him to the nearest hotel and have her way with him.

His nostrils flaring, Onegus sucked in a breath. "What were you thinking about just now?"

"Wouldn't you like to know?" She lifted the menu to hide her flaming cheeks.

With her dark coloring and the amount of makeup she had on it was doubtful Onegus would notice her blush, but she needed a moment to catch her breath and think.

Should she lie? Try to play coy?

Men didn't like to catch their prey too easily. If they didn't have to work for it, they didn't appreciate it as much.

Then again, Onegus had come to her house so he could meet her mother, which none of the men Cassy had ever dated had offered to do on the second date. Then he had taken her to the most exclusive members-only restaurant, which was probably going to cost him thousands.

Guys these days didn't expect to work as hard for a hookup, especially not men like Onegus, who had women throwing themselves at them left and right.

The thing was, Cassandra wasn't playing games to make herself stand out from the crowd. She just didn't want casual sex. She wanted a relationship that led to intimacy, and not premature intimacy that would leave a bad taste in her mouth.

When she lowered the menu, he was still staring at her.

She arched a brow. "What?"

"You asked if I would like to know what you were thinking about, and the answer is yes, I would."

Smiling, she reached over the table and put her hand over his. "I'll tell you after dinner."

He groaned. "You are evil. Why not now?"

She shrugged. "A lady should always be a little mysterious. Otherwise, where's the fun?"

Onegus

Unexpectedly, Cassandra's hard-to-get act was indeed fun.

Onegus loved that she wasn't all over him and was making him work hard to gain her approval. He loved that she challenged him on every front, forcing him to bring forth the best version of himself.

It was like a blast from the past, and it was refreshing, especially since she wasn't doing it just to be difficult or to play games. Cassandra wasn't willing to compromise on what she wanted from a man, and he applauded her for it.

Except, he couldn't give her that, and if he were truly a gentleman, he would have walked away.

Cassandra wanted a relationship, she wanted love and closeness, she wanted a partner she could trust.

Onegus could be none of those things. He might be able to see her a few more times, but eventually, he would have to move on. Unless, of course, he was incredibly lucky and Cassandra was a Dormant.

She hadn't exhibited any paranormal talents yet, and the raw energy he could sense in her could be just a physical manifestation of her assertive character. Some humans projected their feelings with such force that it was uncomfortable being around them, but that wasn't the case with Cassandra. To Onegus, the energy was like an aphrodisiac, an irresistible pull.

Unless she could somehow shape it and wield it, though, it wasn't a paranormal talent.

When they were done with dinner, and they ordered coffee and dessert, he leaned forward and smiled. "You said that you would tell me after dinner."

"Tell you what?" She pretended not to remember.

They'd talked about many things throughout the evening, but he doubted she'd forgotten that flare of arousal he'd scented coming from her.

"I'll jog your memory. When we discussed whether I was cocky or confident, a lovely blush coated your cheeks, and you hid behind the menu. The entire evening, I've been waiting not so patiently for you to tell me what caused that blush."

She glanced around, checking if anyone was listening in. "I'll tell you when we are in the car."

"Na-ah, Ms. Cassandra Beaumont. Stop being a coward. Out with it."

Her eyes narrowed, sending jagged daggers his way. "I'm the opposite of a coward."

She was even more magnificent when her feathers were ruffled. Sexy lady, so full of fire. He couldn't wait to feel the burn.

Crossing his arms over his chest, Onegus challenged her. "Prove it."

She swallowed. "You said that you're just confident, not cocky, and you are right. Your confidence, in addition to everything else you are, makes you very attractive to me." She swallowed again but didn't back down. "The thought that caused that blush was that it would be difficult to force myself to keep you waiting much longer, and I debated who would win the battle, my body or my mind."

Her honesty and courage impressed him, and he wanted to repay her in kind.

"What is your mind telling you?"

Unfolding her arms, she put her hands on the table, her long, elegant fingers splayed, the red nail polish like drops of blood on the white tablecloth. "It tells me that I should get to know you better first. That if we jump straight into intimacy, it wouldn't be as satisfying as having an emotional connection first." She let out a breath. "I'm not built for hookups, but the pull I feel toward you refuses to be denied."

"Then don't." He reached over the table and gripped both of her hands. "I feel the pull and the connection as well, and if I were a better man, I would have taken you home, kissed your cheek, and said good night."

She tilted her head, the dangling silver earring catching the light from the candle. "But you are not going to do that."

He smiled, letting the predator inside of him peek through the thin civilized veneer he wore. "I want you, Cassy, with an intensity that I haven't felt for any other woman, and I've been with many. I feel like I will burn if I don't have you. I won't make empty promises just to seduce you, though. I don't know what tomorrow will bring. Hell, I don't know if I will still be here a week from now. My boss might send me to Europe or the East, and I might be gone for weeks."

The last part wasn't true, but he needed a ready excuse for when he would have to say goodbye and stop seeing her, which was inevitable. But unlike all the other times he'd done so, the thought caused a dull pain in his chest. He hadn't lied or even exaggerated when he'd told Cassandra that he'd never met a woman who intrigued him and ensnared him as completely as she had.

Cassandra

Onegus's message was clear. And honest.

They had just met, and he couldn't promise her forever, but the thing between them was too powerful to deny.

He was strong, physically and mentally, and perhaps with him she could for once lower her shields and let the storm swirling inside her loose.

No, she could never do that. What was she thinking?

She wouldn't risk damaging this magnificent male just to test what happened if she let go of the tight leash that she had over the darkness that swirled and churned inside her.

"I can't make any promises either," she said softly. "Maybe I won't like you the next morning."

His smile was predatory. "Does it mean that you will spend the night with me?"

She nodded. "Your place or mine?"

Wow, talk about a surprise. Onegus had been pushing hard, but until the words left her mouth, Cassandra hadn't expected him to win.

He looked just as stunned at receiving the invitation as she was at issuing it.

"Is your place even an option with your mother there?" he asked.

"Good point. What about your roommate?"

"I have an apartment downtown."

She arched a brow. "A shag-pad?"

He laughed. "It's a brand-new place, and you are the first guest I'm going to take there."

It was on the tip of her tongue to ask where he'd brought the many other women he'd been with, but it was none of her business. She didn't own his past or his future, she could barely stake a claim on his present.

After Onegus paid the bill without batting an eyelid, they were escorted back to the valet station, where his car was already waiting for them.

"I'm afraid to ask." Cassandra reached for the seatbelt after the valet closed her passenger door.

"Ask what?"

"How much was the bill."

Onegus chuckled. "Do you ask all of your dates how much they paid for the meal?"

She cringed. "I can't help it. I hate wasting money even if it's not mine." She cast him a sidelong glance. "Kevin gave me a ten grand budget to buy the dress and accessories for the gala. Guess how much I ended up spending?"

It was probably the least appropriate topic of conversation she could choose on the way to a hookup, but she was nervous, and talking about budgets and money was safe and took her mind off what she was about to do.

"Double," Onegus said. "That dress was almost as exquisite as the woman wearing it."

She snorted. "My mother was right. You're such a charmer. But thank you. Anyway, I spent less than half, and Kevin was mad at me for not spending all of it. I didn't even tell him that the dress I bought was once worn by a celebrity on the red carpet."

God, she was babbling what Onegus probably considered nonsense. What did he care about where she'd bought her dress or how much she'd spent on it?

"Which one?" He smiled. "I can't think of any actress that could look as good as you in that dress."

His compliment sounded utterly genuine, and it made Cassandra feel a little less embarrassed about her nervous prattling.

"I didn't ask."

"But if you bought the dress secondhand, how did you still manage to spend five grand?" There was no judgment in his voice, only curiosity.

"The shoes cost nearly three thousand." She smiled shyly. "I have a weakness for shoes. That's the only wardrobe item that I don't buy at a bargain."

"Kevin is paying you well. Are you saving for something special?"

"I bought the house my mother and I live in, and I want to pay off the mortgage in ten years. I'm also investing in stocks to grow my money."

"Your mother looks very young," Onegus changed the topic unexpectedly.

Cassandra had been wondering when he would bring that up. Everyone who ever met her mother said the same thing.

"If you're asking me how old she is, the answer is that I don't know. The number changes every time I ask."

"What does her driver's license say?"

"She lost it years ago and never bothered with a replacement."

Onegus arched a brow. "How does she get around?"

"Nowadays, she uses Uber. Before I bought the house, we lived in an apartment building that was close to a bus station. She just used the bus." Cassandra glanced out the window, noting the wide boulevard and the high-rises on both sides of it. "My mother has a memory problem. I don't think she would be able to get a new license if she applied for it."

"She's too young to have Alzheimer's."

Cassandra didn't like talking about her mother's condition. It was no one's business. But for some reason, she felt like it was okay to tell Onegus about it. He would never use the information to taunt her or hurt her like some of her school friends had done.

"It's not Alzheimer's. My mother suffered a head trauma a long time ago and had total amnesia. She had to relearn everything from scratch, including speech, and she did, but she still suffers from periodic memory lapses. She tries to cover up for that by making up stories, so if she tells you something outlandish, it's probably made up. The best thing to do is to just nod and pretend that you believe her. Confronting her with the truth just makes things worse for her."

Onegus nodded. "How did she manage to raise you and do such an excellent job of it?"

Cassandra smiled. "She and I are proof that love is more important than anything else. I knew from a very young age that my mother forgot things and that I needed to be alert and help her out. But I also knew that she loved me unconditionally and would do anything for me. She would eat ramen for weeks so she could buy me the art supplies I needed for my drawings and paintings. She also made most of our clothes, buying fabric remnants and creating beautiful things from them."

"No wonder that you are so frugal as well as creative, which is an unusual combination." Onegus turned into the underground parking of one of the high-rises. "Your mother instilled both in you."

"That and many other good qualities. You won't ever hear me complaining about my childhood."

Onegus

The apartment Ingrid had designated for Guardians' use during the wedding celebration was fully stocked and ready for Onegus to move in, which was why he'd decided to bring Cassandra there. Usually, he took his partners to one of the keep's apartments or to a hotel.

The upside was that for now, he was the only one who had access to the apartment, so there was no risk of one of the Guardians claiming it first. The downside was that the surveillance cameras had been already installed, the feed going to the security office in the keep. There was no avoiding the guys seeing him taking Cassandra up to the apartment.

Normally he didn't care, but she was unlike any of the others, and it infuriated him to think about the lewd remarks the guys might make when they saw him with her.

He even considered disconnecting the security feed and sneaking her up there somehow. Except that would bring the Guardians running to investigate, which would achieve the opposite of what he wanted.

"Does anyone live here?" Cassandra asked as they exited the elevator on the nineteenth floor. "Everything smells brand new."

"Not yet. It used to be an office building. The conversion to apartments was just recently completed." He unlocked the door with his phone. "After you, my lady."

Sauntering on her spiky heels, her slim hips sashaying enticingly, Cassandra looked around the professionally decorated living room and then walked up to the wall of windows. "You don't live here," she said, facing the glass.

"No, not yet. But I will be staying here starting Thursday."

Turning around, she arched a brow. "What happens on Thursday?"

He'd misspoken. The upcoming wedding and the clan members, who were arriving soon and would be staying in the building, needed to stay confidential or as confidential as possible.

Fortunately, he'd had many centuries of practice in coming up with convincing lies. "The semi-official opening of the building is this Friday. We have a large list of preferential clients who get to experience the apartments during the week before we open them to the public. I'm their host, and I need to be here to entertain them."

As Cassandra narrowed her eyes at him, the energy vibrating under her skin intensified. "You're not a real estate agent, Onegus. Why are you feeding me stories?"

"I'm not." He pushed his hand into his pocket. "Can I offer you a drink?"

The energy crackled. "What's really going on in this place?"

"Precisely what I told you."

As a faint rattling noise snagged his attention, he started to turn, catching from the corner of his eye a crystal vase swaying on top of the pedestal it was precariously perched on. Lunging for it, he could have caught it before it hit the floor, but instead of falling it exploded, the shards flying toward him like pieces of shrapnel.

Onegus's lightning-quick reflexes had him lift his arm to shield his face, at the same time grabbing Cassandra's arm and flinging her behind him.

He groaned as a volley of shards hit his forearm and thighs, penetrating the fabric of his suit and embedding in his flesh.

Behind him, Cassandra trembled. "I'm sorry. Oh God, I'm so sorry."

Turning around, he inspected her from top to bottom. "Are you hurt?"

Cassandra's eyes were the size of saucers, and instead of the fresh scent of ozone he associated with her, he smelled fear.

"I'm fine." She looked at his arm. "Are you hurt?"

He smiled to reassure her. "The suit absorbed most of it. I'm fine." He wasn't, but once he plucked out the shards in the bathroom, his wounds would heal right away, and no sign of injury would remain.

"I'm so sorry," she murmured again. "I didn't mean it."

"It wasn't your fault." He looked at the pedestal and the crystal pieces that were strewn about. "Cheap, made-in-China crap. It must have had a defect, or maybe the frequency of our voices agitated it into exploding."

She let out a shuddering breath. "I thought that I knocked it over by mistake."

Taking her elbow, he led her to the couch. "Let me pour you a drink."

She looked at his shredded sleeve and the tiny pieces of crystal embedded in his pants. "I should get those out first." She reached for his sleeve.

Onegus caught her hand. "Don't. You'll only hurt yourself. I'll get you a drink and then check the damage in the bathroom."

Cassandra shook her head. "I'm coming with you. You might need help." She lifted her small bag. "I have tweezers."

Damn. He couldn't let her see him heal faster than humanly possible. "I'll tell you what. If you really want to be helpful, find a broom and clean up this mess while I'm in the bathroom."

She opened her mouth, no doubt to argue, but then closed it and nodded. "I can do that."

"Thank you." Onegus leaned and kissed her cheek. "I'll be right back."

In the bathroom, he plucked out the bigger pieces from his sleeve and then carefully peeled the jacket off, wincing as the shards dragged over his skin.

Underneath, his shirt sleeve was soaked with blood. As he looked at the many tiny particles that were embedded in the skin underneath, he thought about Cassandra's offer to use her tweezers.

Hopefully, Ingrid had included a pair in the basket of toiletries, and he wouldn't have to ask Cassandra for hers. She would offer to do the plucking, and if he allowed it, he would have to thrall the memory of his fast healing away, and then he couldn't thrall her again after biting her.

Not a good plan.

When he found the tweezers in the basket, Onegus let out a relieved breath.

It took him almost half an hour to dig all the shards out, and when he was done, he stepped into the shower to wash the blood away.

Cassandra

What a mess.

Cassandra's damn temper had done it again. She should have told Onegus to take her home instead of going with him to his new shag pad.

He hadn't lied when he told her that she was the first one he'd ever brought there, but that was only because he'd just gotten the place. And why the hell had he made up those ridiculous lies about showing apartments to potential clients?

Onegus might not be the head of his family's international conglomerate, but his position in the organization was important enough that he wouldn't have to do the job of a real estate agent. If he'd told her that he was selling the entire building to potential investors, it would have been somewhat believable, but to assume that she'd believe he was tasked with showing apartments to potential buyers had been an insult to her intelligence. It had gotten her so mad that she'd lost the battle of trying to keep her sizzling energy contained, and it had exploded into that crystal vase as if it had been drawn to it.

Even after all the years she'd been dealing with that power, Cassandra still had no idea why it chose certain objects and not others. It seemed that glass, crystal, and ceramic were its favorite conduits. Usually, only inanimate objects suffered the consequences, but that could be dangerous as well.

She shuddered. If Onegus hadn't reacted as quickly as he had, both of them could have gotten seriously injured.

The guy had incredible reflexes.

Still shaken, Cassandra opened the bar cabinet and surveyed the selection. There was also a built-in fridge at the bottom, and it was well stocked. She mixed herself a tall glass of gin and tonic, added a few ice cubes, and drank half of it in one go.

It had way more tonic than gin, so getting tipsy wasn't going to happen, but she felt a little better and went looking for a broom and dustpan.

She found both in the utility cabinet in the kitchen, along with the latest Dyson model. Sweeping in high heels and an evening dress felt ridiculous, but with all the little pieces of glass she didn't dare take her shoes off. Once most of it was gone, she took out the Dyson and vacuumed the rest.

Altogether it hadn't taken her more than ten minutes, but she was starting to worry about Onegus. Maybe he needed help getting the shards out?

If he got seriously injured because of her, she would never forgive herself.

There had to be a way to control those damn power surges. One way she'd found was to go on a run, but that wasn't feasible in most situations. Self-talk didn't help and trying to meditate only added to her irritation.

Should she knock on the bathroom door and ask if he needed help?

After taking another long gulp from the gin and tonic, she dug the tweezers out of her purse and headed to the bedroom. It was just as beautifully done as the living room. A massive four-poster bed took up most of the space and was covered with a cream-colored duvet and a mountain of pillows. Across from the bed, a matching dresser had a large screen perched on top of it, and a chenille settee with two decorative pillows sat in the corner. Even the colors on the area rug and the artwork matched. The room looked like it belonged in a high-end hotel.

In the bathroom, the water was running in the shower.

So that was what was taking Onegus so long. He must have gotten bloodied to need a shower.

As guilt assailed her once more, Cassandra felt the urge to flee. She could leave right now, call an Uber, and never see Onegus again.

A coward's way out.

Eyeing the bed, she thought about all the ways she could make it up to him. Maybe she could kiss and lick all those nicks and scrapes better?

They had only shared that one kiss on the beach, but if that was an indication of the kind of lover Onegus was, Cassandra was up for one hell of a trip.

After she'd made up for the explosion, though. She didn't deserve getting pleasured until then.

Sitting on the bed, she kicked her sandals off and sighed with relief. They were pretty and matched her dress, but they weren't comfortable. Her toes were grateful to her for ending their torment.

Cassandra debated for a long moment whether she should undress or wait for Onegus to get out of the bathroom and peel the dress off her. Eventually, the soft duvet cover won the argument.

Pulling the dress over her head, she tossed it on the settee. The necklace and earrings were off next, and she put them on the nightstand. Leaving the tiny satin panties and matching bra on, she crawled under the duvet to wait for Onegus to come out.

Onegus

As he stood under the spray, Onegus wondered about Cassandra's strange reaction to the vase shattering. She'd kept apologizing as if it had been her fault, but she'd been nowhere near the pedestal when the vase started rocking.

The scent of fear she'd emitted had been strong, but he'd also detected guilt. Had she really thought that she'd knocked into the pedestal? Or had something else caused it to move?

After the accident, Cassandra's energy had seemed dimmed. Was it possible that it had been somehow released into the vase?

Other than Sylvia, Onegus had never encountered anyone with telekinetic ability. Sylvia could fritz out electronics with a thought, and most of the time she could control it, but sometimes her energy just got loose and caused havoc. Was it possible that Cassandra possessed a similar talent? If she did, it was probably on a different frequency than Sylvia's, and she had no control over it.

It should be interesting to find out.

By the time Onegus finished showering, there was no sign of injury anywhere on him. His clothes, though, were ruined.

After removing his phone and his wallet, he wrapped the suit jacket around the bloodied white shirt, and together with the pants, tossed everything into the wastebasket.

Thankful for Ingrid's attention to detail, he pulled one of the two white terry-robes off the hook and shrugged it on.

It would do for now, but he needed a change of clothes to take Cassandra home tomorrow morning. She might want him to take her back tonight, but he had no intentions of being done with her before the sun came up.

A long text to Arwel took care not only of that, but also a change of clothes for Cassandra, courtesy of Jin. Onegus had known that she was staying with her mate at night, and even though it hadn't been approved by him, he hadn't objected.

In appreciation, Jin was more than happy to do him a favor.

Tucking the phone and the wallet into the robe's pocket, Onegus turned to the door. When a soft rustling from the other side hinted at Cassandra's presence in the bedroom, he smiled.

Was it too much to hope that she was waiting for him in bed?

Yeah, it was. She probably waited to see whether he needed help plucking out the crystal shards.

Nonetheless Onegus was hopeful, and as soon as he opened the door, he glanced at the bed. Only her head peeked over the duvet, but her shy smile was the best invitation imaginable.

"What a pleasant surprise." He prowled toward the four-poster.

He wondered if Cassandra would be on board with putting those posts to good use. Imagining her nude and spreadeagled, her limbs tied with soft silk scarves to the posts, Onegus hardened, and his shaft tented the robe.

Commanding it to stand down, he uttered a soft groan.

It was a stupid idea on so many levels. First of all, games like that required complete trust, and Cassandra didn't know him well enough or long enough to play. Secondly, he had no silk scarves on hand. And thirdly, he'd never played games like that before and had no idea why it had even popped into his head.

Smiling nervously, her eyes roaming over his body, Cassandra let the blanket slide down, revealing her small, satin-covered breasts. "You look good in a robe."

"I look even better without." He undid the tie and let the terry cloth part.

Cassandra's eyes widened at the sight of his nude body and the impressive erection that he'd sprung.

Her tongue darted out to lick her lips. "Yes, you do."

Lifting to her knees, she let the blanket drop all the way.

The two scraps of gray satin covering her breasts and her mound didn't leave much to the imagination. Cassandra's body was pure perfection. She was slim and athletically built, but she was all woman, nonetheless.

Her eyes darting to his erection, she walked her knees closer to the edge of the bed. Her intention was clear, but if she touched him, it would become impossible to keep his fangs from punching out, and he wasn't ready to thrall her yet.

As she reached for him, he caught her wrist and lifted her hand to his lips. "Not tonight, sweetheart. I don't want it to be over before it begins."

A lie, but a handy one.

"I want to make it up to you."

"You are." He climbed on the bed and kneeled facing her.

As he reached with his finger and traced the outline of her mouth, her lips quivered, and as he wiped off the silvery, cherry lipstick and slipped the tip of his finger into her mouth, she licked it clean.

"That's one way to take lipstick off." She chuckled.

"There is still plenty of it left." Dipping his head, he licked at her lips while drawing a circle around her satin-clad nipple with his wet finger. "I didn't want to stain your bra."

"Your consideration is much appreciated." She reached behind her and unclasped it.

His breath hitched as it fell on the bed, exposing her perky breasts and stiff nipples. She had no tan lines, and for a brief moment, he wondered whether she tanned in the nude or just used a lot of sunscreen to protect her perfect skin from damage.

Cassandra

As Onegus stared at her breasts, Cassandra could barely breathe, waiting for him to do something, anything to ease the ache, to defuse the energy building up a new storm inside her.

Then his head dipped, and he flicked his tongue over her left nipple, nipped it lightly, and licked the small hurt away.

"Breathe," he reminded her.

As she sucked a breath into her oxygen-starved lungs, he switched sides and licked her right nipple.

She couldn't decide whether what he was doing was pleasure or torture. His tongue and his lips eased the ache but created a new one, and she wanted them everywhere and all at once.

His hands too.

Those large, masculine hands that were touching her so gently as he smoothed them over her back. Then he reached her rear, and the gentleness was gone as he kneaded her ass cheeks.

Letting go of her nipple, he lifted his head and angled his mouth over hers, and that too wasn't gentle.

Her hands shooting to his spiky hair, she pulled him closer, her naked breasts pressing against his powerful chest. His skin was smooth, hairless, but he was all man. She trailed her hands down his back, tracing every muscle, every ridge and valley, learning him.

He was still kissing her when his finger trailed the edge of her panties, teasing.

Please. She was too proud to give voice to the plea.

Then he left her mouth and trailed kisses down her neck, nipping, licking his way down, and as he reached her nipple, his finger pushed the scrap of fabric aside and found her wetness.

He hissed, his wicked finger pressing against that spot at the apex of her thighs, and when he sucked her nipple into his mouth, she bucked her hips and groaned, her head falling backward.

More, she needed more, but Cassandra was too proud to beg.

They were both still on their knees, facing each other, when Onegus's finger pushed inside of her, and the coil that had been tightening sprang free.

The sound leaving her throat sounded like a growl, and as she ground herself on his finger, riding out the orgasm, Onegus chuckled softly. "Greedy minx, aren't you?"

In response, she wrapped her arms around him and pulled him down with her.

His magic finger had gotten dislodged by the maneuver, but having his heavy body on top of her was worth it. His weight on her felt just perfect.

Sturdy, strong, solid.

Cupping her cheeks, he looked into her eyes and smiled. "You are magnificent, my Cassandra." He dipped his head and kissed her softly.

Given the fire burning in his eyes, the lust she'd sensed hiding behind the admiration, the guy had to have the self-control of a monk to kiss her so gently.

A lover's kiss.

Don't read too much into it.

And then he was sliding lower and taking her panties with him, exposing her to him unceremoniously.

"Just look at you." He leaned back on his haunches. "A goddess."

His hands smoothed up her legs, starting with her calves, going up to the outsides of her thighs, and when they circled in, parting her for his heated gaze, Onegus dipped his head and licked her where she needed it most.

A strangled moan left her throat.

It had been so long since anyone had touched her intimately that she felt like a virgin again, and for sure no one had ever touched her with such reverence and skill.

Plunging two fingers inside her moist heat, Onegus licked and nipped, kissed and sucked, and through it all, she wasn't sure who was making more animalistic noises.

He sounded like a tiger as he growled against her flesh, a happy tiger, though. She'd never been with a man who seemed to revel in feasting on her, and knowing that he enjoyed being the giver of pleasure just as much as she enjoyed being the receiver unfurled something inside her.

A ravenous tigress who'd been too shy to purr for others, purred like a well-oiled engine for Onegus.

As the coil inside her tightened until it could tighten no more, Cassandra fisted Onegus's hair, barely aware that she was probably hurting him, and as he closed his lips over her clit and sucked, the coil sprung. The release that barreled down her wasn't a wave, it was an explosion, wresting a scream out of her that would have startled the neighbors if there were any.

Pressing a soft kiss to her folds, Onegus slid back up and cupped her cheeks. "I will never tire of hearing you scream my name." He kissed her hard.

The taste of her was strong on his tongue, but surprisingly, she found it erotic rather than gross.

Cassandra had a feeling that everything this man did to her would feel right.

Heck, she couldn't believe that she'd screamed his name without being aware of it. She'd never screamed a guy's name before. In fact, she couldn't remember ever screaming her climax at all.

Onegus

As Onegus looked into Cassandra's eyes, he wanted to be the man she believed he was. There was awe in her gaze, a dreaminess, and it wasn't just about the two orgasms he'd wrought out of her. There was trust and hope that maybe what they were sharing was more than just a hookup. That it was the beginning of something wonderful.

He wished he could give her that and much more, but for now, all he could give her was pleasure.

Gazing into her expressive eyes, he nudged her entrance, waiting as he always did for the final consent, but not really expecting to be denied.

"Stop," Cassandra said to his great surprise, and put a hand on his chest. "You forgot protection."

"Right." Onegus reared up on his haunches. "Sorry about that." He leaned down over the bed to retrieve his wallet from the robe pocket and took out a packet.

As he tore it open, Cassandra sat up. "Let me put it on you."

If she touched him, he would probably explode in her hand, but he handed it to her anyway.

"Impressive." Her fingers brushed over the sensitive skin.

"You say the nicest things, but if you don't hurry, I'm going to erupt."

She smiled apologetically. "I wanted to take a moment to admire. It's not every day that a girl gets to see such male perfection."

He wasn't sure whether she was teasing or serious. Onegus had enough trouble keeping his fangs from punching out prematurely, which was a bigger problem than coming all over her beautiful breasts if she didn't hurry up.

As her long fingers expertly sheathed him, he wondered how she'd gotten so good at it. If she didn't do hookups and had been in love only twice, those two times must have been long-term.

But now was not the time to think about that.

As Cassandra lay back, he prowled over her, nudged her legs apart with his knee, and settled himself between them.

Some of the momentum had been lost, on her part, not his, but as he kissed her mouth, her neck, and then paid tribute to each nipple, Cassandra's hips started churning beneath him in a blatant invitation.

Lacing his fingers through hers, he laid their joined hands over her head and guided the tip of his shaft into her.

After orgasming twice, Cassandra was slick, but it had been a long time since she'd been with anyone, and she was tight.

Rolling his hips, Onegus pushed a little further, and when she moaned and arched up, he fed her a little bit more.

"You're tormenting me." She arched up again.

Lifting his hips, he didn't let her impale herself. "Patience, beautiful. I don't want to hurt you."

"You won't." She tried to pull her hands out of his grip.

His self-control only went so far, and as he surged into her, seating himself to the hilt, they both groaned.

The fit was tight, but not uncomfortable, and yet he didn't move, letting her get accustomed to the intrusion.

Dipping his head, he took her lips, intending the kiss to be soothing, gentle, but Cassandra was impatient and nipped his lower lip.

"Move," she hissed.

Onegus chuckled against her mouth. "Your wish is my command."

He withdrew slightly, and pushed back in, going slow at first and increasing the tempo and power of his thrusts in small increments to gauge her response. When she was panting, urging him to go deeper by arching into every thrust, he let go of her hands and gripped her hips.

Holding her down, he pounded into her hard and fast, and she melted beneath him, surrendering to him in the most primal way.

He needed her mindless with lust before he could let his fangs punch out, and as the release barreled through her for the third time, he pushed a small thrall to have her accept his bite without fear.

When she turned her head, offering him her neck, the last of his control snapped and as he erupted inside of her, his fangs sank into her neck and she orgasmed again, and again, and again.

And then her eyes rolled back in her head and she passed out.

For long moments, he lay on top of her, holding her tightly to him as if he would never let her go, listening as her breathing evened out and her heart rate slowed down.

When his own heart stopped hammering against his rib cage, he pulled out gently and padded to the bathroom to dispose of the condom.

He was still hard enough to pound nails with his shaft, and as he stood under the spray in the shower, he gave himself another release while replaying what had happened only minutes ago.

That didn't do the trick either, and when he came back to the bedroom with a couple of wet washcloths, Onegus was still sporting an erection that refused to deflate.

He found Cassandra sprawled on the bed in precisely the same position he'd left her, a satisfied smile on her beautiful face. She didn't stir when he gently cleaned her, and her breathing didn't change cadence when he climbed into bed and scooped her into his arms.

Tomorrow, he would have to wake her up early and get her home so she could change into work-appropriate attire, but tonight, he planned to hold her for as long as she let him.

Cassandra

"Good morning," said a familiar male voice as the bed dipped.

A moment later the smell of freshly-brewed coffee registered, and Cassandra opened her eyes.

It was morning?

The room was still mostly dark, the dawn's early light just starting to illuminate the sky.

"What time is it?" She reached for the coffee mug.

"It's five-thirty in the morning." Onegus smiled. "I figured that the coffee smell would do the trick. When I tried to wake you up twenty minutes ago, you pulled the pillow over your head and showed me your beautiful ass."

"I don't remember it." She took a sip from the coffee.

In fact, she was confused, not sure which parts of last night she remembered and which she'd dreamt up. She'd had the most amazing dreams of soaring through the clouds above alien cities and waving to the people below. She'd also dreamt about Onegus biting her neck, but it hadn't been painful. On the contrary, it was the most pleasurable thing she'd ever experienced, and after the number of times she'd orgasmed last night, that was saying something.

"You were tired." He leaned and kissed her cheek. "I wish I didn't have to wake you up, but unless you can call in sick, I need to get you home so you can change."

"I wish I could." She took another sip from the coffee. "But if I'm not there, my snowflakes aren't going to do a damn thing, and I'll have to pull all-nighters to catch up."

He arched a brow. "Your snowflakes?"

"The employees in my department. A bunch of twenty-somethings who think that they are entitled to do as little as possible and not only get paid for it but also get promoted." Cassandra shook her head. "Forgive my rant. I'm cranky in the mornings, especially this early."

"You can rant to me as much as you want."

He flashed her his gorgeous smile and reached for the mug of coffee on the nightstand.

With the cobwebs of sleep dissipating, she noticed that he was dressed in a pair of jeans and a button-down. The closet door had been open when she'd walked into the bedroom last night, and there had been nothing in it. "Where did you get the clothes from?"

"I texted a friend last night and had him deliver a change of clothes for both of us. He left them by the door." Onegus lifted his leg, showing her that the jeans were too short. "Arwel is not as tall as I am, but his girlfriend is about your size, and she lent you a T-shirt and a pair of leggings."

That was embarrassing. Had he planned on her spending the night? Or had he contacted his friend after she'd passed out?

"That's very sweet of her, and please thank her for me, but it's not necessary. The building is vacant, and no one is going to see me leaving with my evening dress on."

"That's true." He smoothed his hand over his curly blond hair. "But since he was bringing things for me, I figured you might want to change into something casual as well."

"It was a nice thought. I appreciate it."

"I wish both of us didn't need to go to work today." He gazed at her from under his blond lashes, his blue eyes vivid even in the dim morning light.

The man was truly beautiful.

Surprisingly, things weren't as awkward between them the morning after as she'd expected. It almost felt as if they'd been longtime lovers, comfortable with each other, but still very sexually aware.

"I wish so too." She took a few more sips of coffee before handing him the nearly empty mug. "I need to use the bathroom."

"Of course." He didn't move.

She had three options. Fling the comforter off and parade naked to the bathroom, wrap the comforter around her body and drag it to there, or ask Onegus to give her some privacy.

Normally Cassandra wasn't shy, and even though he'd seen every bit of her already, it still felt like too much too soon.

Understanding flashing through his eyes, Onegus got up. "I'll get you a robe."

"Thank you." She clutched the comforter to her chest.

Alone in bed, she felt the gravity of what she'd done weighing on her. She shouldn't have gone to bed with him on their second date, or third if she counted the gala. It was too soon. And yet, she couldn't bring herself to regret it.

She would, though, if he never called her again.

Men were hunters, and once they caught their prey, they lost interest. Cassandra had never made it so easy for a guy before. If a man wanted her, he had to work hard on wooing her because she was worth it.

Onegus returned with a robe that was identical to the one he'd worn before. "I'll make breakfast while you get dressed. Any preferences?"

She smiled tightly. "A fresh cup of coffee will do. I usually don't eat breakfast."

"I'll make eggs and toast." He leaned and kissed her cheek again. "You rocked my world last night, Cassy. I want more of that soon."

"Me too."

She waited until he left the room to let out a relieved breath.

This wasn't the end. It was just the beginning.

Emmett

Twelfth day in captivity.

Emmett wondered how long he would keep count. A month? A year? A decade?

Kian had promised to let him out of the cell, conditional on the information he'd provided proving useful in locating his tribe, but Emmett doubted it would be.

The Kra-ell were nomadic by nature.

Their numbers were small, so it wasn't difficult to keep moving from place to place, and it helped keep them hidden. If too many humans started disappearing in one area, people became suspicious, especially of those who were different.

It had been relatively easy to disappear in China, and during his time with the tribe they'd moved several times, never returning to the same spot twice.

Kian's people were not going to find anything at the location he'd given them. Their best chance was to follow the money.

If Jade had sold Kumei there should be a money trail, but he had a feeling that she'd kept at least some control over the company. That was why he'd sent the email there.

What else could he offer Kian in exchange for his freedom?

The sanctimonious prick would never release him to his precious human world, but under the circumstances, the immortal village sounded like a sweet enough deal.

If all the immortal females were as tasty as Eleanor, then he was in for a buffet of treats.

Seducing them wouldn't be difficult. According to Arwel, Emmett's only competition for female attention were the former Doomers, a bunch of crude, uneducated brutes.

Compared to them, Emmett was a catch. Hell, he was a catch compared to nearly all males, human, long-lived, and immortal. He was sophisticated, charming, and a great lover if he said so himself.

The fact that he nibbled on a little blood from time to time was inconsequential, a small price to pay for the incredible physical pleasure he provided his partners, not to mention the intellectual pleasure of his company. Any female should feel honored to be chosen by him.

Perhaps he could offer Kian money, provided that the prick hadn't emptied Emmett's largest bank account already. He had plenty more, but losing what he had in the one he'd given the goddess access to would be painful.

What a powerful compeller the Clan Mother was.

Compared to her, Jade was a weakling. And unlike Jade, the Clan Mother had treated him with respect. But then she'd forced him to give her access to his largest bank account, which was what Jade would have done. She owned everything that their community had, including its members.

But at least Jade never tried to appear as anything other than the ruthless bitch she was. It would be a sad joke if after all of Kian's preaching about morality, fairness, and the importance of consent, he stole the money.

The guy didn't seem to be after Emmett's fortune, but everyone, even a rich guy like Kian, could always use more.

Emmett had a lot more stashed away in foreign accounts, and he owned the Safe Haven property free and clear. Which was another problem he needed to solve. The future profits belonged to him, but if he didn't claim them, they would be lost, squandered by whoever had stepped up to take his place.

Was it Riley?

She was the most qualified, but she lacked charisma and the others wouldn't follow her. Worse, they would try to undermine her, and the internal squabbles would ruin the well-oiled money-making machine he'd created.

As the door mechanism activating snagged his attention, Emmett looked up, curious to see who was visiting him this time. It was probably just one of the Guardians with his breakfast, but as starved as he was for company, even the stoic Alfie would do.

He liked Jay better, but the one Emmett liked the most was Arwel.

The guy was intelligent and well-read, which was a rare find these days. Perhaps it was different with immortals, but young humans liked their information to be served in condensed bites, preferably in color and with sound. And if they bothered to read at all, it was all about I and I and more I. They should be called the I generation, not X or millennials or any of the other terms used to describe them.

When the door finished swinging open, Arwel walked in with a tray in his hands, and Emmett greeted him with a genuine smile. "Good morning. I'm glad it is you and not one of your helpers."

"Why is that?" Arwel put the tray on the coffee table.

"You're more fun to talk to, and I'm bored." He lifted the lid off the container of blood and took a sip. "Lamb." He smacked his lips. "My favorite."

Arwel pointed at the plate of beef tartar and another container of blood. "After you finish everything, brush your teeth and wash your mouth. There is a change of guard later on, and the sight and smell of blood might gross them out."

Emmett paused with the tall container mid-air. "Are you leaving me?"

Arwel chuckled. "Not yet, but soon."

"Why?"

"I'm needed elsewhere. But don't worry, you will like my replacements." He smiled. "Eleanor and Peter are here, and one of them or both will bring your lunch. I'm staying just until they have the routine down."

Eleanor.

As everything that made Emmett a male awakened, and not too gently, his mouth filled with saliva, and not for the animal blood in the cup he was holding in his hand.

But then reality came knocking, and he frowned. "Should I expect trouble?"

"Not unless you cause it. They will not harm you."

"They both have reason to seek revenge, and I'm helpless." He lifted his cuffed arms. "I'm bound by shackles, both tangible and intangible. Your Clan Mother compelled me not to use my powers against her clan members."

"I'm well aware of that. Otherwise, I would have never agreed to have a female guard you."

"Do you think so little of me? I didn't harm Eleanor. I just nibbled a little on her blood, and regardless of what she told you, she was most willing. I didn't use compulsion on her, and the spiked wine had very little effect on her."

Arwel's usually pleasant expression hardened. "She tried to stop you, but you held her down and kept sucking. That's not willing in my book or any other."

They were all a bunch of self-righteous pricks, even Arwel. "Spare me the holier-than-thou sermon. As if all the females you guys bite during sex are consenting to receive your venom. They might sign up for the sex, but not for the fringe benefits they haven't bargained for."

Margaret

"I don't think I can eat one more hamburger or steak without getting nauseous," Ana whispered as Bowen closed the door behind him. "But I don't have the heart to tell Bowen that I'm sick of eating the same thing every day."

"You don't have much longer to suffer through it." Margaret looked at Bowen through the window, her eyes following his movements as he fired up the grill. "You and Leon are leaving Thursday morning."

Ana sighed. "Yeah, I know. I'll probably miss Bowen's cooking when I go back to living on frozen meals."

It would be hard to say goodbye, especially to Bowen, but everyone had to go back to work eventually, including her.

He'd offered to come with her to Safe Haven, but that would be a temporary solution as well, and it would make saying goodbye to him even harder. Bowen didn't belong in Safe Haven, and he didn't belong with her. If she had any decency, she would not only let him go but push him away.

If you love something, let it go. If it comes back to you, it's yours forever. If it doesn't, then it was never meant to be.

She could remove the middle portion of that saying. Bowen was suffering from an acute case of a savior complex, and once he was free of her, he would realize that and forget about her.

Margaret looked through the window at the two men on the front porch. Leaning against the railing, Leon was sipping on a beer while Bowen fanned the charcoal to ignite a larger flame.

He was so handsome, so masculine, such an incredibly good man.

Tearing her eyes from Bowen, she looked at her friend's flat stomach. "Maybe you are pregnant after all. You said that you missed your birth control shot."

"The doctor took a blood test. I'm not pregnant." Ana rubbed a hand over her belly. "But maybe my stomach is still sensitive."

"You've lost weight."

Ana had returned changed from the clinic, and aside from the very strange and sudden weight loss, she didn't look like someone who had to get antibiotics through an IV. Her hair was glossier, her skin smoother and blemish-free, and her eyes practically glowed, especially when she got excited. Ana herself joked about the miracle potion the doctor must have injected her with.

But joking aside, what had actually happened in that clinic?

Ana grinned. "At least one good thing came out from that damn infection. I finally lost those stubborn pounds on my hips and ass that I couldn't get rid of."

"If you say so."

"Or was it two things?" Ana lifted a brow. "You were different when I came back. I have a feeling that things were getting serious between you and Bowen." She smiled. "It's adorable the way he looks at you."

"What do you mean?"

"He follows you with his eyes like a lovesick puppy."

To compare that mountain of a man to a puppy was an insult. Besides, Margaret wouldn't call his fond glances lovesick.

"He does not." She lifted her glass of water and took a sip. "We are just friends."

Liar.

Ana pursed her lips. "Right. Tell it to someone who doesn't know you. Yesterday, when Leon and I returned from our hike, your cheeks were flushed, and you looked like you were floating on a cloud of happiness."

Ana was just fishing. Margaret didn't blush. Or did she?

"I don't know what you're talking about." She felt heat creep up her cheeks.

Damn.

Ana smirked. "Did you two do something naughty when Leon and I were gone?"

"Not what you're imagining, that's for sure."

"Then tell me what you did, and it better not be nothing."

"We kissed. That's all. Just one kiss." Actually, there were two or three kisses, and a lot of caresses.

She'd lost her mind yesterday, allowing herself to indulge in the fantasy for just a little bit.

Those few precious moments would have to sustain her for a very long time. Now that Emmett was gone, Margaret was going to insist on some changes, mainly no more shunning members for abstinence. She had no intentions of inviting anyone into her bed.

"Just one kiss?" Ana glanced out the window. "With that hunk of a man? What's wrong with you?"

"This." Margaret lifted her cast. "What could we possibly do with that?"

She had a few ideas, but she wasn't going to share them with Ana or Bowen. If she made love to the man, leaving him would destroy her.

"A lot," Ana said. "You just need to be creative."

"I'm not that imaginative."

Liar.

Margaret had spent half the night thinking about all the naughty things she could do with Bowen despite the cast, and she had fallen asleep only after giving herself a release while imagining those were his fingers between her legs and not her own.

"I think Bowen is in love with you."

"Think again. Why on earth would he love me? What's there to love?"

Ana looked as if she'd slapped her. "Margaret! I don't want to hear you say such nonsense. You are a wonderful woman, beautiful and compassionate. What's not to love?"

If she only knew.

"Forget I said that. I'm in a mood today." She rubbed her thigh above the cast. "I'm itchy, and I want this thing off already." It wasn't a lie, but it wasn't the truth either.

Her mood had little to do with the cast and a lot to do with the man she had to leave behind.

Ana's eyes softened. "You poor thing. Is there anything I can do to make it better for you?"

"I'm fine. As long as I'm busy, I don't think about it, and it doesn't bother me as much."

"I'll let you work then." Ana pushed to her feet. "I'm going to chop some veggies for a salad."

Margaret waited until Ana was in the kitchen before letting out a breath.

Why couldn't she just let herself enjoy Bowen?

If she could regard him in the same way she had the Safe Haven male members that she'd been with over the years, everything would be fine. Thoughts about the future would be irrelevant, and she could enjoy the days she had left with him, accepting the gift of him without feeling guilty about indulging in what she shouldn't.

Eleanor

"Ready?" Peter put a hand on Eleanor's shoulder.

"Yeah. I'm just wondering if we should go in together. The idea is for me to get close to Emmett, which is not going to happen with you smirking from the sidelines. Maybe you should stay with Arwel and watch us through the feed."

"How is that different from me being in there with you? You will know that I'm watching, and so will Emmett."

She turned to look at Arwel, who was sitting on the couch with earphones on, learning Chinese.

At least he wouldn't listen in.

Maybe that was the solution. "Can you watch without the sound on? Arwel is busy, but I'm sure he wouldn't mind."

"He's still the boss. We need to ask him if that's okay."

Arwel waved a hand. "Go ahead. The Clan Mother compelled Emmett to behave. Just watch your neck. She didn't tell him not to suck blood."

"Very funny." If Eleanor wasn't holding a tray, she would have flipped him off. "By the way, do I want to know what's in here?"

"Just hamburger patties," Arwel said. "I didn't want to gross you out on your first visit, but you'll have to get used to the blood."

She grimaced. "I'll live."

"Come on." Peter walked out into the hallway. "I'll open the door for you, but I won't come in."

"Thank you."

When the door to Emmett's cell swung open, Eleanor took a deep breath, plastered a bored expression on her face and sauntered in.

Emmett rose to his feet and dipped his head. "It's a pleasure to see you, Eleanor. Can I relieve you of the tray?"

He looked different without the beard and the long, majestic hair. Gone was the charismatic cult leader, and in his place was just a very handsome, attractive man, who was still pretty damn charismatic even without the props.

"So gallant all of a sudden." Eleanor put the tray on the coffee table.

Behind her, the door started to swing closed, and she had a moment of panic thinking about being locked in with Emmett in the small room.

"I'm always gallant." He motioned for her to take a seat on the couch. "Are you going to join me for lunch?"

She snorted. "I'm not going to be your lunch, that's for sure."

He laughed. "Touché. I promise to never bite you without your permission again." He sat next to her, unfurled a paper napkin as if it was a fancy fabric one, and draped it over his pants.

"From what I understand, you couldn't bite me even if you wanted to. The goddess compelled you to behave."

"Ah, Eleanor." He lifted the lid off the container. "As a compeller, you should know that the wording needs to be very precise. Otherwise, it's possible to find loopholes."

"Where is the loophole here?"

"The Clan Mother commanded me not to harm any members of her clan, but I don't consider a bite that delivers pleasure harmful, nor the little nibbling I do. I took very little from you." His dark eyes flashed turquoise for a moment. "Your taste was exquisite."

Remembering how it had felt, a shiver ran down Eleanor's spine. And if she cared to be frank with herself, the momentary terror she'd felt when she couldn't dislodge his hands had only added to the fuel of her arousal. Or was it something else?

That's why she was here, to find out what caused that strange, unwanted desire she felt for Emmett.

She still missed freaking Greggory, and if he hadn't been such a jerk, she would have wanted him back. But that chapter was closed, and all she could do was to look forward.

Emmett speared a hamburger patty with a fork and transferred it to a paper plate. "Can I offer you at least one? They are not bad."

She looked at the nearly raw meat and shook her head. "I'll have lunch later. Go ahead, eat. Don't mind me."

Next time, she was going to bring a meal for herself as well. If she was to seduce him into trusting her, she needed to spend time with him. The trick was not to make herself too obvious.

That shouldn't be a problem.

Eleanor wasn't the flirtatious type, and Emmett was a hunter to the core. If she showed no interest, he would try to seduce her, and after a while, she could pretend to succumb to his charm and charisma.

Again, that wouldn't be difficult.

She looked around the small room and noted the pile of books stacked on top of the dresser. "I see you've been busy reading."

"There isn't much else to do here." He wiped his mouth with a napkin. "What do you do to pass the time?"

"I train."

"How about that partner you've talked about and Peter has mentioned? Do you spend time with her?"

She laughed. "That was a made-up story. Kri, my friend and trainer, was supposed to come with me to Safe Haven, and we pretended to be a couple. Kri is happily mated to a fellow Guardian in training."

"What about you?"

Her smile faltered. "I had a boyfriend, but things didn't work out between us. We ended it a few days ago."

"I'm sorry to hear that." He didn't look sorry at all. In fact, he looked like the cat who was about to abscond with the cream. "Did it have anything to do with what happened between us?"

She shrugged. "If he couldn't handle what I needed to do on the job, he wasn't the right guy for me."

"I agree a hundred percent."

Bowen

"Tea?" Bowen clicked the electric kettle's switch on.

Margaret nodded. "I would love some, thank you."

As usual, Ana and Leon had gone on a hike right after lunch to give him and Margaret some alone time.

The kiss had changed things between them, but he wasn't sure if it was for the better. They could no longer pretend that their relationship was just friendship, which was what he'd wanted, but Margaret seemed to cling to the pretense as if her life depended on it.

She hadn't said a word about the kiss they'd shared the day before, and her smiles had been guarded, polite. She had, however, put a little more effort into her appearance, which gave him hope. Her hair was no longer hanging limply down her shoulders and was instead styled in soft waves that shone thanks to Anastasia's curling iron. It wasn't much, but combined with the healthier-looking skin color and the little weight she'd gained, her beauty shone through.

If he only had more time, he would peel away her layers despite her resistance and uncover the diamond buried underneath. But even after all the time they'd spent together, he didn't even know what those layers were about.

What was she trying to protect?

Her heart?

What was she afraid of?

He was running out of time, and accommodating Margaret's avoidance was not an option. He had to confront her, to get her talking, and he wished he was better equipped for the task. Margaret needed someone with Vanessa's skill set and experience, not a Guardian of a few words.

When the water boiled, Bowen poured it into the two cups, added teabags, and put a few chocolates on each saucer.

Margaret glanced at the chocolates and smiled. "Are you still trying to fatten me up?"

"Not trying. Succeeding." He sat next to her. "But my work is not done." He dipped the teabag in the hot water. "If you insist on going back to Safe Haven on Sunday, I need to come with you to make sure you are not forgetting to eat."

She lifted her phone. "I'm not going to give this up, and Ana showed me how to set up timers with reminders. I will not forget to eat."

The phone was clan issue, and Kian would not want it falling into enemy hands. The device had restricted access, but someone could realize that it wasn't an iPhone or any other known brand and try to reverse engineer it.

"I'll have to get you a new one. This device belongs to the organization I work for."

"Oh." She cradled it in her palms. "That's a shame. I've gotten attached to this marvelous thing. Now that I know what it can do, I can't imagine life without it."

He was so damn jealous of that piece of technology. She couldn't imagine life without it, but she had no problem imagining life without him?

"I wish you thought that way about me," he murmured.

Her smile wilted and a tear slid down her cheek. "Oh, Bowen. I will miss you terribly, but it's for the best."

"How can you say that? You can stay with me. We can explore our feelings for each other, let them grow. It's not like either of us is leaving someone so we can be together. There is no upside to you going back there without me, nothing worthy of the sacrifice, it's just your stubbornness that's in the way of our potential happiness. Why don't you want to give us a chance?"

She looked down, her wavy brown hair cascading and creating a curtain to shield her face from him. "Safe

Haven is not the right place for you, Bowen. Eventually, you will need to get back to work, and saying goodbye will be even more difficult. That's why I said it was best if we parted now."

"I don't intend to leave Safe Haven without you." He reached for her hand and clasped it. "My plan is to make you fall in love with me and leave together."

She chuckled sadly, but still didn't look at him. "Falling in love with you is easy, Bowen. You are handsome, and wholesome, and everything that is good. I'm not worthy of you, and sooner or later you are going to realize that and leave."

"If you think that your opioid problem makes me think any less of you, you are wrong. It's in the past, and I will never hold it against you. On the contrary, you overcame the addiction and have stayed clean ever since. It shows a remarkable strength of character, and you should be proud of yourself for achieving something that many fail to do."

She shook her head. "The shame is not about the addiction itself. It's about how I got addicted in the first place, and what I did to support it."

His gut clenched as he thought about the trafficking victims he rescued. Most of them were addicted to drugs not because they chose them but because their captors forced them to use, so they would later do anything for a fix without giving them any trouble.

Had Margaret sold her body to support her addiction?

"Whatever you did, it's in the past. You've spent your years in Safe Haven helping countless people deal with their demons. It's time you forgave yourself."

"I can't."

When he opened his mouth to argue, she lifted her hand. "Please, Bowen, let it go. It's difficult enough for me as it is." She looked at her phone and sighed. "I need to get back to work. Immersing myself in it is my way to cope. If I give it up, this one thing that makes me feel good about myself, I will have nothing left."

Cassandra

Cassandra closed the garage door and took a deep breath before opening the door to the laundry room.

This morning she'd managed to dodge her mother's barrage of questions about her date with Onegus, but there was no escaping it now.

She could have stayed late at work, hoping that Geraldine wouldn't be home by the time she got there, but she was tired, and finishing up what she needed to do while sleep-deprived was easier done in her pajamas.

"I'm home." She dropped her overstuffed satchel on the kitchen counter and walked over into the family room, where one of her mother's soaps was playing.

"You're home early, Cassy." Geraldine grinned. "We can have dinner together for a change." Her smile turned into a frown as she glanced at the bloated satchel. "I see that you brought work home."

"I always do." Cassandra leaned to kiss her cheek.

"You should have called. I would have prepared something."

"That's okay, Mom. We can order takeout." She headed for the stairs.

"You promised to tell me about your date with Onegus." Geraldine pushed to her feet. "You can do it while I make us something to tide us over."

Letting out a sigh, Cassandra turned around. With all the things her mother was forgetting, couldn't she have forgotten about that?

She walked over to the fridge and pulled out a soda. "He took me to a really fancy restaurant, we ate, we talked, we even danced a little, and then he took me to his place."

Geraldine grinned. "And how did that go?"

"I got angry and shattered a vase." Cassandra popped the lid and took a sip.

Her mother paled. "Oh, dear. I hope it wasn't irreplaceable."

"Is that what worries you? It was a crystal vase, and it exploded. The shards flew at us, and if not for Onegus's lightning-fast reflexes, both of us would have gotten hurt." She sighed. "I'm seriously contemplating taking relaxants again."

Pulling out a pack of frozen ravioli from the freezer, Geraldine shook her head. "You can't. They make you sleepy and dull your creativity. You should take up meditation, or yoga, or just learn how not to get angry over things you can't control."

"I don't have the patience for meditation or yoga, and I'm doing my best not to get angry." Cassandra took out her earrings and stuffed them in her pocket.

They'd had that same conversation many times. Geraldine might have forgotten she'd already given Cassandra that advice, but it didn't make it any less valid.

"Did Onegus suspect that you had something to do with it?" Her mother filled a pot with water from the filter and put it on the stove.

"He was very gracious about it. I took the blame, saying that I accidentally knocked it over. But he said there must have been a flaw in the crystal, and some frequency of our voices resonated with it. He also said that it was cheap Chinese crap, so at least I didn't feel guilty about ruining something valuable."

"What did you get angry about?"

"He lied to me. You know how much I hate that."

"About what?"

"About the apartment he took me to. It was brand new, and in a newly renovated building that no one lived in. He said that he's supposed to show it to prospective clients, but that was a bullshit story. I don't know why he lied about it."

Geraldine pulled out a stool next to Cassandra and leaned her elbows on the counter. "And yet you spent the night with him."

There was no disapproval in her mother's tone, only curiosity.

"I felt so guilty and grateful as well. He saved me from the flying shards, and his expensive suit got ruined. I don't know how he didn't get injured, but he could have, and he did it to protect me." She lifted her hands. "How could I have denied him after that?"

Her mother gave her a lopsided grin. "I'm sure that gratitude was your only motive to hop into bed with that gorgeous hunk of a man."

Cassandra's lips twitched with a stifled smile. "Well, there was that too."

"How was it?"

The thing about having a young, unconventional mother was that they were more like sisters and could talk about everything. And that was also a problem. Cassandra didn't want to discuss her sex life with Geraldine, but her mother would be offended if she brushed her off.

She had to give her something. "Spectacular. I feel so calm." She put a hand over her chest. "Instead of a stormy sea, it's a placid lake in here."

It was as if all of her excess energy had gotten discharged when her body had detonated with one climax after the other.

Geraldine laughed. "That's your cure, Cassy. You don't need relaxants or meditation, just great sex with Onegus."

Onegus

"You are home early." Connor removed his headphones. "I didn't make anything today." He tapped his finger on his tablet. "Brandon gave a mile-long list of things he didn't like about my score for *The Destroyer*. Until I'm done, it's going to be sandwiches from the café."

"You don't need to apologize." Onegus walked up to the fridge and pulled out a beer. "I wish I could tell you that I'll take over the cooking, but I'm moving into the new building on Thursday, and I'm going to stay there until the festivities are over."

Connor smirked. "Not to mention the new lady friend you're seeing. What's her name?"

The guy was the epitome of a busybody, but he wasn't a distributor of gossip, only a collector. Onegus trusted his roommate not to spread rumors about the new lady in his life.

"Cassandra Beaumont. She works for Kevin Brunswick, the founder of Fifty Shades of Beauty. His company donates cosmetics to the sanctuary and halfway house, and he's also contributing funds to the charity."

"Is he related to Josephine Brunswick, the cellist?"

"He's her husband."

"I know her. She's a sweetheart." Connor shook his head. "Dating a lady who works for one of our contributors is dangerous. She's not just a random chick you picked up in a club."

"I'm well aware of that."

Connor eyed him with speculation gleaming in his smart eyes. "She must be something. Since you and I moved in together, it's the first time I've seen you return from a date in the morning, and you are done with work early the second day in a row, which means that you are taking her out again. You're asking for trouble."

"I know what I'm doing." Onegus pointed with the bottle. "I thought that you were pressed for time. Go back to your composition."

"Just don't fall for her." Connor put the headphones back on.

Onegus had never fallen for a woman before, and he wasn't about to now. Cassandra was one of a kind, but if she wasn't a Dormant, he had no business pursuing a relationship with her.

And even if she was a Dormant, she wasn't necessarily his one and only. Hell, he had no desire to get shackled with a mate, and not for the reason other males avoided commitment. Giving up other females would be a relief rather than a hardship, but he liked his autonomy. Having to share everything with another, to not be able to just get up and go when he pleased, and for whatever reason, that was definitely a hardship.

It was crippling. He'd seen it happening to all of his head Guardians. So yeah, the bastards were happy, but that happiness came at a price. For them, the gain must have been worth much more than the pain, but for him it was the opposite.

That being said, it wasn't going to be easy to let Cassandra go.

They clicked, and it wasn't just physical, although sex with her had seriously rocked his world. He liked her assertiveness, her no-nonsense attitude, her work ethic, her drive, her talent...

Damn, there was a lot to like about Cassandra Beaumont. So much so that he was inclined to reevaluate his gain versus pain ratio. She felt different than other women he'd been with, and that strange energy field she emitted might be an indicator that she was more than just human.

It was worth investigating, and it gave him a good excuse for seeing her again.

Walking toward his bedroom, he pulled out his phone and dialed her number.

"Hello," she answered after six or seven rings, pretending once again that she hadn't recognized his number.

He could play along. "Hello, beautiful. Are you still at work?"

"I'm home, but I brought work with me."

"Can you take a break?" Onegus sat on the bed and leaned his elbow on his knee.

"To do what?"

He couldn't thrall her again so soon, but he needed to be with her again, see that perfect body of hers naked and writhing in pleasure. He should have enough self-control to hold off biting her until the next day.

"I can come to your place and bring takeout, or we can go out."

"How about I come to your place instead? Not that apartment you took me to yesterday, but your real home."

Aha, so that was what she was after. She still doubted him and wanted to make sure that he didn't have another woman in his life.

"I thought that you were short on time."

"Do you live far away?"

"Quite. It's an hour's drive. Besides, I have a nosy roommate who thinks that he's my mother and asks too many questions."

"He sounds like fun. In fact, I would love to meet him."

Onegus's suspicions were confirmed. Cassandra either didn't believe that he actually had a roommate or didn't believe that his roommate was a he and not a she.

"I can put him on the phone." Onegus rose to his feet and walked back to the living room. "His name is Connor."

"What about me?" Connor took the headphones off.

"Cassandra wants to talk to you." He activated the speaker function.

"About?"

Onegus shrugged. "I think that she doesn't believe me that you are a guy."

"I didn't say that," Cassandra bristled.

He put the phone on top of Connor's tablet.

"Hello, Cassandra. As you can tell by my voice, I am male, but if you want, we can switch to Zoom, and you can see my handsome face. I'm much better looking than this giant brute."

"I'm sure you are." Cassandra's tone lost its edge. "But I'm in my pajamas, and my hair is a mess, so no video."

"That's such a damn shame." Connor looked the picture of disappointment. "I was just joking about being better looking than my brawny, blond-haired, blue-eyed housemate." He cleared his throat for emphasis. "I was curious to see the lady who has him wrapped around her little finger."

Onegus shook his head. It had been a mistake to give the phone to Connor.

She laughed. "He's too big to fit around my little finger."

Connor barked out a snort. "If I value my life, I'm not going to respond to that. Anyway, I wanted to tell you that I know your boss's wife. If you see Josephine, tell her that Connor says hi."

"How did you meet her?"

"I write scores for movies, and she was the soloist for one of my compositions. She's a lovely human being."

"Josie is amazing. She'll be tickled silly that you are Onegus's roommate."

"Housemate. We don't share the same room. That would be just awkward."

Cassandra chuckled. "Naturally."

"Say goodbye, Connor." Onegus took the phone back.

"Goodbye, Cassandra."

"Bye, Connor. It was nice talking to you."

Onegus turned the speakerphone off. "Are you convinced now?"

"I didn't doubt you before."

He laughed. "Liar. Ask your mom what kind of takeout she wants."

"You are serious. You want to eat dinner with my mother and me."

"It would be my pleasure."

"Chinese. My mom loves Chinese food. Orange chicken is her favorite."

"Chinese it is. I'll be there at eight."

"Thanks. I'll see you later."

When he ended the call, Connor was still grinning at him. "She sounds nice. Do you have a picture?"

"I do." Onegus pulled out one that he'd taken on the beach and handed the phone to Connor.

Connor whistled. "She's a knockout. No wonder you are smitten." He enlarged the photo with two fingers. "But she looks a little bitchy, pardon my French." He handed the phone back.

"I admit that Cassandra has an attitude, but that's one of the many things I like about her. She has spunk."

"A spunky lady to spank." Connor waggled his brows.

"Pervert." Onegus turned around to hide his smile, that and the erection that had popped up behind his zipper as he imagined his hand on Cassandra's perfectly rounded bottom.

Cassandra

Cassandra absentmindedly sketched the layout for the cover of the brochure that would go in next month's Surprise Box, years of honing her skills making it possible for her to create while her mind was busy elsewhere.

She knew what the finished product should look like even before putting down the first stroke, and it was just a matter of tweaking the layout and the colors, choosing photos, and adding flourishes.

Despite the calm that usually accompanied her creative work, an echo of unease churned in Cassandra's stomach, and she couldn't figure out what it was. It had something to do with Onegus, something she knew that she should remember and couldn't. The feeling was like trying to recollect a line from a movie, or an actor's name that was on the tip of her tongue yet eluded her.

Had he said something she couldn't remember?

It felt like it was something important, and not being able to bring it up terrified her.

As panic threatened to choke her, Cassandra tried to beat it down by reciting the self-reaffirming convictions that usually helped in situations like that.

Her mind was orderly and sharp. She wasn't going to end up like her mother, losing entire chunks of her past or hours from her day. Her mother's memory issues were the result of head trauma. Cassandra's were just ordinary memory lapses everyone experienced from time to time.

Sometimes, though, she wondered whether Geraldine hadn't invented the trauma and resulting amnesia as well. It had happened long before Cassandra had been born, and given how young her mother was, it must have happened when Geraldine was still a child. She claimed not to remember her family, and yet she'd never mentioned a foster home or an orphanage either. Someone must have taken care of her, a child who'd had to relearn everything from scratch, including language.

When Geraldine mentioned it, which she rarely did, she talked about it as if she'd been an adult while it happened.

Heck, who knew? Her mother refused to reveal her age, claiming that a lady never should, but maybe she was in her fifties and only looked young?

Perhaps crazy people aged slower?

It was frustrating to know so little about the most important person in her life and the only family she had, or rather knew of. But whenever Cassandra complained, her mother just hugged and kissed her and said that 'love is what matters and everything else is just background noise.'

Respecting her mother's wishes, Cassandra hadn't dug into Geraldine's past even though she'd been tempted. When she'd started making good money, she'd even thought about hiring a private eye to look into it, mainly because she wanted to find out whether she had any family out there. But doing so behind her mother's back felt wrong. It would have been a huge betrayal of trust, and her mother didn't deserve that from her.

The woman had dedicated her life to raising Cassandra as best as she could, finding work that she could do from home and doing most of it at night, so her child wouldn't have to fend for herself during the day.

Whatever dark secrets her mother hid from the world and from herself, they belonged to her.

As someone who had her own skeletons in her proverbial closet, secrets that she couldn't share with anyone, she had no problem walking a mile in her mother's shoes. Cassandra wouldn't have wanted anyone digging into them or forcing her to seek psychological help.

The difference was that Geraldine knew her darkest secret, but Cassandra didn't know her mother's.

Perhaps that was how it was supposed to be.

If she ever had children, Cassandra would do her best to hide her witchy powers from them. Until she learned to control that energy, though, she had no business having kids. What if she got angry or frustrated and hurt them?

The thought was terrifying enough to consider getting her tubes tied.

"Cassy." Geraldine peeked into her study. "You should get ready. It's quarter to eight."

She glanced down at her jeans and flip flops. "I am ready. We are not going out. It's just a takeout dinner at home."

Her mother shook her head. "At least change your T-shirt. You have paint smudges all over it."

She chuckled. "It's not smudges, Mom. It's the shirt's design. I got it on sale, but the original price was close to two hundred dollars."

Geraldine's expression was doubtful. "If you say so. Just wear something nice for Onegus. It doesn't have to be fancy, but a lady does not accept guests in flip-flops and jeans."

Her mother sometimes seemed to forget what era they were living in, but arguing with her would only upset her and make things worse. The memory issues became much more obvious when Geraldine was upset.

"You have such old-fashioned ideas about propriety, but fine. I'll change."

Her mother beamed happily. "Now, was that so hard to do?"

"Not at all." Cassandra pushed to her feet. "Just do me a favor and don't spin tall tales or embarrass me in any way during dinner."

"I don't know what you mean." Her mother pushed her chin out. "It's one thing to talk freely and joke around with my daughter, and it's another thing altogether to do so in front of a gentleman caller. I plan to be the perfect hostess."

Cassandra stifled the urge to roll her eyes.

Her mother had embarrassed her plenty of times in front of her friends from school, until she'd stopped inviting them over.

"Since I've never had a *gentleman caller* before, you don't have practice being the perfect hostess, and your book club doesn't count. I heard you and your friends discuss romance books, and you were far from proper." She pulled a summer dress out of the closet. "Let's agree on a sign. If I clear my throat, you will stop whatever you're talking about and change the subject or let me do that. I don't want to talk over you and appear rude."

Geraldine huffed out a breath as if to say that Cassandra was offending her for no good reason. "I'll let you get dressed and go set the table."

"Thanks, Mom."

"You're welcome." Her mother hesitated for a moment. "I know that you are all grown up and that you don't need advice from your crazy mother. But just try not to seem too eager. Men like to chase, and if they catch you too easily, they don't appreciate you."

Geraldine had given her that same advice so many times that it was hardwired into her brain. Nevertheless, Cassandra pretended it was the first time she'd heard it. "Thanks for the advice, Mom." She walked up to her mother, kissed her cheek, and once she left, closed the door and sighed.

Her mother's advice sounded so outdated, so old-fashioned. Even anti-feminist. Why should women play hard to get when they wanted sex just as much as men did?

They shouldn't.

But the world was not fair, and people played all kinds of games to get the upper hand. Cassandra hated playing games, but she hated losing even more.

Onegus

The door opened even before Onegus had a chance to knock, but it wasn't surprising given that the guard had called the house before letting him through the gate.

He was glad that Cassandra and her mother lived in a gated community. Home invasions were much more commonplace than most people realized, and two women living alone were an easy target.

"Hello, Onegus." Geraldine beamed at him, or rather at the bag he was holding in his left hand. "The orange chicken smells delicious."

In his right, he was balancing a bouquet of flowers and a bottle of wine. It never hurt to go the extra mile, so to speak.

"Good evening. I hope it is as good as it smells." He handed her the bottle and flowers.

Geraldine looked lovely, her dark hair swept to the side and secured with a comb, and a pale blue summer dress accentuating her delicate build. The cat-eye eyeliner and pale pink lipstick made her look like a fifties model, but she was way too young to have grown up in that era. In fact, she looked no older than Cassandra, maybe even younger, because Geraldine's expression was softer.

Perhaps she wasn't Cassandra's birth mother?

Nah, that didn't make sense. No agency would let a young, unmarried woman adopt a child. Unless she was Cassandra's older sister. Perhaps siblings were allowed to foster their younger sisters and brothers?

But that didn't make much sense either.

Applying Occam's razor, the simplest explanation was that Geraldine had Cassy as a teenager, and she'd been lucky enough to age well.

He followed her inside. "Is Cassandra still working?"

"You guessed it. She insists on creating a new design for each new monthly Surprise Box, says it keeps them fresh, but that means that she has to reinvent the wheel every month anew."

It was a very lucid insight from a woman who was supposedly a little off.

He put the bags on the kitchen counter. "Cassandra knows what she's doing. Kevin is lucky to have her."

"Onegus." Cassandra flew down the stairs, her dress billowing around her hips, earrings dangling, and a bright smile on her gorgeous face.

"Cassy." He opened his arms, and she went right into them, wrapping her arms around his neck as if welcoming her mate returning from a long trip.

It felt too right.

Her enthusiastic welcome shouldn't make him feel so damn happy.

As he embraced her lightly and kissed her forehead out of respect for her mother, Geraldine cleared her throat.

"Let's eat before everything gets cold."

For some reason, Cassandra chuckled. "My mother seems uncomfortable with our display of affection. She's a little old-fashioned."

Geraldine smiled sweetly. "It's not that. I just can't wait to dig into my orange chicken." She took the bag and started putting boxes on the dining room table that was already set up for three.

He leaned and whispered into Cassandra's ear, "You look beautiful. Good enough to eat." The last sentence was delivered in a tone an octave lower than the first, and he interpreted the answering gleam in Cassandra's eyes as a *yes, please.*

"Later," he whispered.

Her mother cleared her throat again. "Cassy, could you please bring sodas from the refrigerator?"

"Of course." She winked at him before letting go and heading into the kitchen.

"I want to thank you," Geraldine said.

"You're welcome, but it's nothing." He waved a hand at the takeout boxes. "I hope you enjoy it. The Golden Dragon is my favorite place for Chinese."

"I'm sure Cassy and I will love it. But what I really wanted to thank you for is making my daughter happy." She narrowed her eyes at him. "Don't hurt her."

The message was clear, and he didn't doubt the potency of the unspoken 'or else.' The same energy he'd felt swirling inside Cassandra was also inside her mother, just at a much lower voltage.

He wondered whether sensitive humans picked up on that the way he had and what they made of it. In days long passed, mother and daughter could have been accused of witchcraft. Thank the merciful Fates those days were over, hopefully never to return, but one never knew with humans.

The us-versus-them chimp mentality was hardwired into the human race, as was blindly following their leaders, whether clergy, and or politicians. Nowadays there were also internet and social media influencers to follow. The twenty-first century was a brainwashing fest like no other, but the impetus hadn't changed. It had always been about power and money, and it was still about leaving as little of it as possible in the hands of the masses.

As long as it didn't lead to wars, though, Onegus didn't care. The problem was that at some point, someone always figured out that they could shift even more money and power from others to themselves by taking it forcefully.

"What are you thinking about?" Cassandra smoothed a finger over his forehead. "You're frowning."

He hadn't noticed that she'd returned with a six-pack of sodas and wine glasses for the wine he'd brought.

"Just random thoughts." He smiled. "Thank you for sharing your home with me tonight. I'm honored." He dipped his head to Geraldine.

"It's our pleasure." Cassandra's mother smiled sweetly as if she hadn't threatened him just a moment ago.

Cassandra

They were almost done with dinner, and so far Geraldine had behaved, but Cassandra had a feeling that her luck was about to run out when her mother smiled mysteriously, put her fork down, and pushed her plate away.

"This was excellent, but not as good as the one I had in Washington while dating Cassy's father."

Cassandra cleared her throat.

Disregarding her, Geraldine continued. "He was an analyst for the Ethiopian embassy."

So today, her father had been just the analyst. The other day he'd been the ambassador himself, and other times he hadn't been from Ethiopia but from Yemen or Senegal. And that was when he wasn't a visiting professor, a surgeon, or an astronaut.

As her mother lifted a paper napkin and dabbed it at her lips, Cassandra cast Onegus an apologetic sidelong glance.

"He was a descendant of the legendary Queen of Sheba." Her mother chuckled. "Or so he claimed." Her eyes became dreamy. "He was certainly majestic enough. Tall, broad-shouldered, and his smile." She fanned herself with her hand. "It was as beautiful as yours, Onegus."

Eager to interrupt the fantasy trip, Cassandra pushed to her feet. "Ready for coffee and dessert?"

Onegus followed her up. "I'll clear the table."

Geraldine remained seated for a moment longer, that dreamy expression still on her face. It would almost be a shame to bring her back to reality, but Cassandra feared that one of these days her mother would float away on the wings of her imagination and never come back.

"Mom, isn't Gwen supposed to pick you up at ten? It's nine-fifty, and you still need to change into something warmer."

Her mother shook her head. "I'll grab a sweater on my way out. It's not like we are going anywhere. We are just going to watch a movie at Gwen's."

"As you wish."

Geraldine pushed away from the table. "Do you need me to help clear the dishes?"

"No. We are fine, Mom. Go have fun."

"Thank you." She smiled at both of them. "It was a lovely dinner."

When Geraldine headed upstairs to get her sweater, Onegus smirked like a cat who had realized that the canary's cage was open. "We will have the house to ourselves," he said softly. "I feel like a teenager waiting for my girl's parents to leave, so I can have my wicked way with her."

Cassandra filled the carafe with water from the filter. "I'm sorry about my mother's stories about my father." She poured it into the coffeemaker. "I don't know if she makes them up because she can't remember who he was, or because she enjoys the fantasy." She smiled at Onegus. "For some reason, he's never just a schoolteacher or a plumber, which would make her stories more believable."

Onegus glanced toward the stairs, but her mother wasn't coming down yet. "As long as the fantasies don't make her dangerous to herself or others, they are harmless. Geraldine sounds lucid most of the time, she is intelligent, friendly, and seems to have an active social life."

"Yeah, she belongs to a book club that meets twice a week, sometimes three. My mother has a much more active social life than I do." Realizing how pathetic that sounded, Cassandra added, "But she doesn't work eighty hours a week and has the time to be social."

Onegus sighed. "We are a lot alike, you and I. I have never taken a proper vacation. I consider traveling for business my time off."

Leaning against the counter, she crossed her arms over her chest. "Do you enjoy what you do?"

"Very much so." He cast a glance at the hissing coffeemaker, which was spewing dark brew into the clear carafe. "Sometimes I don't even notice that I've been in the office for twelve hours straight."

"That's why you don't take a vacation," Cassandra said. "You enjoy working more than you enjoy time off."

It was also a sign of loneliness.

Cassandra hadn't taken a vacation since she'd started working for Kevin either. Neither of her two boyfriends had offered to take her on one, and going alone was just sad. After her high school friends had gone to college and she'd gone to work for Kevin, Cassandra had lost touch with them, so that wasn't an option either. Besides, they were no doubt married by now and chasing gaggles of kids around.

When the coffeemaker was done, she poured them both a cup. "Where would you go if you had someone to go with?"

He was about to answer when her mother came down the stairs.

"I'm off to Gwen's." She kissed Cassandra's cheek and then did the same to Onegus. "I hope to see you again." She tilted her head as if it was a question.

"I'm not going anywhere anytime soon."

Hopefully, that wasn't a lie.

"Good." Geraldine beamed happily.

Cassandra wondered if her mother was going to remember Onegus once he stopped coming over.

Probably not, which would be a blessing.

The guy was too good to be true, and something in his tone had told her that he wasn't planning on sticking around for long despite what he'd told her mother.

There were other indicators as well.

If he was serious about her, he would want to show her off to his friends, not take her to a deserted building where no one could see them together. So yeah, he'd taken her to his cousin's restaurant, and they'd even danced a little, but he hadn't introduced her to his famous cousin or anyone else.

Having her speak with his roommate on the phone didn't count.

If there was another date, she would insist that Onegus invite her to his house, the one he shared with the composer, or that he invite some of his friends to join them on an outing. If he tried to wiggle out of it, she would have proof that her hunch had been right, and she should end things before getting attached to him.

It would still be hard as hell to say goodbye to Onegus, but she could at least save her dignity and avoid even more pain down the line.

Onegus

As soon as the door closed behind Geraldine, Onegus pulled Cassandra into his arms. "Let's skip coffee and dessert. I'd much rather snack on you." He smacked his lips.

Her smile was tense. "I still have work to do tonight."

"So do I, but there is always time for a quickie." He dipped his head and kissed her softly. "I can either eat my dessert here, sprawled on the dining table, or on the couch, or you can take me to your bedroom."

She hesitated for a couple of seconds. "Let's go to my room." She took his hand and led him up the stairs.

"That's my mother's room." She pointed at the double doors leading to what was no doubt the master bedroom. "And this is mine." She opened the next door and turned the lights on.

The room was small, but like the rest of the house, it was uncluttered and beautifully done. A queen-sized bed with a wrought iron headboard took up most of the space. The bedding was cream-colored cotton with embroidered accents, and a colorful quilt was folded at the foot of the bed. There was space for only one nightstand and a dresser that was tall and narrow, and there were no knick-knacks or framed photos like in most females' bedrooms. Cassandra also had no television or any other electronics in her room, not even a landline phone, and instead of pictures, an intricate quilt covered half the wall across from the bed.

The room was designed to promote peaceful sleep and nothing else. He applauded her decorating approach. Living in a city that had suffered a number of powerful earthquakes, having nothing in her bedroom that could fall over and break was a smart decision.

"You don't work in here," he stated the obvious.

She chuckled. "I wouldn't be able to sleep at all if I had my work stuff here. The next bedroom over is my study, but I use its closet to store half of my clothes. There is not enough room in this one."

She sounded a little nervous, so he ran his hands over her back in soothing circles. "You bought the house, and yet you gave your mother the master bedroom. How come?"

She shrugged. "My mother worked very hard to raise me on her own. She deserves a little pampering from me. Besides, I only sleep in here, and I use the other bedroom as well."

He put his hands on her waist. "Under all your bluster, you are very sweet."

She scrunched her nose. "I am not sweet. I'm spicy."

He licked his lips. "Let's put it to the test."

He gathered her dress until it was bunched around her middle. "Lift your arms."

Smiling seductively, she did, and he pulled the dress over her head.

"Gorgeous." He lifted her by the waist, laid her on the bed, and then stood at the foot of it and just feasted his eyes on her.

"Get the lights, Onegus," she whispered.

"Are you being shy, Cassy?"

"No, but it's more romantic in the dark."

"If you say so." He walked over to the light switch and flicked it off.

Plenty of moonlight streamed through the open window, bathing Cassandra in a silvery light that made her skin glow like burnished copper.

Her bra and panties were white satin, simple yet elegant, just as the gray set she'd worn the day before. The woman had impeccable taste, and she paid attention to the smallest of details.

Even the bottle of moisturizer on the nightstand matched the color scheme of her room.

It gave him an idea. "Turn around on your belly. I'm going to give you a massage."

She grinned. "With a happy ending?"

"Of course."

As Cassandra turned over, he sucked in a breath. Her panties weren't a thong, but they didn't cover much either. The narrow triangle of satin barely covered the valley between her cheeks, and they were so enticing that he just had to kiss each one before sliding those panties down her long legs.

"I love your ass." He kissed each cheek again before reaching for the lotion.

"Only my ass?" Reaching behind herself, Cassandra popped the clasp of her bra, pulled it off, and tossed it on the floor.

"I love your breasts too, and your legs, and your arms." He squeezed out a dollop, rubbed it between his hands, and smoothed them over the back of her thighs. "I also love those pouty lips of yours, and your eyes, especially when they sizzle with power."

Cassandra stiffened. "What do you mean?"

"Your spunk, your energy." He smoothed his hands over her perfect bottom and kneaded. "You are strong, determined, uncompromising, and I find it sexy as hell."

"Some would summarize it as bitchy," she murmured.

"Not me." He slid a finger down her feminine folds, eliciting a throaty moan.

"What would you call it?"

He paused for a moment, thinking how to put into words the way he saw her. "I would call it majestic, my beautiful queen."

Cassandra

Cassandra laughed. "You are such a charmer, Onegus. But you are not original. I've been called a queen bitch before."

The smack landing on her bottom caught her by surprise. "What was that for?"

It hadn't been more than a love tap, and given how big and muscled Onegus was, he had barely touched her. Was it part of the foreplay?

"I just couldn't help myself." Another one landed on her other cheek, and then he was kneading them with his strong fingers, spreading the heat around. "This ass is driving me crazy. Men would go to war over this perfection."

"You're obsessed." Smiling into the pillow, she wiggled her bottom.

He smacked it again. "You're damn right I am. Can you blame me? Have you looked at that ass in the mirror?"

She laughed again. "I sure did."

Being playful in the bedroom was a novelty. The other men Cassandra had been with, the whole two of them, had taken sex way too seriously. She never would have expected to enjoy the banter with Onegus so much.

"Once or twice. But you promised me a massage, and all you're doing is talking and playing with my butt."

"Apologies, my queen."

She heard him squirt another dollop, and then his hands were on her calves, massaging, kneading.

Her toes curled as her muscles eased.

After strutting in high heels all day, her calf muscles were tight, and having his strong fingers on them felt almost orgasmic, which she freely expressed with several delighted moans.

He chuckled. "And here I thought that you would be hard to please." He lifted her foot and massaged each toe separately.

"If you promise to do this every night, I'll marry you as soon as we can get to a chapel." She regretted her words as soon as they'd left her mouth, and even more when his hands stopped massaging. "I'm just joking, Onegus. I have no intentions of marrying you or anyone else. I'm married to my job."

Liar.

She loved her work, but that didn't preclude having a man in her life, or even children—provided that she mastered her energy so it never acted out when it shouldn't. Her mother would help her raise them, and she could hire a nanny to help her. Geraldine would be thrilled to have babies to take care of. And as for her long workdays, Cassandra could do most of the work from home.

Kevin wouldn't mind. In fact, he would probably be overjoyed. It would save him from having to manage all the complaints from the other creatives about her bitchy attitude and her so-called unreasonable demands for timely production.

Yeah, dream on.

Time wasn't on her side as far as having children was concerned. If she didn't find someone soon, as well as learn to control her power, that would remain just a dream.

"I kind of liked the idea." His hands moved back to her calves. "But regrettably, I'm in the same boat as you. And on top of that, I also travel for work. Not a lot, but enough to make my lifestyle unsuitable for marriage. Unless my hypothetical future wife worked with me in my office and came along on my business trips, she would be alone most of the time."

Onegus had told her as much, so at least she knew that he wasn't making it up to explain why she shouldn't think of him as husband material, but it hurt nonetheless.

Cassandra let a single tear slide into the pillow, and then she shut her damn brain and heart down and concentrated on the sensation of his hands on her body.

He started a slow track up her thighs, his fingers tracing the inner side with feather-light strokes.

As her core responded, igniting with need and flooding with heat and moisture, she shamelessly parted her legs a little to invite more. If this was all he could give her, she would make the most of it as long as it lasted.

His fingers dipped lower, skimming the edge of her swollen petals and providing absolutely no relief.

This was dangerous.

The sexual frustration combined with the irritation from before provided combustive fuel for the volatile energy building up inside her.

When the bottle of lotion on the nightstand started shaking, she whispered, "Onegus."

"Yes?" His fingers continued their barely-there strokes.

The bottle fell down to the floor, the hard plastic making a thudding sound but not a splattering one, which was a relief.

"Touch me before I explode."

He chuckled. "That's the idea."

The lotion was the only item in her room that could have fallen victim to her energy. If he didn't defuse it somehow, Onegus would be next.

"I'm not joking."

Something in her tone must have gotten through to him, and those teasing fingers glided into her.

Her moan was one of pleasure and relief.

Then his mouth replaced his fingers and he gripped her hips, lifting her bottom to allow him better access.

Grinding herself on his tongue, his lips, she groaned into the pillow.

His grip on her hips tightened, holding her in place as his tongue found that most sensitive spot and flicked over it.

Behind her eyelids, her eyes rolled back in her head, and as his mouth closed around that needy, pulsating bundle of nerves, the climax exploded out of her in a rush.

"Onegus!" She shouted his name into the pillow.

Kissing her folds softly, he caressed her sides as the ripples subsided and her panting slowed.

She expected him to drop his pants and spear into her, but instead, he kissed her ass cheeks one at a time.

"No rest for the weary." He lightly slapped her bottom. "You have work to do."

She flopped around. "What about you?"

"I'm the master of delayed gratification."

"Are you sure?" She glanced at the erection pushing against his zipper.

He smacked his lips. "I got my dessert. I'll have a full five-course meal tomorrow."

Vlad

As the plane touched down on the runaway at Milwaukee airport, Richard opened his eyes and yawned.

"Good morning." Vlad unbuckled his seatbelt.

Since Kalugal had given Richard only one day off, they'd decided to save time by taking the red-eye. They'd left Los Angeles Tuesday night, and were going back today. Unless Wendy's father wasn't where he was supposed to be, it should be enough time for what they were about to do.

Richard had slept through the entire flight, but Vlad had been too strung out to even close his eyes. The taser idea hadn't worked out because they couldn't take the device on a commercial flight, and getting one in Milwaukee would be too much of a hassle.

Vlad would have to rely on his willpower to refrain from killing Wendy's father. Richard wasn't strong enough to hold him back, and even if he was, Vlad didn't want to put him in the position of having to muscle down his mate's son.

The other thing that had kept him awake was that he still hadn't told Wendy the big secret about his own father. She was his mate, and he was supposed to tell her everything, and the more time passed since his mother had revealed the truth to him, the more guilty he felt for not sharing it with Wendy.

The truth was that there was no reason to keep it from her. The weak excuse he'd come up with to justify it was that he didn't want to add to her burden.

What he was about to do weighed heavily on both of them, and he figured that it would be better to save his news for after his mission was done.

Neither he nor Richard had checked-in luggage or even carry-ons, and since the airport wasn't big, they were out the door within minutes after landing.

As they waited for the Uber that Richard had called, his partner-in-crime checked the app for the car's progress. "It's five minutes away, or so it says. The damn thing keeps updating." Richard looked up. "I hope we catch Roger Miller at home. If he leaves to run an errand, we will be stuck waiting for him and might miss our flight back."

Roni had gotten all the latest details on Wendy's father. His address hadn't changed since Wendy had left home, and he was working as an insurance agent for a local company. Fortunately for their plans, most of the week he did it from home, working from the company's offices only on Tuesdays and Fridays.

It was only a little after nine in the morning in Milwaukee, so he should be awake. Vlad had debated long and hard whether it would be better to attack while Roger was asleep, getting into his head when he had no barriers up.

The problem with that was accessibility of long-term memories. Short-term memories were easy to access, but memories from nearly two decades ago would be buried deep, unless Roger thought about what he had done to his wife and daughter often and in detail.

Since that was unlikely, Vlad would have to use more crude persuasion methods to get him to reveal what he had done. If Roger resisted or tried to lie, he could then enter his mind and pluck the memories that the interrogation would undoubtedly bring up to the forefront of the maggot's mind.

He would do his best not to kill Wendy's father, but he probably wouldn't leave him unscathed.

"I wish we had Yamanu with us," Richard said as the Uber dropped them one street over from Roger's house. "What if he's going to scream murder? Can you thrall him not to do that?"

"I'm a good enough shrouder to put the three of us in a bubble of silence." Vlad felt his fangs elongate. "No one is going to hear him scream."

"Easy, kid." Richard put a hand on his shoulder. "Don't work yourself up before we even get there. You need to keep calm." He looked around him. "Maybe I should find something I can clobber you over the head with."

He was only teasing, trying to get Vlad to loosen up, but it wasn't a bad idea.

"When we get inside his house, look for something you can use. Just don't smash my brain. Even immortals can't recover from that."

"Got it."

As Vlad's phone buzzed in his pocket, he didn't need to look at the screen to know it was from Wendy. It was still early morning in Los Angeles, and she'd probably just woken up.

Are you there yet?

He typed back. *We are walking toward the house. We will be there in less than five minutes.*

Don't kill him.

I won't.

Her return text was a row of hearts.

I love you too. I'll call you when we are done.

Onegus

As Ingrid walked into the apartment she'd designated as the chief's operation center, her eyes immediately zeroed in on the barren pedestal.

"What happened to the crystal vase that was there?" She pointed an accusing finger.

"It's gone." Onegus rose to his feet. "I bumped into it, and it fell before I could catch it."

Hand on her hip, Ingrid narrowed her eyes at him. "What really happened to it?"

He sighed dramatically. "Is it really important? It was just some Chinese-made crap that probably didn't cost more than twenty bucks."

"It was eighty-six bucks, and it wasn't crap." She tossed her purse on the entry table and sauntered toward the kitchen. "But I know that your reflexes are too fast to allow it to fall. Did you bring someone up here?"

He followed her into the kitchen. "It's none of your business, but yes. Cassandra must have bumped into it, and I was too late to catch it."

That wasn't how it had happened. The vase just exploded, and he had a feeling that Cassandra's ire had something to do with it, but he wasn't sure.

Arching a perfectly shaped blond brow, Ingrid pulled a soda out of the fridge. "Cassandra Beaumont? The one you danced with at the gala?"

"How did you know?"

She leaned against the counter. "Your pictures were plastered all over the tabloids. You're the chief, and you don't need my advice, but you shouldn't have brought her here. She's not some random chick you picked up at a club. You've been photographed together. Being seen with her again is asking for trouble."

"No one saw us coming up here aside from the guys in security." He rubbed a finger over the cleft in his chin. "I sense something special about her."

"Oh, yeah?" Ingrid's eyes sparkled with interest. "Do tell."

There was no harm in telling her his suspicions. She was a smart woman, and she wasn't prone to gossip. She would keep whatever he shared with her confidential.

"Cassandra emits energy like a high-voltage wire, especially when she gets agitated or excited. I have a feeling that the vase just exploded because Cassandra got mad at me."

"What did you do?"

"Nothing." He leaned on the counter next to her. "She thought this was my shag pad." He crossed his arms over his chest. "Cassandra has standards. She demanded that I introduce myself to her mother before agreeing to get closer."

"That's kind of old-fashioned. Did you actually do it? Or did you thrall that idea out of her head?"

He cast her an amused glance. "I'm the chief. I don't thrall humans willy-nilly. I met with her mother."

"And?"

"She's almost as lovely as Cassandra, and she emits similar energy, just not as potent."

"Do you think that they are Dormants?"

He smoothed his hands against his spiked hair. "I feel a pull to her that I haven't felt toward any woman before, and it scares the shit out of me. I wasn't looking for a mate."

Ingrid's lips twitched with a stifled smile. "Is the big bad Onegus afraid to face his feelings? Or are you afraid of the beautiful and bewitching Cassandra Beaumont?"

He chuckled. "When you meet her, you might be scared too. That strange power of hers is like a keg of dynamite, and she has a very short fuse."

"Well, if she feels so special to you, go for it. Try to induce her."

"I don't think that I'm in love with her yet. And until I do, I'm going to use damn protection."

"What happens once you realize that she's the one? Since you've already had fun with her, I assume that she's susceptible to thralling?"

"She is, but I don't want to overdo it and cause damage." He sighed. "I can't stay away from her, and it's driving me crazy. Spacing our encounters is torment."

"Yeah." Ingrid pursed her lips. "You need to get her somewhere secluded, tell her the truth, get her consent, and then have fun until she transitions. And if she doesn't, thrall the memory away. We also have the option of Kalugal compelling her silence. Even Eleanor would do for that."

Onegus shook his head. "I'm not overly keen on involving others in my private affairs." He cast her a sidelong glance. "I don't know why I'm even telling you all this."

She patted his arm. "Because even the chief needs someone to talk to. But if you don't want to involve anyone else, the vacation option is still there." She smiled. "The cabin becomes available soon. Leon and Anastasia are coming to the village tomorrow, and Anastasia's friend is going back to that cult place Sunday evening. If you are willing to do the cleaning yourself, you can take Cassandra to the cabin on Monday. The Odus have their hands full with driving the guests around and serving the Clan Mother."

"I can't take a vacation until everyone goes home."

"Then invite her for the next weekend. It's not like there is a rush." She chuckled. "Except for your insatiable craving for her, that is."

Vlad

"Take a deep breath," Richard said as they walked up to Roger's front door.

"I'm okay." Vlad fisted his hands inside his pockets.

That's where his hands were going to stay unless Richard couldn't handle Roger on his own, which wasn't likely with his immortal strength. They'd agreed that Richard would do the physical intimidation while Vlad reached into Roger's mind.

Secretly, he hoped that Richard would kill the bastard. Then blood wouldn't be on his hands, but Roger would be dead and unable to hurt anyone else.

There was no answer when Richard knocked on the door. He rang the bell.

"Hold your horses," Roger shouted, and a moment later, the door opened.

The guy was still handsome for a drunkard who was in his late forties, but Vlad could sense the monster inside even though he wasn't particularly empathic. Given Richard's icy demeanor, he felt it too.

"Roger Miller?" Richard asked.

"What do you want?"

"We have a few questions for you." He flashed the fake FBI ID that he'd printed from the internet. It wouldn't have fooled a ten-year-old, but Vlad reached into the maggot's mind and made him believe it.

"About what?" Roger still blocked the door.

"Your daughter." Richard took a step forward. "Let's get inside."

Reluctantly, Roger moved, letting them into his house.

The place was a mess. Newspapers and magazines covered every surface, including the couch and one of the armchairs facing it. Several pairs of dirty socks littered the carpet, and there were empty beer cans everywhere.

Roger collected the newspapers strewn over the couch to make space.

"The housekeeper quit on me." He motioned for them to sit down. "Did anything happen to Wendy?" There was a note of concern in his voice that surprised Vlad.

The monster who'd abused her until she'd managed to escape him couldn't possibly care for her.

"That's what we are trying to find out." Richard sat down and pulled a little notepad and pen out of his pocket. "When was the last time you saw her?"

"I've already answered all those questions. I haven't seen her since she was recruited. I have no idea where she is, and why she's thrown away a well-paying job. It was probably for some dick." He ran a hand over his thinning hair. "I did everything I could to raise her so she wouldn't grow up to be like her drug-addicted, whoring mother, but she turned out to be exactly like her."

Vlad's fangs punched out, but as he lunged for the maggot, Richard got in the way. "Stop right now, kid. I've got it."

"No, you don't." Vlad pushed him aside.

"What the hell?" Roger's horrified expression probably saved his life. "What are you?"

The satisfaction of seeing it cooled Vlad's murderous intentions. "I'm your worst nightmare."

Instead of tearing the jerk's throat out, he took hold of his mind, clamping invisible fingers on his cognition and bending it to his will. He had never done that before, but it came naturally to him. If he wanted, he could have fried Roger's brain, turning him into a vegetable. Would Wendy be mad at him if he did that?

Forcing his mental fingers to ease the pressure, he asked, "What did you do to Wendy's mother? Where is she?"

Roger sucked in a breath. "I don't know, and I don't care. She was a druggie and an unfit mother. I told her to stay away from me and from Wendy or I'd end her miserable life. I thought that I was protecting Wendy by removing the bad influence, but apparently that shit was in her genes and there was nothing I could do to fix that."

"Did you kill your wife?"

He shook his head. "She still had enough brain cells functioning to never show her face in this house again. Either that or she died from a drug overdose. I don't know where she went after I kicked her out."

Reaching into his mind, Vlad looked over the memories Roger had summoned. The abuse and humiliation he'd inflicted on the poor woman were enough to have Vlad's blood boiling in his veins, but he didn't see Roger killing Wendy's mother. Was it possible that he'd suppressed the memory of that?

Perhaps his monstrosity hadn't crossed the line into murder?

"And you think that you were a fit father?" Richard asked. "You abused your daughter."

"I was strict with her, so she wouldn't turn out like her mother. I did the best I could, but it wasn't enough."

"Why did you keep her if you didn't want her?" Richard asked.

"Who said that I didn't want her? I wanted to raise her right, to make sure that she never touched drugs, that she did well in school, and that she didn't sleep around. But despite my best efforts, she ended up being a disappointment."

"You consider abusing her your best effort?"

Roger waved a dismissive hand. "I don't know what she told those shrinks in the government program, but I never hit her in the face or did anything to disfigure her. What I did was nothing compared to what my father did to me, and I turned out all right." He lifted his shirt and turned around. "That's a souvenir from my asshole of a father."

Roger's back was crisscrossed with old welts, but that wasn't an excuse for what he had done to his wife and daughter.

Richard winced. "Your father was a worthless worm, and you followed in his footsteps." He clapped his hands. "Here is the applause."

Tired of the excuses, Vlad squeezed his mental fingers, knocking Roger out.

When the guy slumped, Richard reached to check his pulse.

"I didn't kill him. I just knocked him out. I'm debating whether turning him into a vegetable would upset Wendy."

Richard arched a brow. "I didn't know it was possible to do that with a thrall."

"Neither did I." Vlad pushed his bangs out of his face. "Maybe it's something that I inherited from my father."

"What did you see in his mind?"

"A lot of crap I wished I could un-see, but I didn't see him murder Wendy's mother."

"Did he abuse anyone else since?"

"I don't know. He didn't summon those memories, and I can only see recent ones."

"What do you want to do with him?"

"Kill him. Even if he's not a murderer, he's a twisted, sadistic monster. I'd be doing the world a favor."

Richard shook his head. "You promised Wendy that you wouldn't. Thrall him, make sure that he never hurts anyone again, and erase the memory of us ever being here." He smiled evilly. "You can always come back at a future time and finish the job."

Cassandra

"You're in a good mood today." Kevin perched on the edge of Cassandra's desk. "You haven't snarled at anyone yet. What gives?"

"I finished the design for the new brochure and handed it over to Brenda to put into production. Then I started working on next month's box. I made good progress, and I'm finally ahead instead of being behind."

Last night, after Onegus had left her satisfied but puzzled, she'd taken a shower and worked until two in the morning.

Why hadn't he wanted her to return the favor?

Or just finish what he'd started and make love to her?

What kind of man brings a woman to a shattering orgasm and just leaves?

"Why didn't you send the brochure to me for approval?"

She crossed her arms over her chest. "Since you never bother to check them, I stopped doing that months ago. Hadn't you noticed?"

Kevin's expression turned sheepish. "I didn't. You should remind me."

"Fine." Cassandra uncrossed her arms and picked up her pencil.

He didn't make a move to leave and was still looking at her as if she'd dyed her hair green. "Do you need anything? Or were you just bored and decided to waste my time?"

Kevin smiled. "And she's back. I just wanted to check on the design for the eyeshadow line ad campaign. Did you send that to me and I missed it too?"

"Not yet. I'm still playing around with it. And I need to run a comparison test to choose the best performing creative. I'll send it to you when it's done." She twirled the pencil between her fingers. "I almost forgot. Tell Josie that Connor says hi."

"Who's Connor?"

"A score composer she's worked with before. He's Onegus's roommate."

Kevin grinned. "That's what the good mood is about. Did you snag the most elusive eligible bachelor that all the socialites have been pursuing for years?"

She frowned. "How come no one did?"

"He's a mysterious fellow. He shows up for those big charity events and then disappears for months." Kevin leaned closer. "To tell you the truth, I thought that he was gay, but apparently I was wrong."

She snorted. "Very wrong."

"Do you know where he disappears to?"

Onegus had told her the truth about his position in the family business, but she wasn't going to betray that even to Kevin.

"He told me that he travels a lot for business. I thought that it was just an exit strategy for when he dumps me, but maybe it's true and that's why he's gone most of the year."

"Why would he dump you?"

Cassandra leaned back. "A guy like him is expected to marry an heiress or the daughter of a high-ranking politician. What would his family think if he brings home a woman who doesn't even have a college education?"

That was regrettably true even if he wasn't the head of the operation. He was still a member of an incredibly rich and influential family.

Kevin shook his head. "If that's a sore spot for you, you should just get that damn degree. You can do it online." He leaned closer and whispered, "That's what I did."

"I know." She rolled her eyes. "I don't have time for that, and I don't need it. But people judge you if you don't have it."

When her cell phone rang, she snatched it off the table and smiled. "It's him." She waved her hand at Kevin. "Go. Find someone else to bother."

"Fine." He pushed off the desk and walked out of her office.

She waited for him to close the door before answering. "Hi."

"Hi, yourself. I have a question. Can you take a vacation starting the following Monday?"

"No. Why? Are you going somewhere?"

"Not unless you are coming with me. I want to spend time with you away from work and all the hustle and bustle. I will be very busy starting tomorrow and all through next week, and I don't know if I will be able to make time to see you."

So that's what this was about. He was letting her down gently.

Cassandra wasn't going to make it hard for him. It was better to end this on a good note and at least keep fond memories from their very short time together.

That was what her brain said. Her heart, on the other hand, felt as if Onegus had stabbed it with a rusty knife.

She rubbed her chest. "I can't take more than one day off. I just have too much to do."

"You have a department full of employees. Have them earn their money."

Was he insisting because he knew she couldn't go?

"They won't lift a pencil if I don't tell them how to do it and when. I don't have anyone who can take over for me. I haven't taken more than a day off since I got promoted."

"That was more than ten years ago."

"Tell me something I don't know."

"I'll call your boss and admonish him for overworking you and hiring the wrong people for your department. I want you all to myself for at least a week."

He sounded sincere. Maybe she'd misjudged his intentions?

"Out of curiosity. If I managed to get away for an entire week, where would you take me?"

"My family owns a secluded cabin in the mountains. It's very romantic, and there are no other homes for miles around. We will have complete privacy."

As Cassandra's anger flared red hot, the pencil holder on her desk started rattling.

She'd expected Onegus to say Paris or Milan, and if not that, then at least New York. But a damn cabin in the woods?

"I see. You want to take me to another place where no one will see us together. What's the matter, Onegus? Embarrassed to be seen with a pleb?"

"What kind of nonsense is that?" He pretended to get mad. "Where have you gotten that idea from? I danced with you at the gala and our pictures were splattered all over the tabloids and the internet. I took you to the fanciest restaurant on the West Coast, or maybe even the entire country, and we danced there as well. How can you think that I'm embarrassed to be seen with you?"

"The gala was nothing. You didn't come with me and you didn't leave with me. And the restaurant was dark, and no one paid any attention to us. The damn place belongs to your cousin, and you didn't even introduce me to him."

"That's because Gerard is a prick, and if I had walked into his kitchen, he would have thrown a knife at me. You are being ridiculous, Cassandra."

"Am I? I invited you to meet my mother and introduced you to her, but you couldn't even invite me to your home and introduce me to your roommate?"

"I let you talk to him on the phone."

"Whoopty doo. I'm the kind of woman a guy should be proud to be seen with, a woman he would show off to his friends and introduce to his parents. I'm not a shameful secret to be brought in the middle of the night to an unoccupied building." She paused to take a breath. "I told you that I don't do hookups, and if that's all you have to offer, then I'm not interested. Goodbye, Onegus." She disconnected the call.

The tears started a moment later.

Cassandra really liked the guy, and pushing him away hurt, but everything she'd told him was true. If he wasn't willing to show her that he was serious about her, she wasn't going to waste any more of her time on him, or worse, fall in love with a man who didn't appreciate her.

Onegus

Dumbstruck, Onegus stared at his phone. He couldn't believe that Cassandra had hung up on him without waiting for his reply.

The woman was nuts, and she had a huge chip on her shoulder. How could she think that he was embarrassed to be seen with her?

She was gorgeous, successful, smart, talented, had superb taste, and she was a potential Dormant. Naturally, she wasn't aware of the last one, but she was well aware of everything else. Had he really given her a reason to suspect he thought otherwise?

The woman was more than confident, she was prideful, and she had a shitty attitude.

For a brief moment there, he'd thought that she might be the one for him, and he'd even contemplated ways he could have a mate without compromising his work standards. But he'd been wrong about her, and she wasn't the one for him. Onegus didn't need the drama, and he didn't need tantrums. What he needed was a coolheaded, reasonable woman who had a life of her own and wasn't needy or dependent.

Aside from the short fuse, he'd thought Cassandra was all those things, but it seemed like that short fuse was a much bigger problem than he'd anticipated.

Angry and hurt, he threw the phone on the desk and headed out.

Ingrid intercepted him in the hallway. "I programmed the locks of all the rooms with the guests that will be staying in them and emailed everyone their room assignments. That will save us the trouble of handing out keycards and showing them to their rooms."

"Good." He kept on walking.

"What happened?" She fell in step with him, her high heels clicking along.

"Nothing."

"Don't nothing me, Onegus. I'm not one of your Guardians, and I smell girl trouble. Did she turn you down for the vacation idea?"

He stopped and turned to her. "She practically slammed the phone down on me."

"Why? What did you say to get her mad?"

"Nothing. She asked me where I wanted to take her, and I told her about the cabin. She exploded, accusing me of being embarrassed to be seen with her and hiding her from my friends and relatives."

Ingrid winced. "I can see her point. You didn't introduce her to your friends or family, just not for the reason she thinks."

"So, what am I supposed to do? Bring her to the village?" He turned and kept walking toward the elevators.

Ingrid rushed after him. "You could invite her to the wedding. That will put an end to any talk about you hiding her from the important people in your life."

"Are you serious?" He pressed the button.

"Completely. Gerard's human staff is serving at the event, and Yamanu is going to take care of their memories when it's over. He can do the same to Cassandra."

The elevator arrived, and the door opened, but Onegus didn't step inside. "If Yamanu will erase her memories, then what's the point of inviting her to the wedding? She won't remember it."

"Good point." Ingrid put a hand on her hip. "You will need to do it and only remove the incriminating stuff and where the event was held. You will also need to get her drunk so she will blame the holes in her recall on the booze."

"Too risky."

"Not really. The same was done with Nick when Eva insisted on inviting him to her and Bhathian's wedding.

And just like in Nick's case, it's only a temporary fix until Cassandra transitions."

"What if she doesn't?"

Ingrid laughed. "She will. If the mighty chief is obsessing about a female, then she must be a Dormant."

Vlad

"You need a drink." Richard stopped at the corner of the street and pulled out his phone to call an Uber.

"Am I back to normal?" Vlad glanced down at his mother's mate. His fangs had retracted, but he had a feeling that his eyes were still glowing.

Richard chuckled. "You are back to looking as normal as you usually do."

"Thanks." Vlad grimaced. "And I don't mean it sarcastically. You were a great help in there. If not for you, I don't think I would have walked out of that house with his heart still beating."

"You're welcome, kid." Richard clapped him on the back. "We have three hours until our flight back. We can have that drink at the airport."

Vlad nodded. "I need to call Wendy."

"Wait until we are inside the car, and then do your silent bubble trick. It's a forty-minute drive to the airport."

Wendy was probably biting her nails, worried about what he might have done to her father and what he'd discovered about her mother. The good news was that Roger hadn't killed her mother. The bad news was that they still didn't know whether she was alive and if she was, where to find her. Roger hadn't lied about not knowing where she'd gone after he'd kicked her out of the house. Vlad had double-checked by going through the memories he'd brought back, looking for any clue, but there had been none. Roger had never bothered to search for the mother. In his mind she'd been as good as dead, most likely from a drug overdose.

As the Uber driver pulled up to the curb, Richard opened the back door and signaled for Vlad to get in. He then took the front passenger seat and started chatting with the driver about the best restaurants and bars in Milwaukee, keeping the guy's focus on himself and not on the strange dude sitting in the back and talking without making a sound.

After snapping the sound bubble around himself, Vlad dialed Wendy's number.

"Is he dead?" she shot at him.

"Regrettably, he's still breathing."

She let out a breath. "Thank God."

He chuckled. "It should be, thank Richard. He kept me from losing it."

"You sound like you are in a good mood. Did you find out what happened to my mother?"

"He didn't kill her, and he doesn't know where she went after he kicked her out. He told her that he would kill her if she didn't stay away from you and him."

"Why?"

"He said that she was a drug addict."

"Yeah, that's what he told me too, but I didn't believe him."

Vlad pinched his brows between his thumb and forefinger. "She was, but I don't blame her for escaping the nightmare of living with him in any way she could. It's a miracle that she didn't off herself."

"Maybe she did," Wendy whispered. "Otherwise, she would have come back for me."

"She might have been too scared. Roger meant it when he told her that he would kill her if she ever came back. And from what I've seen of his memories, he nearly did it several times, beating her up so badly that she ended up in a hospital."

"How did they let him get away with that? Why did no one intervene?"

He was quiet for a moment, remembering what she'd told him about her father. "You know how he did that. The same way he fooled your teachers and the nurse and anyone else who noticed that you weren't doing so well, or the people who you actually turned to for help."

"I don't get it. He's not a compeller."

"No, but he's a handsome, all-American-looking guy, and he knows how to play the part of the harmless, charming, ordinary man. People don't want to see the monster hiding behind the façade. They prefer to believe the lie and keep their heads in the sand."

"Yeah, I know. So what do we do now? We are back to square one, we can't find my mother, and you made the trip for nothing."

"Not for nothing. I made sure that the maggot will never hurt anyone again."

"How?"

"I thralled him to feel severe chest pain if he even thinks of hurting anyone. Anytime he has violent thoughts, he will be gripped by that pain and believe that his heart is going to give out and he's going to die."

"That's clever. How long is it going to hold?"

"Depends on how strong his brain is. I plan on reinforcing it from time to time."

"I don't want you to ever see him again."

"I won't. It can be done over the phone."

She was quiet for a moment. "I didn't know that thralling works long distance."

"It doesn't, but compulsion does."

There was another long pause. "Are you going to ask Eleanor to do that for us?"

"I think that I can do it myself. I discovered today that my thralling ability comes with a strange twist. I need to figure out exactly what it means."

"How come you didn't know you had it before?"

Telling her about his Kra-ell ancestry over the phone was far from optimal, but it was time. "There is something that I've been meaning to tell you after this thing with your father was over, but I wanted to do it in person. Can you wait until I'm back?"

"No way! You have to tell me now. I can't stomach another moment of stress and anxiety."

"My father wasn't a human. He was a Kra-ell hybrid."

"A what?"

"Kra-ell, like the Krall, like the cult leader the clan captured."

"How is that possible? And what does it have to do with your newly discovered ability?"

"To answer the first question, my mother had a thing with one of them and kept it a secret until the cult leader was found and their existence became known to the clan. And as for your second question, apparently my strange new ability, as well as my superior strength, came from my father. I was always aware of the latter, but not of the former."

Margaret

After lunch when Ana and Leon had gone on their daily hike, leaving Margaret with Bowen, she ducked into the bathroom like the big coward she was.

Yesterday she'd been saved from his probing questions by their return, but now they were gone, and he would no doubt use the opportunity to keep digging into her shameful past.

She should never have agreed to stay through the weekend. Tomorrow, Ana and Leon were leaving the cabin and going their separate ways for a while. Strangely, neither looked too distraught about that, so maybe their separation period was going to be short.

Margaret wished them the best of luck, and she also wished that they would stay until Sunday and not leave her alone with Bowen with no buffer.

If all he wanted was sex, she could've dealt with that, but he wanted so much more than that. She would have loved to give him all of it and more, but he wouldn't want any part of her if he knew how horrible she really was. A lifetime of helping others couldn't compensate for what she'd done, and once Bowen found out, he would want nothing to do with her.

She could keep it from him, pretend that the past didn't exist, and he would never find out. But she would know, and it would forever eat at her from the inside. Hiding it was akin to deceiving him, and it would cost her the last shreds of her dignity.

Margaret didn't have much left, and she desperately clung to the little she had. If she lost it, it would be the end of her. She would either find a way to end her miserable existence or succumb to the false oblivion drugs offered.

A soft knock on the door startled her.

"Are you okay?" Bowen asked. "You've been in there for almost an hour."

"I'm okay." She put a hand over her racing heart. "I'll be out in a moment."

"I'll make coffee."

"Okay."

Sitting on the edge of the tub for a moment longer, she tried to think of a good excuse for why she had to leave tomorrow. Perhaps she could call Riley again and ask if she was needed?

But what if Bowen insisted on coming to Safe Haven with her?

She needed to end his inexplicable infatuation with her. Bowen had a heart of gold, and his need to save her was clouding his judgment.

It was time he learned the truth about the woman he believed was such a saint.

Easier said than done, though.

The only one who had known all of her sins and hadn't judged her for them was Emmett. Her savior who had turned out to be a sinner himself.

No wonder he'd been so understanding.

God, she missed him. Not as a lover, but as a leader, a teacher, the man who had shown her a way to rise from the ashes and make something of herself. He'd been harsh, demanding, but by doing so he'd pushed her to do better, to excel, and to feel pride in her work when it had finally gotten his approval.

After flushing the toilet that she hadn't used, Margaret washed her hands, splashed some water on her face, and toweled it off. Taking a deep breath, she leaned on her crutches and hobbled out of the bathroom.

Bowen regarded her with worry in his eyes. "You look pale. Are you sure that everything is all right?"

Margaret nodded and took a seat at the counter. "I'm fine. I was thinking about Ana and Leon leaving, and I realized that we should leave as well. We've hogged this cabin for long enough. Maybe some of your cousins would like to use it over the weekend."

She was such a damn coward. She'd always been one, which was the main reason her life had turned out as horrible as it had. If she had been more assertive and less fearful, she would be in a much better place today.

Shaking his head, Bowen poured coffee into two cups and brought them to the counter. "Are you scared of being here alone with me? Is that why you want to leave early?"

"I'm not scared of you, Bowen. I never was. You are the best human being I know."

He chuckled. "Compared to the bunch of goody two-shoes you've lived with for the past decade or two, I'm probably the wickedest person you know."

"Not even close." She put a spoonful of sugar in her coffee, added milk, and stirred. "It's time, Bowen. You need to get back to your life, and I need to get back to mine." She swallowed. "I need you to book me a flight for tomorrow afternoon."

Bowen

Bowen wasn't buying it. Margaret was scared, the scent of her fear was unmistakable, but he didn't know what she was scared of. If it wasn't of him, then of what?

"If I'm booking you a flight, I'm booking one for myself as well." He rose to his feet and scooped her into his arms.

"What are you doing?" Her arms instinctively went around his neck.

"I'm getting to the bottom of this." He carried her to the couch and sat down with her in his arms, positioning her in his lap sideways, so her legs, the good one and the one in the cast, were stretched out comfortably. "What are you afraid of, Margaret?"

Avoiding his eyes, she looked down. "Of your reaction once you learn the truth about me."

"Unless you murdered someone in cold blood, there is nothing that would change my opinion about you."

That got a small smile out of her. "What if I murdered someone not in cold blood? What if it was a crime of passion?"

"Then I will hear you out and determine whether it was justified."

"You are very forgiving."

"Not at all. But I know you better than you think. You are incapable of hurting anyone."

"You might be right, but sometimes inaction is just as bad. I'm a coward, and my cowardice is at the root of all that has happened to me."

Cupping her cheek, he gently guided her head so that her other cheek was resting on his chest. "Tell me what happened to you."

"I'm ashamed."

"Don't be. I'm not going to judge your choices or what you had to do to survive."

Heaving a sigh, Margaret closed her eyes. "My mother died when I was sixteen of a viral infection that she'd picked up in a hospital while having a minor operation. My father didn't last long after that. He died from heart failure. The only family I had was an uncle whom I didn't know and who lived in another state. He didn't come for me, and I was sent to foster care. It wasn't as bad as people think, and the couple who took me in were okay. But I was lonely, and frightened, and I used the only assets I had, which were a pretty face and a nice figure. I met a guy who was more than a decade older than me, had a paying job, and proposed after dating me for two months. I thought that my troubles were over, but they had just begun."

Suspecting where Margaret's story was going, Bowen's arms tightened protectively around her. "Go on."

"He started hitting me when I got pregnant. At first, it was just a shove here, a slap there, but it got progressively worse. He never hit me in the stomach or punched me in the face, it was always in places that I could hide under clothing, and like an idiot, I did. I was ashamed, I was scared, and I didn't know who to turn to for help. He always apologized, blaming it on the booze or on stress at work. And each time he promised that it would never happen again, but it did. Over and over, and no matter how hard I tried to please him, to avoid his wrath, he always found reasons to knock me around."

Bowen's fangs were itching to elongate, but he tamped down the urge. It wasn't about him and the rage he felt. This was about Margaret pouring her heart out and him showing his support.

He kissed the top of her head. "I'm so sorry for all that you've suffered. And I'm glad that you somehow managed to escape. It must have been very difficult."

She heaved another sigh. "When our daughter was born, he fell in love with her, and the violence stopped for a while. I hoped that we'd turned a new page and that we could be a normal family, but I should have known better. It started again soon enough, worse than before."

She lifted her head and looked at him. "I wasn't clumsy, and those broken bones were not accidents. That was how I got addicted to opioids. It started with the first hospital visit and a prescription that I abused. It was easy back then to get more. There was no awareness of how dangerous opioids were and that they were just as addictive as street drugs. I became an expert at manipulating the system and getting more prescribed, and when that failed, I bought them from dealers. I pinched pennies, skimming from the household budget. I barely ate, saving on groceries. I got nice baby outfits and toys second-hand for next to nothing and claimed that I'd spent a lot of money on them." She sighed. "I became very creative."

Bowen had a feeling that Margaret wasn't telling him the worst of it, but he wasn't going to press. She was finally confiding in him, and his heart broke for her. He would take only what she was willing to give, but he could encourage her with his support.

"You did what you had to do to survive. I'm not judging you."

She huffed out a breath. "That's not the worst part. I needed more and more to get that disassociated floaty feeling going, and saving on groceries and other household expenses wasn't cutting it." She swallowed. "He wasn't blind to what was going on, but he couldn't lock me in the house to prevent me from getting more, and beating me up was just making things worse. Eventually, he hired a nanny to take care of our daughter when he was at work because he didn't trust me with her." Margaret's eyes were full of tears when she looked up at him. "That's the only thing I was ever grateful to him for. I was spacing out, and I was afraid of being alone with our baby. The nanny was a young woman who didn't speak a word of English, and even as out of it as I was, I noticed that something was going on between them. When I confronted him, he put me in the hospital again."

Bowen couldn't help the growl that rose from his throat, and as Margaret looked up, she gasped. "Your eyes are glowing."

Thankfully, he was still able to control his fangs. "It's a light effect. Go on."

She lowered her eyes to her hands. "I was given opioids again," she whispered. "I had a Eureka moment, and a pattern began. As soon as I ran out, I provoked him into beating me up badly enough to get me hospitalized so I could get more. At some point, I just wished he would finish the job, and I wouldn't wake up again."

Bowen didn't know what to say to that. The things she was telling him were even worse than what he'd suspected. In a way, it would have been better if she'd prostituted herself to get the drug money. It would have done less damage.

"Anyway," she continued. "He almost did. He told me that if I didn't get my act together, he would have me committed to a psychiatric hospital, and he would make sure that I didn't ever see my child again. He searched the entire house and threw away every pill he could find, but I had more stashed away for an emergency. I tried to quit, but I was too weak to do it without help. When he found out, I was sure he was going to kill me. He nearly choked me to death. The baby screaming for me in the next room must have gotten through to him and he let go and stormed out of the house. The next morning, he waited for me in the kitchen with a bag that he'd packed for me. He told me to run and hide because if he found me, he was going to finish what he'd started the night before. I believed him. He wasn't drunk, he was completely lucid, and he had murder in his eyes. Nevertheless I cried, and I begged, and I pleaded, and I promised to go to rehab, but it only got him more furious, and the things he said..."

Margaret shook her head. "I was afraid that he would hurt our daughter to punish me. He loved her as much as he hated me, but he wasn't right in the head." She snorted. "And neither was I. I figured out that she was better off with him and the nanny than with me, and I left. I had no money, no friends, and nowhere to go. But I still had a full packet of Percocet stashed away. I decided to end my life and took all of them at once. Someone found me passed out behind the supermarket dumpster and called an ambulance. They pumped my stomach and called him. He did his usual shtick, pretending to be the wronged husband who had to deal with a horrible, druggie wife who whored herself out—that's how he explained the marks on my neck and the black eye he'd given me, it had been an unsatisfied client, not him. His act must have been convincing, or maybe they thought that it had been my fault, and I was sent to mandatory rehab. He came to visit once, just to deliver the same message. If I ever came anywhere near him or Wendy, even unintentionally, he was going to make sure that it was the last thing I did."

Bowen frowned. Her daughter's name was Wendy?

Suddenly, the pieces of the puzzle started falling into place. That was why Margaret had seemed familiar when he'd first seen her. She'd reminded him of Wendy. The big brown eyes, the smile, the face structure. But Wendy was short and plump, while Margaret was tall and slim.

Perhaps it was just a coincidence.

He didn't know Wendy's last name, but he could easily find out. He could call Wendy herself, but if his suspicion proved incorrect, it would upset her. He could probably get the information from Jin or from Eleanor.

"Did you change your last name?"

Margaret lifted her head. "Why do you ask?"

"I'm just curious. Your ex sounds like a dangerous scumbag. If I knew you back then, I would have advised you to get a fake identity so he could never find you. He could've changed his mind later and come after you."

Bowen would have killed the scum to keep her safe and get her daughter back to her.

"That was what Emmett said when I told him my story and he got me a new identity." She swallowed. "I never got a divorce because I never dared to contact Roger. Legally, I'm still married to him."

"Not for long. What was your married last name?"

"Miller. But what do you mean by not for long?"

"I have friends who can take care of that," he lied.

"How?"

"Hacking into official databases." That might have been true, but it wasn't how Bowen planned to end Margaret's marriage.

He was going to make her a widow.

Margaret

Bowen hadn't reacted as Margaret had expected. He hadn't been appalled by her drug addiction and what she had done to support it, not even by her greatest sin, which was leaving her daughter behind and running away and hiding like the coward she was.

He didn't regard her as a piece of trash, and his arms were still around her, supporting, encouraging.

Perhaps he hadn't internalized the gravity of her cowardice yet. A man like him could never understand a spineless mouse like her. He was strong, brave, he would have fought against all odds.

Why hadn't she?

"He might have divorced you," Bowen said. "I don't know much about the subject, but I'm sure no one expects a wife gone missing for eighteen years to sign divorce papers. One of my cousins is an attorney. She can check it for you."

Margaret shook her head. "I'm afraid to do that. What if he gets notified that someone checked? He will know it was me, and it's best that he thinks that I'm dead."

"There are ways to do that without alerting him. My cousin is very good at what she does."

Panic gripping her, Margaret felt her throat close up and breathing became difficult.

"What's wrong?" Bowen looked at her with worry in his eyes.

"I can't breathe," she croaked, her hand going to her throat.

"Don't be scared." He took her clammy hand in his. "I will never let anything happen to you. You are safe. No one is going to get you."

Slowly, his words penetrated the haze, and the tightness in her throat eased. When she sucked in a breath, Bowen released one as well.

"If you feel such acute panic after eighteen years, I can't imagine how scared you were back then."

"I'm still terrified. Why do you think I never left Safe Haven? When you took me to the hospital, it was the first time since my arrival there."

He frowned. "I thought that you were allowed to leave for doctors' visits and the like."

"Theoretically, yes, but I never needed to see a specialist. We had a doctor that came twice a year to give everyone a physical, and Shirley took care of the colds and the flus and the sore throats. The furthest I'd gone away from the lodge was the beach in front of it."

"Weren't you curious about Wendy?"

Here it was. Now that Bowen realized the extent of her cowardice, he would despise her.

"Of course, I was. We had no access to the outside world in Safe Haven, but I begged Emmett to check for me. He said it was dangerous, that any internet inquiry can be tracked, and looking for information about a minor would trigger some safety features that would alert Roger and enable him to find me. Emmett said it wasn't worth the risk to me and to the rest of the community. He said that Roger sounded insane, and that he might come with a machine gun and kill everyone in his path."

As the choking sensation started again, Bowen squeezed her hand. "Emmett lied to you, Margaret. Or rather exaggerated. It's true that everything you do on the internet can be tracked, but someone has to have a very good reason to do that, the resources, and the knowhow. Looking for information about Wendy wouldn't have triggered any traps unless your maniacal ex was a computer expert and a master hacker or has enough money to pay for one."

"Why would Emmett lie about that?"

"For the same reason he didn't allow community members access to the internet or even radio and television. By controlling the information, he controlled the community."

What he said made sense, but Emmett wouldn't have done that to her. Or would he?

Maybe he'd thought he was protecting her?

Or maybe he'd checked despite what he'd told her and found out that something had happened to Wendy?

As the panicky sensation threatened to steal her air again, Margaret tightened her grip on Bowen's hand. "Can you help me find out about my daughter?"

He hesitated. "I have a cousin who is an expert on those things. I can call him."

"Can you do it now?"

His eyes were full of pity as he looked at her. "To call him, I will have to let you out of my arms, and you are shaking like a leaf."

She hadn't been aware of how cold she was until he'd pointed it out. "I don't know why I'm so cold."

"Telling me your story was emotionally draining, and it has awakened old fears. You are in a system overload." He caressed her arm. "Close your eyes and rest your head on my chest."

His voice was so soothing, so compassionate.

She did as he instructed. "How come you don't hate me for what I did?"

"Why would I hate you? You were a victim. How old were you when your daughter was born?"

"I had just turned nineteen."

"You were still a child yourself, alone, abused, and frightened." His voice sounded as if it was coming down a tunnel, but his words eased some of the heaviness in Margaret's heart.

Heaving out a sigh, she drifted away, pieces of their conversation floating disjointed in her exhausted mind.

How had Bowen known that she'd left eighteen years ago? Had she told him that? Margaret couldn't remember, and as cognition faded, focusing on any one thought became impossible.

Bowen

When Margaret's breathing had slowed and deepened, Bowen pushed to his feet with her in his arms and gently laid her on the couch. Remembering that she'd been cold, he covered her with the throw blanket before heading out to the front porch.

He needed a moment to breathe some fresh air and calm the fury her story had evoked. She'd been victimized for years, first by her husband, who'd abused her and robbed her of her child, and then by Emmett, who'd lied to her and compelled her to panic every time she thought about finding out what happened to her daughter.

The cult leader's motives might have been benevolent if he'd truly believed that he was protecting Margaret and his community from her psychotic husband. Or, they might have been malevolent, meant to keep Margaret from leaving.

Although why he had deemed her so important was unclear. She didn't have any money, and her work for the community could have been done by others.

Had her blood been a delicacy he hadn't wanted to lose?

Leon had told him that Emmett claimed Eleanor's blood was particularly tasty and potent. Perhaps that was also true of Dormants' blood?

It hit him then. If Margaret was Wendy's mother, she was a confirmed Dormant. Eleanor had been right about her.

Pulling out his phone, he dialed her number.

"Bowen, what a nice surprise," Eleanor answered. "Are you calling to congratulate me on my promotion?"

"What promotion?"

"Kian put Peter and me in charge of guarding Emmett. We've temporarily moved to the keep."

He couldn't care less who was guarding the guy, but he didn't want to hurt Eleanor's feelings by ignoring her unexpected promotion. It must be a big deal for her.

"Congratulations. How did that come about?"

"It was Kri's idea. She said that Emmett might tell me things he wouldn't tell the guys. I suggested it to Kian, and he liked the idea. I'm now officially a Guardian in training, including the salary that comes with the position."

"I'm happy for you. How is it going with Emmett so far?"

"I've only seen him twice. Once yesterday and once today. I'm taking it slow, so it won't be too obvious."

"What exactly are you planning to do? Seduce him?"

"It's an option."

She'd tried to sound nonchalant, but Bowen detected the nervous undertone. "That's going above and beyond your job description."

"I know. If I do that, it would be for me, not for the job."

"Then I wish you good luck. I have a question for you."

"Ask, and I shall answer."

"Do you know Wendy's last name?"

"Yeah, it's Miller. Why?"

Should he tell her before he told Wendy and Margaret? It didn't feel right, but he needed a woman's perspective and advice on how to handle the situation.

"I think that Margaret is her mother."

There was a long moment of silence, and then Eleanor huffed out a breath. "Is her last name Miller?"

"It was before she had it changed, and she has a daughter named Wendy who she left behind with her abusive husband."

"Did you tell her your suspicion?"

"No, not yet. I wanted to make sure first."

"Good. Miller is a very common name, and so are Wendy and Margaret. It might be a coincidence. Before we raise their hopes, we need to make sure."

"How?"

"Blood test. Bridget already has Wendy's, and if she needs a fresh sample, she can make up an excuse for why she needs it. Julian or Gertrude can go to the cabin and collect Margaret's."

"Were you involved in Wendy's recruitment?"

"No, Simmons recruited her himself. Why?"

"Do you know her father's given name?"

"It was in her file, but I don't remember. Maybe Jin or Jacki know, but I doubt it. Wendy was a loner, and she didn't interact with the other trainees. But maybe Richard knows. He was her and Vlad's roommate until he moved in with Stella."

"I'll call him. If he says that the father's name is Roger, I think that's proof enough."

"Probably. But there is still a small chance that there is another Miller family that has a Margaret, a Roger, and a Wendy."

"Perhaps, but given that we suspect Margaret is a Dormant, the chance of coincidence is reduced to practically zero."

"Probably, but we don't know whether Margaret is a Dormant for sure. A blood test will be conclusive proof that she is Wendy's mother, and then you can bring her to the village without having to go through all that nonsense of inducing her and waiting to see if she turns."

"You are talking about a DNA test, and those take time. I need to know as soon as possible."

Eleanor sighed. "Do they look alike?"

"Not enough. They have the same eyes and smile, and the same hair color, but Margaret is tall and slim."

"That's not good enough. You need at least one more piece of information that can be verified."

"Like an address. Provided that her father didn't move, and if he did, that Wendy knows the old one."

"Did Margaret tell you where she's from?"

"I didn't ask. Right now she's asleep after I helped her relax with a little thrall." He ran a hand over the back of his head. "It was an emotionally draining experience for her."

"I bet. If I remember correctly, Wendy is from Milwaukee, but I'm not sure. I can ask her, make some excuse about why I need to know."

"I'll just call Vlad. I don't know why I didn't think of calling him first. Wendy is working at the café, so it's not likely that she will overhear the conversation."

"Good luck."

"Thanks. And do me a favor, don't tell anyone until Wendy and Margaret are told."

"Obviously."

Vlad

Vlad was nursing his second beer at the airport bar when his phone rang.

"Wendy again?" Richard asked.

Vlad frowned at the screen. "It's Bowen." He accepted the call. "This is Vlad. Did you dial my number by mistake?"

"No mistake. I need to talk to you. Are you anywhere near Wendy?"

"No. Why?"

Vlad didn't elaborate on where he was at the moment. The less people knew about his and Richard's excursion, the better. He'd promised Richard to keep it confidential.

"I think that I found her mother, but I want to make sure before I tell either of them and raise their hopes for nothing. I need us to compare notes, so to speak."

Richard arched a brow. "I'll be damned."

Vlad lifted his face heavenward, wondering about the Fates' twisted sense of humor. Couldn't Bowen have called him a day earlier? He wouldn't have gone to pay Roger a visit and would have been spared from looking into the guy's ugly memories. Then again, his visit ensured that Roger Miller never hurt anyone again, so it wasn't a complete waste of time. Besides, Bowen could be wrong.

"What do you want to know?"

"Wendy's parents' names."

"Margaret and Roger Miller."

The Guardian let out a breath. "That's a match. Where is Wendy from originally?"

"Milwaukee."

"That's what Eleanor thought. I haven't asked Margaret yet, but I will when she wakes up."

"How did you meet her?"

"Do you know about the Safe Haven Cult rescue mission?"

"Yeah, the cult leader kidnapped a Guardian, and a bunch of you went there and rescued him."

"Correct. But do you know why the Guardian was there in the first place?"

"Something about an heiress that Turner was hired to retrieve. I don't know all the details."

"The heiress's name is Anastasia, and she turned out to be a Dormant and has already transitioned. She didn't go to the village yet because she wanted to stay with her best friend Margaret, who's recuperating in the cabin from an injury she sustained during our rescue mission."

"Our Cabin? The one Wendy and I stayed in?"

"One and the same."

"So, Wendy's mother was in the cult all these years?"

"It's a long story, but her husband abused her and then kicked her out and told her that if he saw her again, he would kill her. She ran to Safe Haven, the cult leader took her in and nursed her back to health. What he also did, though, was to compel her to fear looking for any information about her daughter. She suffered a panic attack when I suggested a simple internet search. She actually couldn't breathe."

Vlad shook his head. The Fates weaved a complex tapestry. He just wished he knew what their end goal was.

"How did you connect the dots?"

"From the very first moment, Margaret seemed familiar to me. I didn't know why until she told me her story about leaving a daughter with her abusive husband. Everything clicked into place the moment she told me that her daughter's name was Wendy. I just needed to make absolutely sure before I told Margaret that her daughter was safe and that she could see her today if she wanted."

"I can give you their home address. Roger Miller hasn't moved since Wendy was a baby. If Margaret gives you the same address, then that's the final proof."

"That's great news. Eleanor suggested we have them both take a blood test, but those things take time, and I'm running out."

"Why? What's the rush?"

"Margaret wants to return to Safe Haven tomorrow. But if she's indeed Wendy's mom, then she's a confirmed Dormant, and I can tell her everything and bring her to the village."

Finally, Vlad connected the dots. He'd been too distraught over the earlier interaction with Wendy's father to pick up the clues, but Bowen's comment about bringing Margaret to the village had been like a light beam through the haze.

"Is she your one?"

"I think so."

Vlad chuckled. "Welcome to the family, Bowen. I've always liked you."

"Same here, kid. Text me that address, will you? And also a picture of Wendy, or even better, the two of you together. If Margaret confirms the address, I want to be able to show her the beautiful, happy woman Wendy is today. And since a lot of it is thanks to her mate, Margaret should see a picture of her son-in-law as well."

Vlad wasn't sure about that. He wasn't what a human mother pictured as husband material for her daughter, but maybe it would be better if she was prepared.

"I will send the address and the pictures as soon as we end the call. Let me know if she confirms the address and it's conclusive. I would like to tell Wendy the good news."

There was a brief moment of silence before Bowen said, "Don't tell her yet. I have a feeling that it will be a shock for Margaret, and she will need some time before she'll be able to face Wendy."

Vlad looked at Richard, who nodded sagely, agreeing with Bowen.

"I'll wait until you tell me it's okay."

"Thank you."

"I need to thank you. Earlier today, I thought that Wendy's mother would never be found. The Fates have a strange sense of humor proving me wrong only a couple of hours later."

"Indeed. Sometimes I think that they push us around like chess pieces on a board and having free will is just an illusion."

Margaret

"Margaret." A warm hand caressed her arm. "I need you to wake up for a moment."

She opened her eyes to Bowen's handsome face hovering a few inches above hers. "I'm awake." She tried to sit up, but her head hurt and she put it back down.

While she slept, Bowen had brought her a pillow from her bedroom and covered her with a blanket. He was still taking care of her, even after learning what a rotten person she was.

"I'll make you coffee, but first, I need to ask you something."

At that point, she had no more secrets to hide. She'd laid herself bare for him, expecting him to recoil with disgust, but he was still there, still looking at her with soft eyes that seemed just a little troubled.

"What do you need?"

"Do you remember the address of the house you shared with your ex?"

How could she forget?

"Why do you need to know that?"

"I just do."

She put a hand on his forearm. "You can't go kill Roger. As bad as he is, Wendy doesn't have anyone else."

"That's not why I need the address."

She looked at him skeptically. "I saw your eyes when I told you what he'd done to me. You saw red. I know that you are a soldier, and that you've seen combat. You're a good man, a protector, and it's an instinct for you to take out the bad guys."

"I swear on my honor that I don't need the address so I could go kill your ex."

She had a feeling that honor meant a lot to Bowen. He wouldn't swear on it in vain. But just in case, she would start with the street name and omit the house number. "It was on West Tesch Avenue in Milwaukee, Wisconsin. But he might have moved since then."

"He didn't." Bowen sat next to her on the couch. "I have something important to tell you."

"What is it?" She pushed up, leaning against the armrest.

Bowen opened his mouth to answer when the door opened, and Ana came in with Leon.

"Are we interrupting in the middle of something?" Ana asked.

Bowen nodded. "Can you give us a few more minutes?"

"I'll just grab a couple of water bottles from the fridge." Leon headed to the kitchen.

"Get two for Margaret and me as well."

"No problem."

As Leon tossed him the two bottles on his way out, Margaret was sure at least one of them would hit her, but Bowen caught both like a circus performer.

When the door closed behind the two, he uncapped one bottle and handed it to her, then did the same for his.

"What were you going to tell me?" She took a sip.

"Wendy is no longer with Roger. She is safe and sound in our village, mated to one of my cousins. I needed the address to confirm that you are really the mother of the Wendy I know." He lifted his phone and showed her a text message from someone named Vlad.

She must be still sleeping, and this was a dream.

Margaret lifted the bottle and took another sip. If it was a dream, it was damn realistic. "Can you pinch me? I must be dreaming because that's just impossible."

He sighed. "It's fate. Do you want to see her picture?"

Margaret swallowed, her throat suddenly dry even though she'd just drunk water. "Yes, please," she whispered.

He tapped on his phone and handed it to her. "This is Wendy today."

Tears started streaming down Margaret's cheeks. The beautiful, smiling young woman in the picture was her Wendy. She had absolutely no doubt. Wendy was a perfect mix of her and Roger, who had been as handsome on the outside as he was twisted on the inside.

"She's perfect."

"I agree."

"Do you know her?"

"Quite well. She and her mate stayed in this very cabin with Leon and me."

Her eyes widened. "They were the couple you guarded?"

He nodded. "They found love here. Just like Anastasia and Leon." He wiped away her tears with his thumbs. "And just as we did."

"Knowing what I did, how can you love me?"

"What you told me didn't change anything. I feel the same as I did this morning and as I felt the day before, and the one before that. And now that I know your story and how the threads of our lives were weaved into one tapestry, it is clear to me that the Fates have been planning this for a very long time." He took her hand and kissed it. "We belong together."

Bowen

It must have been too much to process, and Margaret just fell apart. Sobbing uncontrollably, she pushed at his chest, and when he yielded, she flung both legs around and hopped on her one good leg toward the bedroom, nearly falling on her face if not for Bowen's quick reflexes.

She let him help her to the bed, but then lifted her hand. "Please. I need to be alone for a little bit."

"I understand." He didn't, but he did as she asked nonetheless.

She should have been overjoyed, her tears should have been of happiness and not of devastation.

The front door opened a crack, and Anastasia poked her head inside. "Is it safe to come in?"

"Yeah." He walked to the refrigerator and pulled out a beer.

"What happened?" Leon asked.

"You're not going to believe it." Bowen gave them a quick summary, omitting many of the details he thought Margaret would prefer to keep private.

"I'll be damned." Leon shook his head. "How did I miss it? She looks a lot like Wendy."

"Who's Wendy?" Anastasia asked. "I mean apart from being Margaret's daughter, who I never knew existed."

When Leon was done telling his mate an abbreviated version of Wendy's story, Anastasia walked to the kitchen, pulled out a bottle of wine, and uncorked it. "Let me handle this." She took a glass, filled it to the brim, and took it to Margaret's room.

"Let's give them some privacy." Leon pulled out a beer for himself and headed out the front door.

As Bowen followed, he heard Anastasia huff out, "Oh, Margaret, just stop it and grow a set. Bowen has a lot he can tell you about Wendy."

Closing the door, he didn't hear Margaret's response.

"Congratulations." Leon offered him his hand. "You found your mate."

Bowen shook it. "Who would have thought that when I gave Wendy fatherly advice, I would one day become her stepdad." He grimaced. "Not that it's going to happen anytime soon. Margaret is too fragile to handle any more surprises right now, and I don't know whether she should even attempt transition in her state."

"The timing is actually perfect." Leon leaned against the railing and crossed his legs at the ankles. "The Clan Mother is here for the wedding and birthday celebrations, and she'll still be here two weeks from now. If you hurry, Margaret could enter transition while Annani is still here, and if things turn south, the Clan Mother can give her a blessing."

"The blessing is good only for giving the mates hope." Bowen took a long swig from his beer. "It doesn't do shit for the transitioning Dormant."

"I disagree. Each time the Clan Mother has given her blessing, the Dormants have enjoyed a miraculous recovery. Coincidence? I think not."

Bowen shrugged. "Nothing is going to happen between Margaret and me during the next two weeks. I just can't bring myself to make a move on a woman recovering from surgery. The cast needs to come off first."

Surprisingly, Leon nodded in agreement. "It didn't occur to us before, but we should have remembered that the body needs to be healthy before transition can occur." He lifted his bottle in a salute. "But at least you can now tell Margaret the truth and bring her to the village. There is no doubt that she's a Dormant."

If only things were as simple as that. Bowen had thought that he understood people, men and women, but he hadn't foreseen Margaret's reaction. Her response to his declaration that they had found love in the cabin had been to start sobbing. She hadn't denied it though, so maybe she felt the same and had just gotten overly emotional.

"I can't tell Margaret anything right now because she's already overloaded and won't be able to process it. The problem is that she wants to return to Safe Haven tomorrow, and I can't let her do that." He shook his head. "Well, I can, but I will have to go with her, and she doesn't want me to."

"Why the hell not?"

"She thinks that she's not good enough and I don't know how to convince her otherwise." He took a long swig from the beer, emptying it. "I've never had problems with women. I thought I understood them, but apparently I'm just as clueless as the rest of my gender."

Leon nodded in commiseration. "Maybe she needs more time. She's just learned that her daughter is within reach, and then you drop the love thing on her. It was too much?"

"I thought that you and Anastasia were giving us privacy."

"We tried, but other than sticking fingers in our ears, we couldn't help hearing you talk."

The door opened and Anastasia stepped out, holding the half-empty glass of wine in her hand. "Margaret has calmed down a little, but she wants to stay in her room and think. She says she's not ready to face Wendy." Anastasia joined Leon, leaning against the railing. "She's scared that Wendy will reject her."

"It's possible," Leon said.

Bowen frowned. "Do you think that I should talk to Wendy first? Explain why her mother never contacted her?"

Anastasia shook her head. "It's Margaret's story to tell."

"But she doesn't know the whole story, and if I don't tell her about Emmett, she won't know it before talking to Wendy."

"What does Emmett have to do with anything?" Anastasia asked.

"He compelled her to be terrified of looking for her daughter."

"Are you sure?" Leon asked.

"Every time I mentioned searching for information about Wendy on the internet, Margaret had a panic attack. Maybe that's why she's so scared of meeting her."

"We need that guy who helped Peter," Anastasia said. "He can remove the compulsion like he did for him. If it's still messing with Margaret's head, no wonder she's so spooked."

Bowen pushed away from the railing. "I need to check with Kalugal to see if he's willing to do it. He's a character, and he might demand my firstborn in exchange for the favor. But maybe he can do something over the phone. A video call should be enough."

Margaret

Margaret had stopped crying long enough for Ana to leave, but as soon as the door closed behind her friend, she grabbed a pillow and pressed it to her face to muffle her sobs.

It was hard to breathe, but she welcomed the suffocating sensation. If only she was strong enough to go all the way and end her miserable life.

How could she possibly face Wendy? She wasn't strong enough to survive her daughter's anger, her anguish. It would have been so much better for Wendy to believe that her mother was dead.

That was what she probably believed already, no doubt thanks to Roger, and she'd made peace with that, laid it to rest. Digging up her not-so-dead mother would only cause her pain.

Wendy would wonder why Margaret had left her, and why she hadn't cared enough to come back to check on her.

All the literature that Margaret had read claimed that antagonizing abusers could have catastrophic results, and that it was best to seek shelter before proceeding with legal action. The problem was that sometimes that wasn't good enough, and the abusers found their victims and hurt not only them but also the people who sheltered them.

But those were all excuses, and Wendy would be justified in scoffing at them.

Had Roger abused Wendy as well?

He'd loved her as a baby, so perhaps he hadn't, and Wendy had grown up in a decent home? Maybe Roger had divorced Margaret in her absence and married the nanny? She'd been kind to Wendy. She would have made a good stepmom.

Nevertheless, Margaret should have fought for her daughter and not run away like a spineless coward, hiding away and hoping that Roger and Wendy thought her dead, convincing herself that it was best for everyone's sake that they did.

When the bed dipped on her left side, Margaret nearly jumped out of her skin. With the pillow over her head, she hadn't heard the door open.

"I brought you tea," Bowen said.

She clutched the pillow to her face. "Please, leave."

"I'm not going anywhere. Talk to me, Margaret."

What could she possibly tell him? All she wanted was to be left alone so she could crawl back to her little hideyhole in Safe Haven, where she was as good as dead to the rest of the world.

"Don't you want to meet your daughter?"

Panic seizing her throat in a choking sensation, Margaret flung the pillow away. "Did you tell Wendy about me?"

"No, not yet."

Letting out a breath, she slumped back on the pillows. "Thank God for small mercies. Don't ever tell her that you've found me. She's better off believing that I'm dead."

"How can you say that?" Bowen lifted a corner of the duvet and wiped the tears off her face. "She is getting married in a few months. Don't you want to be at her wedding?"

Margaret's eyes widened. "She's getting married? Is she insane? She's too young."

"At her age, you were already a mother."

She winced. "Yeah and look where it got me. Marrying at eighteen was the worst mistake of my life, and I'm still paying for it."

"Your mistake was marrying the wrong man. You were just a kid, alone, with no one to guide you, to offer you advice, or to see past Roger's veneer. You can't keep punishing yourself for what he did."

"I'm not punishing myself. I'm trying to save my daughter even more anguish. Believing that her mother is dead is better than knowing she was abandoned."

"You shouldn't decide that for her. After hearing your story, she might forgive you or she might not. But I believe she will. Wendy is a good kid. She was a little moody when I first met her, but she's changed so much after moving in with Vlad. She's happy."

"How do you know that? Maybe she's faking it?"

Bowen shook his head. "She's not. She doesn't need to. I know Vlad well, and he's the kindest, most mellow guy you can imagine. He's studying to become a graphic artist, and in the meantime, he works part-time in his best friend's bakery. Wendy works at the village café, so I see her almost every day. There is always a smile on her face. She's confident, friendly, and everyone likes her."

Bowen's description of Wendy's life eased some of the heaviness in Margaret's chest. "It sounds like she's really happy, which is more reason not to dump my existence on her head. The best thing I can do for her is to remain dead."

Bowen

Frustrating woman.

Bowen wished he had some psychological training, something that would help him get through to Margaret. But all he knew was what would have worked for him, and that would probably not work for a woman who'd spent half of her life in hiding, hoping the world had forgotten about her and thought her dead.

Perhaps telling Margaret about her possible immortality and Wendy's transition would change her perspective? Make her less fearful and more hopeful?

After all, Margaret had lost nearly eighteen years of Wendy's life, but if she transitioned, she would have eternity to make up for it. Nothing could compensate for Wendy's entire childhood that she'd missed, but that was water under the bridge.

Margaret had to grow a set, as Anastasia had put it, and face the music.

Since he was taking her with him to the village no matter what, she was going to meet her daughter whether she wanted to or not.

"Then Roger wins." He thrust the mug at her hands. "Drink."

She winced, either at his tone or at what he'd said about her ex winning, and then looked at the tea suspiciously. "What's in it?"

"It's just tea, but if I could pour courage into it, I would."

More tears ran down her cheeks as she lifted the mug to her lips with trembling hands, took a sip, and sighed. "How did you meet Wendy? And how did she end up in this cabin with Vlad, you, and Leon?"

Was this progress? Or was it an evasive maneuver to steer the conversation away from facing her daughter?

"It's a long story, and it's not mine to tell. Wouldn't you prefer for Wendy to tell you her story in her own words?"

"I'm terrified," Margaret admitted. "She might refuse to see me. Or she might agree to meet me only to spit in my face and tell me to go to hell. I deserve both, but I wouldn't survive it." She touched a trembling hand to her temple. "Whatever I managed to piece back together with Emmett's help would shatter. I wouldn't survive the rejection."

"I have a friend who might help you." Bowen pulled out his phone.

He'd spoken with Kalugal, and the guy had graciously agreed to help, telling Bowen to call him when Margaret was ready.

She shook her head. "I don't want to talk to a shrink."

"My friend is not a psychologist. He's a hypnotist and a motivational speaker. He will help you calm down and be less fearful."

"I don't want to lean on yet another crutch."

"It's not like that. Give him just one minute of your time." When she kept shaking her head, he added, "For me."

Lifting her sad eyes to him, she nodded. "I'll do it for you."

Bowen dialed the number. "I have Margaret with me here, and you are on speakerphone. Do you need me to activate the video function?"

Margaret's eyes widened, and she shook her head vehemently while pointing at her face.

"No need. My voice is enough. Hello, Margaret. My name is Kalugal. How are you doing today?"

She sagged. "Hello. I've been better."

"I bet. I want you to listen to me and repeat what I say. Are you ready?"

She nodded. "Yes."

"I have no reason to be afraid. Say it and believe it."

She whispered it.

"I am surrounded by friends who care for me, protect me, and will not let anything happen to my daughter or me. Say it."

This time around, her voice was a little above a whisper.

"Now say this. I am strong, I am a survivor, and I can handle anything life throws at me."

As she repeated the words, out loud this time, Margaret straightened her back.

"That's it. My job is done," Kalugal said. "Best of luck with the rest of your life." He ended the call before Margaret murmured a thank you.

Lifting her eyes to Bowen, she took a deep breath. "He's really good. I actually feel stronger, more confident."

Later, after he'd told her the entire story, Bowen would explain what Kalugal had actually done, but for now he was going to take it one step at a time.

"Can I call Vlad now to have him deliver the good news to Wendy?"

Margaret shrank into the pillows, but she didn't say no. "Does he know about me?"

"Yes. He gave me the address to verify that it was really you. I asked him not to tell Wendy until you were ready."

"Thank you." She put the mug on the nightstand and wrung her hands. "Do you think that's the best way to do it? For her boyfriend to tell her?"

"I'm not sure. Would you like to consult with Anastasia and Leon?"

"Yes, I think that's a good idea."

Margaret

After washing her face, brushing her teeth, and combing her hair, Margaret felt a lot better. Or maybe it was the result of the short, yet very effective pep talk she'd gotten from Bowen's friend?

He must be a powerful hypnotist to effect such profound change in less than a minute. For lack of a better description, it felt as if he'd unlocked something inside her, some hidden reserve of courage or maybe zest for life that Margaret had thought was lost forever.

Though still terrified of Wendy's rejection, she no longer experienced the choking sensation that usually accompanied any thought of contacting her daughter, even checking on her covertly from afar.

When Margaret opened the door and stepped into the living room, her friends were waiting for her with fresh coffee and a plate of sandwiches.

"Feeling better?" Ana asked.

She was sitting in Leon's lap and looking stupidly happy and in love, especially for someone who was leaving tomorrow and parting with her boyfriend for at least a little while.

"Much better. Thank you."

Bowen got up and helped her to the couch.

Glad for the help, Margaret didn't shoo him away like she usually did. The meltdown and following sobbing fest had left her so exhausted that she could barely hold on to the crutches.

She glanced longingly at the coffee. "I don't know how Kalugal did it, but I feel like I've gotten a new lease on life."

Bowen poured her a cup, added milk and sugar, and handed it to her. "I'm very thankful that he agreed to help."

"Thank you." She took a sip. "What he did for me was nothing short of a miracle. He must be making a fortune selling his services."

Leon chuckled. "Kalugal is rich enough not to need to sell those particular services, and he's not kind enough to offer them for free either. You are lucky he's our cousin."

"How many cousins do you guys have?"

Ana chuckled. "A lot. They call every extended family member a cousin. I met a few of them, and I can't wait to meet the rest." She grinned at Margaret. "I'm moving in with Leon."

"I thought that you wanted to go back to law school."

"I might do that later." She kissed Leon's cheek. "Maybe I'll even finish my degree online. I can't be apart from my one and only, the love of my life."

As envy and regret gripped Margaret's heart, she glanced at Bowen, who had an unreadable expression on his face. He'd told her that they had found love in the cabin, and instead of telling him how she really felt about him, she'd had another panic attack and had run off sobbing.

Well, hopped off. She wouldn't be running anytime soon.

Tearing her gaze from him, she looked back at Ana. "So what do you think? What's the best way to break the news to Wendy that her mother is not dead?"

Ana leaned against Leon's chest. "I vote for a surprise reunion. Vlad can bring Wendy over here under false pretense, something about visiting Bowen and Leon for old times' sake. That way, you get to tell her your story yourself. If I were in Wendy's shoes, I would like that better. It will spare her all the guessing and agonizing on the way here."

"What if it's too much for her to process?" Leon asked. "If Vlad warns her, she'll be better prepared."

Ana shook her head. "This cabin holds fond memories for her. Wendy and Vlad fell in love here. Besides, if she needs to clear her head and cool off, this is the perfect place for that. There is nowhere to run to, she will have to face you."

Margaret nodded. "Either way is not perfect, but I'd rather tell her my story myself. There is so much I need to explain."

"We are here for you," Ana said. "I can attest to the influence Emmett had on you, and how he was able to convince you that hiding and letting the world believe you were dead was your best option and in Wendy's best interest."

"How did you know that he did that?"

Ana shrugged. "I figured it out. One way or another, he did that to all the community members. He convinced me that my father would destroy my life if I let him. There was a kernel of truth in that, which was why I believed him, but I didn't need to hide in Safe Haven to assert my will and not let my father dictate how I lived my life. I could have done it on the outside just as well, probably better."

"Emmett had the same hypnotic quality as Kalugal," Bowen said. "Think how easy it was for Kalugal to free you from fear. That's how easily Emmett instilled it in you."

The truth of his words slammed into Margaret with a force that had her slumping against the couch pillows. "Why would he do that to me?"

"Control," Bowen said. "As long as you were terrified of leaving, you were his to exploit."

"I'm not such a great find."

Bowen growled. "You were twenty years old when you got to Safe Haven."

He was right. She was pretty back then, and Emmett had shown a lot of interest in her. At first, it had been to help her heal, but once she'd gotten better, his interest had turned more carnal in nature.

Over the years though, the guilt and sorrow eating her from the inside had turned her into a walking skeleton, making her look older and more haggard than her years or type of work justified. Emmett's interest in her had slowly faded along with her waning beauty, but the fear he'd instilled in her had remained.

Margaret shook her head. "How am I going to explain that to Wendy?"

"You are not alone." Bowen wrapped his arm around her shoulders. "We are here to support you."

Vlad

Vlad wasn't sure at all that Bowen's idea to surprise Wendy was the best way for her to be reunited with her mother.

He hated lying to her, although technically he wasn't. He was just omitting what he knew about Bowen's new girlfriend.

The excuse for driving up to the cabin at night, right after his return from his trip to Milwaukee, was a reunion with the Guardians who'd been assigned to her and Richard after she'd betrayed their other location to her uncle.

"Remember not to mention my trip to Milwaukee to Bowen or Leon. Richard wants to keep it hush-hush."

"I know." Wendy curled up in her seat. "When did they come up with the reunion idea?"

"Today. They are leaving the cabin tomorrow afternoon, so today was the last day to do it. They were talking about us and how we fell in love at the cabin, and Leon wanted Anastasia to meet you. Just don't say anything about immortals because Anastasia's friend doesn't know yet."

Wendy's eyes sparkled. "Yet? Is she a potential Dormant?"

Vlad just nodded.

"I'm so happy for those two." She shifted in her seat to face him. "Leon and Bowen were really nice to me when they had no reason to be." She chuckled. "After you told me about being immortal, Bowen gave me a fatherly-sounding speech. I thought he was going to warn me not to hurt you again or else. Instead, we talked about people changing, and about my fear that you might become controlling or violent. You know how terrified of relationships I was. He helped me realize that I shouldn't be."

Not knowing how to respond to that, Vlad nodded again.

"Anyway, Bowen did a good job of reassuring me. He said that you're golden and that immortals were good people. He was also the one who told me about fated mates. I really hope that Anastasia's friend is a nice person. Bowen deserves to be happy."

"I'm sure she is."

"What's her name?"

"Margaret."

"That's easy to remember." Wendy turned to look out the window. "I don't think we are ever going to find my mother. She probably died from a drug overdose like my father said."

Vlad had told her a watered-down version of what he'd seen in Roger's mind, but perhaps he shouldn't have. If Wendy knew what her mother had suffered, she might be more forgiving.

"That maggot doesn't deserve to live. If not for my promise to you, I would have killed him, bled him slowly while he screamed in pain."

Wendy recoiled, and he regretted what he'd said even though it was true. He, who had never hurt a fly, would have delighted in tormenting Roger Miller for days, paying him back for all he had done to his wife and daughter.

"I'm sorry." He put a hand on her thigh. "It's still fresh in my mind. I didn't tell you the half of it, but just so you know, your mother had good reason to run and hide and never come back. He would have killed her on sight, and in his rage, he might have accidentally killed you as well, even though he loved you."

In his own twisted way, Roger Miller had believed that he cared for Wendy.

Wendy shivered. "I don't believe that he's even capable of love. In my mind, I don't blame her. But in my heart." She put a hand over her chest. "I ache because I've been abandoned by my mother. My life is good now, and I have no complaints. I just want to know whether she's alive and whether she found happiness elsewhere."

"Your wish might come true sooner than you think," he murmured.

"What do you mean? How?"

"The Fates work in mysterious ways."

Margaret

Margaret was on her third glass of wine when Bowen got up and walked up to the front door. "They are here."

A moment later she heard the car engine, and her stomach did a somersault.

"It's going to be okay." Ana sat next to her on the couch and took her trembling hand in hers. "Try to act natural, see if she recognizes you."

"How could she? Wendy was a baby when Roger kicked me out. She won't remember me, and we don't look alike enough for her to figure it out. What am I going to say to her?"

"It will come to you." Ana patted her hand. "Don't freak out."

Easier said than done. Her entire body was trembling.

"I have no reason to be afraid," she murmured quietly. "I am surrounded by friends who care for me, protect me, and will not let anything happen to my daughter or me. I am strong, I am a survivor, and I can handle anything life throws at me."

Margaret kept repeating the words Kalugal had given her like a mantra in her head until Wendy walked in the door, a very tall, gangly young man at her side.

Then the words left her, lodged in her throat like a rock, and tears started streaming down her cheeks.

"What's wrong?" Wendy walked up to her. "Why are you crying?"

Margaret was trembling so badly that Ana had to pry the wineglass out of her hand because it was sloshing all over her.

"Wendy," she whispered. "My sweet Wendy."

Confusion in her eyes, Wendy crouched in front of her. "Do I know you?"

Margaret nodded. "I'm your mother."

For a long moment, no one talked, no one breathed, and the oppressive silence was choking the life out of Margaret.

As her vision started to tunnel, Wendy pushed up and wrapped her arms around her. "Breathe, Mom. I've got you."

Margaret sucked in a breath, and with the oxygen in her lungs replenished, she started sobbing on her daughter's shoulder. "I'm so sorry. So, so sorry. I didn't want to leave you. I'm sorry, so, so sorry."

"Shh, it's okay. I understand." Wendy pulled back a little and smiled, and it was the most beautiful smile Margaret had ever seen. "I thought that you looked familiar. Now I know why. Have you been hiding in that cult for all these years?"

Margaret nodded. "I'm sorry for being such a coward. I thought that you'd be better off thinking that I was dead."

"I've never believed that you were." Wendy sat on the couch on Margaret's other side, wrapped her arm around her shoulders, and looked at her fiancé. "How long have you known?"

He pushed his long bangs aside, revealing a pair of mismatched eyes. There was boundless love in them as he looked at Wendy. "Bowen called me today and told me that he might have found your mother. He needed a little more information to make sure that it was her. He called me later and told me that the information checked out but asked me not to tell you. He wanted to tell Margaret first. Then he called me again and asked me to bring you here but not tell you the real reason. Your mother wanted to tell you her story in person."

Ana rose to her feet. "I know it's dark outside, but let's go for a walk and give these two privacy."

Margaret gripped her hand. "Don't go. I'm done being scared and ashamed, and you are my friends. I trust you with my ugly secrets." She turned to Wendy. "Unless you prefer otherwise."

Bowen

By the time Margaret had finished telling Wendy her side of the story, all three ladies had tear-stricken faces, the men were fighting a losing battle with their fangs, and other than Margaret and Wendy, everyone had eaten several sandwiches and drunk a shitload of alcohol, even Anastasia.

Bowen's decision to end Roger Miller's life had solidified, and not because he wanted to terminate her marriage. He was going to do that regardless of whether Roger had divorced Margaret in her absence or not.

"I can't believe how forgiving you are." Margaret wiped at her tears. "How did you grow up to be so kind?"

Wendy glanced at Vlad. "I didn't. I was either scared or apathetic, selfish and indifferent, and I vowed never to fall for a man. All of that has changed thanks to Vlad. He showed me that not all people are bad, he showed me a community of people who had each other's backs, and they welcomed me even though I wronged them terribly."

Margaret's eyes widened. "How? What could you have possibly done?"

Wendy sighed. "I almost got some of them captured, and I still have nightmares about what would have been done to them if they hadn't managed to escape."

"Captured by whom? And why?"

When Wendy looked at Bowen, he nodded. "It's okay. You can tell your mother everything. I think she can handle it now."

"Isn't it something a mate does? I don't want to deprive you of the privilege."

"Margaret and I are not there yet, we are just getting to know each other, and this is a unique situation. I think you deserve the honors more than I do."

Wendy huffed. "Don't be ridiculous. If not for you, I wouldn't have found my mother, and you are her mate. You deserve to do it."

Margaret watched the exchange with curiosity mixed with fear in her expressive eyes. "Would someone please tell me what's going on? And why is everyone referring to a significant other as a mate?"

Bowen waved at Wendy. "Let's do it together. You start, and I'll supply details and proof when needed."

Chuckling, Anastasia patted Margaret's good knee. "My advice is to keep an open mind. I was in your situation just a few days ago, and I can tell you that everything is true, and no one is pulling your leg." She rose to her feet. "In the meantime, Leon and I will serve dinner."

Wendy took in a long breath. "So here goes. I have a low-level paranormal talent. I'm an empath, which means that I can read people's emotions." She smiled. "Do you have any special talents?"

Margaret shook her head.

"Usually, paranormal talents run in families. Anyway, dear Uncle Simmons had one day shown up at our house and offered me a very lucrative government job at their new paranormal talent department."

Simmons was Wendy's uncle?

Bowen shot a glance at Vlad, who nodded. "I only found out after Jacki's wedding, and it no longer mattered."

Margaret bared her teeth. "Edgar was my uncle, and the bastard didn't even bother to show up at his sister's funeral."

"I'm not surprised," Wendy said. "He was a selfish, power-hungry pedophile."

"What did he do to you?" Margaret whispered, her eyes filled with horror.

"Nothing. But I'm an empath. I saw what he wanted to do to me. That was revolting enough."

As Wendy continued her story, Bowen walked to the kitchen and pulled a couple of beers out of the fridge. He handed one to Vlad, who followed him there.

"You're in the way." Anastasia shooed them out.

It took another fifteen minutes for Wendy to get to where Vlad had revealed who and what he really was.

Margaret looked shell-shocked, but she heeded Anastasia's advice and didn't voice disbelief. There was awe in her eyes as she glanced at Vlad, then Leon, and finally when she leveled them at Bowen.

"How come I didn't see anything?" she whispered. "Did you thrall me?"

"Twice, but both times were to put you to sleep. Once when we took Anastasia to the clinic, and the other one was earlier today after you told me your story."

Anastasia dragged Leon into the living room. "I can demonstrate if you want." She kissed him hard, and when she let go, his eyes were glowing and his fangs had elongated, but not fully.

Margaret gasped.

There were many more gasps as the story continued, and when it ended, it was past midnight.

"You should spend the night here," Margaret said to Wendy and Vlad. "It's too late for you to drive home."

"It's okay, Mom." Wendy leaned and kissed her cheek. "Immortals only need a few hours of sleep, and our night vision is excellent. For Vlad and me, and these three." She waved her hand over Leon, Anastasia, and Bowen. "Midnight feels like eight in the evening. You have nothing to worry about."

"When will I see you again?"

Smiling, Wendy glanced at Bowen. "You'll see me tomorrow when Bowen brings you to the village. Did you think that you were going back to Safe Haven after everything that I told you?"

"I guess I can't." Margaret wrung her hands. "What am I going to do in your village?"

"Anything you want." Wendy kissed her again. "The important thing is that we are a family again, and we have all the time in the world to get to know each other."

Bowen's gut clenched.

Margaret was thirty-eight years old and not in the best of health. Transition would be difficult for her. Then again, he had to believe that the Fates wouldn't take Margaret away from him and Wendy after going to all the trouble of maneuvering them all together.

Margaret had definitely suffered enough to earn the reward of a true love mate, and Bowen hoped that his many good deeds had earned him some goodwill from the Fates as well.

Cassandra

After Cassandra had ended things with Onegus the day before, he had called at least five more times. Not right away, and not before she'd cried her eyes out in her office and snarled at anyone who'd dared to knock on her door. His first call had come at seven in the evening, but she'd let it go straight to voicemail. He called again, and after letting that one go as well, she'd checked whether he'd left a message, but he hadn't.

After three additional calls, she'd turned her phone off and had tried to go to sleep. It had been a miserable night, but at least nothing had exploded. She wasn't angry, just sad, and the swirling energy inside of her felt subdued.

She'd finally found an antidote.

Depression.

Thank you, but no thanks.

She would let herself mope around for a couple of days, eat excessive amounts of ice cream, and then shake it off.

Sounded like a good plan when she'd tossed and turned throughout the night, but when she turned her phone back on in the morning, a message from Onegus was waiting in her voicemail, and ignoring it was not happening.

Sitting cross-legged on her bed, she pressed play.

"Upon further reflection, I realized that I might have given you the wrong impression. Nothing could be further from the truth, and I'm going to prove it to you. Call me."

How was he going to prove it? Invite her to meet Connor?

She'd pass.

Except, her bravado didn't last long, and after drinking three cups of coffee and feeling like she could personally power the entire state with the energy swirling inside her, Cassandra called Onegus back.

He answered right away. "Give me one moment, please."

It was noisy in the background, people talking, phones ringing, but it was fading as if Onegus was walking away from the source of the noise.

"Thanks for calling me back. I was ready to drive over to your office and make a scene."

She chuckled nervously. "Then I'm glad I called."

"You hurt my feelings yesterday," he said softly. "No one has ever hung up on me before. That was rude."

"I know, and I apologize for acting so immaturely, but I felt hurt too."

She still did, and he hadn't told her how he was going to prove to her that she'd gotten the wrong impression, but there was hope in her heart that hadn't been there before.

"You punished me for an imagined crime that I haven't committed," Onegus said softly. "I owe you a spanking for your ungrounded accusations and for hanging the phone up on me."

He hadn't sounded mad, which was a huge relief, and his teasing affected her in a most unexpected way.

She laughed. "First, you will need to prove your innocence as well as my guilt."

"I can do that in one fell swoop."

"How?"

"I'm inviting you to a family wedding. My cousin is getting married, and the entire clan is gathering to celebrate. I will introduce you to everyone as my partner. Will that end the nonsense about me being embarrassed to be seen with you once and for all?"

And then some.

"Yes."

"Then it's settled." He sounded smug.

"When is the wedding?" If he said a year from now, she was going to hang up on him again.

"This Saturday."

Oh, wow. She needed to get a new dress.

"Where?"

"I can't tell you for security reasons. It's a private affair, and we don't want anyone outside the family to catch wind of it."

Aha. It was probably a tiny thing, and his entire so-called clan meant twenty people.

"Is it a small wedding?"

He chuckled. "Is over seven hundred guests considered small?"

"You have a big family."

"I told you that the entire clan was gathering. A clan implies a large family."

She had run out of rebuttals and had to concede defeat. Her bottom clenched, and not in an unpleasant way.

"Are you going to pick me up?"

"I have to be at the venue early to make sure everything is ready. I'll send a car for you. Or is that not good enough either?"

"No, that's fine. I guess I need to rush to get a dress. You didn't give me much notice."

"More complaints?"

"No. I think I'm done for a while."

"Good. Plan to be ready by eight on Saturday."

"Will I see you before that?"

He chuckled. "Are you eager for that spanking I promised you?"

"Nope. Saturday is good."

CASSANDRA & ONEGUS'S CONTINUES
The Children of the Gods Book 51
Dark Power Unleashed

Turn the page to read the excerpt—>

Join the VIP Club
To find out what's included in your free membership, flip to the last page.

Dark Power Unleashed

Cassandra's power is unpredictable, uncontrollable, and destructive. If she doesn't learn to harness it, people might get hurt.
Onegus's self-control is legendary. Even his fangs and venom glands obey his commands.

They say that opposites attract, and perhaps it's true, but are they any good for each other?

Kian

Six o'clock in the morning was too early for a smoke, but since Kian hadn't actually slept, it could be argued that it wasn't really morning for him. Syssi was in the shower, and while he waited for her to get ready for breakfast, he could sneak outside for a few minutes and get his fix.

As usual, too much was going on all at once, and his mind was spinning in circles trying to make sense of it.

What were the damn Fates up to this time?

"Good morning, master." Okidu bowed. "Would you like a fresh cup of coffee? It has just finished brewing."

"Yes, please."

A steamy mug of coffee in hand, Kian opened the living room sliding doors and walked out into the backyard. Sitting down on his favorite lounger, he put the mug on the side table and picked up his box of cigarillos.

Lighting up, he took a grateful puff and leaned back.

The Fates had played another of their games, bringing yet another Dormant into the clan's fold, and not just any Dormant, but Wendy's long-lost mother.

The text message from Bowen had arrived a couple of hours ago.

The Guardian probably hadn't expected Kian to read it right away, so he hadn't elaborated beyond the basic facts. But Kian could piece it together from what he already knew.

The irony wasn't lost on him.

Margaret had been under their noses for nearly two weeks, but Bowen had figured it out on the same day Vlad and Richard had traveled out of town to have a talk with Wendy's asshole of a father and find out what he'd done with the mother.

If Bowen had figured it out a day earlier, he would have saved them the trouble.

Had Wendy's bastard of a father been left to sully the earth with his presence for another day?

If Vlad had managed not to kill him, the kid had much better self-control than Kian. If he were in Vlad's shoes, Kian would have torn the jerk's throat out, and no one would have been able to stop him. It wouldn't even have mattered if Wendy's father had killed her mother or not. He deserved to die for the abuse he'd inflicted on his family. But Vlad was a gentle soul, and he'd made a promise to Wendy not to kill her father, so maybe the scum was still alive.

In any case, Kian wasn't going to ask or even hint that he knew about Richard and Vlad's trip.

Plausible deniability and all that.

Then there was Onegus and his unconventional request to bring a date to Sari and David's wedding. The chief had met the lady at the annual charity ball, and it seemed like he was seriously smitten, which was uncharacteristic of him. Onegus was a player who never hooked up with the same woman more than twice, which was how it was supposed to be for immortals engaging with humans.

As Kian heard the sliding door open, he turned and smiled at his wife. "That was quick." He extinguished his cigarillo.

"Isn't it too early for a smoke?" She lowered herself onto his lap with effort, her pregnant belly nestling against his. "What's troubling you?"

"Nothing major. Just many little things." He wrapped his arms around her to keep her warm. "Isn't it too cold for you out here?"

Syssi leaned her head on his shoulder. "Not when I'm lying on top of you. You are like a furnace." She lifted her eyes to him. "Are you nervous about Sari and David's arrival?"

Their flight was scheduled to land at LAX at twelve-thirty in the afternoon, and instead of them taking a taxi to the newly renovated building across from the keep, Syssi had insisted on picking them up at the airport.

"I'm nervous about most of the clan being here for their wedding. It's a logistical nightmare to keep everyone's arrival unnoticed. But that's just one in a long list of things keeping me awake at night."

"What else? The Kra-ell?"

"Yeah. That too. I want to get a move on it, but I have to wait until after the festivities. On top of that, Onegus has invited a human date to the wedding, and I was so shocked by the request that I said okay before thinking it through."

Smiling, Syssi cupped his cheek. "It was nice of you to allow it, and it's not a big deal. Gerard's human crew is serving at the wedding, and their minds will need to get wiped at the end of the night. One more human will not make a difference."

"True. But that's another annoyance. There will be too many humans working in the bowels of the keep to prepare and service this wedding, and later, having their memories wiped. Then there are the Chinese crews building our village, who will have to be wiped as well."

"You had every one of them checked for responsiveness to thralling, so it's not like some might be immune. You're fretting for no good reason." She lifted her head and kissed his cheek. "Relax, enjoy. These are happy times for us and for the clan."

Kian shook his head. "I feel like I've become complacent, and I'm taking too many risks." He ran his hand over her back. "The Kra-ell are wise to keep their communities small. They can pick up and go with ease."

"Perhaps they are nomadic in nature." Syssi put a hand on her belly. "I like staying in one place, and despite being an introvert, I love having a big community of people to interact with when I'm in the mood for it. I think I would have gone nuts with just a couple dozen people to talk to. For some reason, that seems more intimate and more intrusive." She rubbed her belly again.

"Is Allegra kicking?" Kian put his hand over hers.

"She's sleeping. I just like touching her. It's so cool that I can feel the contours of her little body through my belly." Syssi shifted, finding a more comfortable position. "Onegus's date must be special if he invited her to the wedding."

"He claims that he can sense some sort of strange energy from her that intensifies when she gets angry or excited. He says that her mother emits similar energy, but not as strong."

"Fascinating." Syssi sat up and put her hands on the small of her back. "I'm going to ask Lisa to sniff Onegus's date out at the wedding. After all, she was right about Anastasia being a Dormant."

Kian moved Syssi's hands aside and started massaging her back. "She was, and I regret not sending her to sniff out Anastasia's friend as well."

It was a gentle way to break the news to Syssi. He didn't want her getting overly excited in her condition.

"Why? Is she a Dormant too?"

"Confirmed."

Syssi turned wide eyes to him. "Did she transition and no one told me?"

There was no way to soften the delivery of what he had to tell her, so he attempted a softer tone. "Margaret is Wendy's mother."

Syssi gasped. "Impossible. How?"

"Apparently, she escaped her abusive husband when Wendy was a baby and has been hiding in Safe Haven ever since. Bowen somehow connected the dots, mother and daughter had an emotional reunion last night, and Bowen is bringing Margaret to the village today."

Syssi tried to push out of his arms. "We have to prepare lodging for them."

He tightened his arms around her. "There is no rush. Ingrid is too busy to deal with that right now, and if we let someone else do it for her, she'll throw a tantrum. Bowen and Margaret can stay with Vlad and Wendy for a week or two. I'm sure Wendy and her mother have a lot of catching up to do."

Cassandra

Cassandra glanced up at the rearview mirror to check her makeup. She'd been in a rush this morning and it showed. There wasn't much she could do about it while driving, though, except perhaps fixing her lipstick. Reaching over the central console for her purse, she was rummaging for the tube when her phone rang.

The familiar number popping up on her car's display brought a smile to her face. "Did you forget something?"

"Are you driving?" Onegus sounded like a stern schoolteacher, displeased with her supposedly reckless behavior.

"Yes, but don't worry. I'm not holding the phone, my hands are on the wheel, and I'm looking at the road."

Given that she'd had her hand in her purse and was about to apply lipstick while driving, Cassandra had been guilty of intent but not of actual infraction. So technically, she hadn't lied.

He chuckled. "How did you know that I was worried?"

"Your tone. You sounded like a policeman or a schoolteacher about to give me a lecture."

"If it turns you on, I can get into either of those roles with ease." His tone was teasing, but his voice had dropped by half an octave, stirring interest in her lady parts.

"I bet." She shifted in her seat.

On the face of things, Onegus appeared charming and easygoing, but she could sense the steel he was hiding under all those panty-melting smiles of his. He had a dominant streak, which would normally put him on her do-not-call list, but he wasn't overbearing and seemed more concerned with her pleasure than his own, so she didn't mind.

In fact, it was a big part of the attraction.

He was the kind of guy a woman could lean on, rely on, and he certainly wasn't a man who would fold under the slightest pressure.

Besides, he could handle her and wasn't intimidated by her, which was no small feat.

"Did you tell your mother about the wedding?" he asked.

"I didn't see her this morning, so no, I didn't tell her yet."

"Don't tell her or anyone else about it. It's crucial that the event stays confidential."

"Are you worried about paparazzi?"

He sighed. "I wish that was the extent of my worries. Our family has enemies, old feuds that go generations back. They would love to find out that nearly the entire clan is gathering in one location."

What the hell was he talking about?

Mafia wars came to mind. "You are kidding, right?"

"I wish I was, and before you jump to the wrong conclusion, it's not a mafia turf war. It really goes back many generations in time."

Onegus had a very slight Scottish accent, but Cassandra wasn't aware of any active feuds between Scottish clans. Then again, she wasn't a history buff, and what she did know came from her mother's Highlander romance novels. Not the most reliable source of information.

"Should I be worried?"

"Not with me by your side. I'll keep you safe."

She chuckled. "A warrior billionaire. It sounds like the title of a bodice-ripper."

"What's a bodice-ripper? It sounds intriguing."

"It's a sexually explicit romantic story that takes place in a historical setting. Highlanders are very popular in that genre."

"Is that so?" He let his Scottish accent come out full force. "I'm up for ripping your bodice anytime and in any setting."

She laughed. "I'll keep that in mind when shopping for a dress to wear to the wedding. No bodice."

"That sounds even more intriguing and fashion forward. But then I'd have to kill all of my male family members for looking at your breasts, and that would ruin everyone's fun."

"We don't want that." She chuckled. "A dress can cover up everything without having a bodice. How formal is the event?"

"As formal as they get. But you don't have to get a new dress. You can wear the same one you wore for the gala. You looked stunning in it. I'll be the envy of all my bachelor cousins."

She couldn't help the grin splitting her face. "Just the bachelors?"

"Yes." His tone changed from teasing to gruff. "We are a very traditional and loyal bunch, and mated males don't stray, not even with their eyes. Once we commit, it's for life."

"That's commendable, but I doubt it's factual. Forty percent of marriages end in divorce."

"Not in our community."

Cassandra had no idea what the official religion of Scotland was, but she was pretty sure it wasn't Catholicism.

"Are you Catholic?"

"It has nothing to do with religion."

"A code of honor then?"

"It's just the way it is. You will have to make do with just the bachelors' admiration."

He sounded cold, and Cassandra didn't like it. She liked the smile in his voice, his light-hearted banter. Had she put her foot in it again?

Perhaps Onegus had a history with an unfaithful girlfriend, and it was a sore point for him.

"I was just teasing. I hate players and cheaters with a passion, which was why I got so mad when I thought that you didn't want to be seen with me. That's the number one sign that a guy is dating several women at the same time. They don't want to get caught, so they find excuses for not going out."

"Has it ever happened to you?" His tone had warmed up a little, but he still sounded serious.

"Yeah, there is no avoiding it. It's not like guys have it written on their foreheads or in their dating app profiles. But as soon as I noticed the signs, I booted the two-timers out so fast that they didn't know what hit them."

"Good for you."

"What about you? Did you ever have a two-timing girlfriend?"

"I've never had a girlfriend."

She rolled her eyes. "Fine, a lady friend then, a woman you've dated. I don't care what you call them."

"I've never been with the same woman more than once, so the only terms that apply are one-night stands and hookups."

Great. So, he wasn't a two-timer, just a serial player. It was almost as bad.

"Fear of commitment much?"

"I just haven't met the right woman before."

Oh, he was smooth. "And I am her?"

"You are the first one I'm willing to explore the possibility with. When I commit, it's forever, Cassandra. I need to make absolutely sure that I'm committing to the right woman. My one and only."

Margaret

Margaret stayed in bed long after waking up, afraid to go out of the room and face the others.

What if it had all been a dream? Or a drug-induced fantasy?

Except, she was clean. She hadn't touched opioids in over a week. Margaret also wasn't creative enough to dream up what she'd learned the day before. Somehow, Wendy had been turned immortal, and so had Bowen, Leon, and Anastasia, but Margaret didn't know how it had been done. Last night, she'd been too overwhelmed to ask.

Supposedly, they all had special genes that could be activated.

Anastasia had been turned with ease, so the activation process couldn't be too bad, and Wendy hadn't mentioned anything terrible either. Maybe it was as easy as getting some miracle elixir intravenously. Ana had joked about the doctor putting a miracle drug in her IV, and maybe that was what had been done to activate her dormant immortal genes.

If that was all it took, Margaret was willing to give it a try.

But did she really want to live forever?

Life was hard. Why would she want to drag it out indefinitely? Didn't the immortals get tired of living?

She wanted time to get to know her daughter, and maybe to explore a relationship with Bowen, who was actually much older than her but looked a decade younger.

Her mortal lifespan was long enough to do both.

If she became immortal, would the process reverse her aging and turn her young and beautiful again?

Could she start anew?

Margaret chuckled softly. The transition might shave ten years off her appearance, but unless Bowen thralled her to forget her ugly past, there was no getting rid of the memories she'd accumulated, and not many of them were good.

She'd learned not to feel too much, not to think about what she'd lost or about how meaningless it all was. She didn't want eternity to ponder the depressing reality of existence.

Margaret had learned to live in the moment, to keep so busy that she didn't have time to think. Idle moments were her enemy, as were the moments before falling asleep.

That was why she'd worked so hard, why she'd kept reading and researching material until her eyes burned from exhaustion and she knew that she would fall asleep as soon as she closed them. Anything less than that meant staying awake for hours and agonizing. To spend eternity like that would be hell.

When a soft knock sounded on her door, she wiped the few tears she'd shed with a corner of the duvet. "Yes?"

"Can I come in?" Ana asked.

"Sure."

Her friend walked in with a cup of coffee in hand. "Bowen is worried about you. He sent me to check on you." She sat on the bed and handed Margaret the cup. "How are you feeling this morning?"

"Strange. Did last night really happen, or did I dream it all up?"

"It happened." Ana smiled. "Your beautiful daughter came. She wasn't angry at you, she hugged you and kissed you, and she called you Mom. It doesn't get any better than that."

"It doesn't." Margaret took a sip from the coffee.

"So why were you crying?"

She shrugged. "I'm not sure that I want to live forever. I mean, I want time with Wendy, but I'm not old. I still have many years left to make up for those I lost."

Ana regarded her with puzzlement in her eyes. "Why wouldn't you want to live forever?"

"Because life is hard, and it's sad. Why drag out the misery?"

"It doesn't have to be miserable. You can learn to be happy." She leaned closer and whispered, "You have an amazing guy who wants to spend that eternity with you. What can be better than that?"

"Does he? When Wendy called him my mate, he told her that we were not there yet."

Anastasia rolled her eyes. "That's because you haven't had sex yet. It's like marriage. It needs to be consummated to be official. Bowen is in love with you, and you are in love with him. It's time you let yourself feel it."

Margaret opened her mouth to refute Ana's claim, to tell her that she wasn't in love with Bowen, but she closed it when she realized that Ana was right.

She'd fallen in love with Bowen from almost the very first moment. When he'd brought her to that ambulance and stayed with her, she'd felt the pull, the yearning. But she hadn't allowed herself to internalize it, in the same way she hadn't allowed herself to internalize anything else.

She'd been existing, not living.

To open her heart would have opened the gates not only to love, but also to misery, to the self-loathing, and to the horrible memories, and Margaret wouldn't have survived it.

Her capacity for pain had been maxed out a long time ago.

"You need to get up and get dressed." Ana patted her arm. "We can leave as soon as you are ready."

Margaret swallowed. "Do you mean the four of us?"

"Of course. There is no reason for us to stay here any longer. We are going to the immortals' village." Ana grinned. "I can't wait to see it. Leon has told me so much about it, and it sounds like a real haven, not the fake one Emmett created." She pursed her lips. "Which reminds me that there is one more piece of information that might shock you."

As panic constricted her throat, Margaret lifted her hand to her neck. "I don't know if I can handle any more shocking news."

"I think this piece will explain a few things, or at least make you see them more clearly. The clan has captured Emmett, and they have him locked up in their dungeon. Apparently, he's also an immortal, just from a different breed, and he used compulsion to make you and the others worship him. The guy who helped you, Kalugal, is not a motivational speaker. He is also a compeller like Emmett, and all he did was override what Emmett has done to you. The leader you admired so much compelled you to get panic attacks every time you thought of contacting Wendy or even just seeking information about her."

Syssi

By the time Okidu parked the limo in the underground garage of the building, Lisa and Ronja had talked up a storm, updating Sari and David on the latest village gossip.

Luckily, mother and daughter weren't aware yet of the one item that would most likely bother Ronja the most once she found out about it.

Syssi wasn't sure what kind of a relationship Ronja and Bowen had, or if it had developed into anything romantic, but even if it hadn't, the news about Bowen's newfound love would probably be upsetting to Ronja. Now that he belonged to another woman, he wouldn't be spending time with her like he used to.

Anandur, Brundar, and Kian had been busy talking about security and didn't pay attention to the prattle, but she'd caught Okidu stealing glances at Ronja through the rearview mirror.

Lately, he'd been acting even stranger than usual. Well, stranger for an Odu, but less strange for a human. Could it be that he was developing real feelings? Was he concerned for Ronja?

The butler knew everything that was going on, heard all the gossip, and stored it in his cybertronic brain.

Syssi shook her head. She was being silly, and it was all in her head. She'd gotten so used to Okidu that he seemed human to her.

"This building needs a name," Lisa said. "I'm tired of calling it the building across the street from the keep."

"What would you suggest?" Anandur asked.

Lisa shrugged. "I don't know. Anything would be better than that. Name it after one of the presidents or something. The Adams building, or Madison, or Monroe. Or the Shangri-La."

Syssi chuckled. "I like Shangri-La, but don't forget that we intend to lease these apartments at some point. I don't think prospective tenants would like their building to be called after a fictional place."

"We can discuss this upstairs." Kian opened the passenger door at the same time Okidu opened the one on the other side. "Mother and Amanda are waiting for us with lunch."

As the eight of them headed toward the elevators, Okidu lifted Sari and David's luggage from the trunk and followed behind them.

"I shall wait for the next elevator, master." He bowed.

"Thank you for getting our luggage." Sari patted his arm. "I left Ojidu home to take care of those who volunteered to stay behind."

The perpetual shroud around the castle meant that those in charge of maintaining it couldn't leave. Usually, that wasn't a problem, but it was a shame that they couldn't take part in the celebrations. It was time to replace the shroud with technology, but, for some reason, Sari was dragging her feet about it.

Perhaps she wanted to move out of there. She had refused Kian's offer to join the village because she liked her independence, but that didn't mean that she couldn't move her people to another location in Scotland. The castle was beautiful, but it was old, and there was only so much that could be done to bring it into the twenty-first century.

"Your apartment is on the top floor." Kian pressed the button to call the elevator. "It's not a penthouse, because the building wasn't designed with residences in mind, but you'll still have a nice view."

Sari cast him an apologetic glance. "You've gone to so much trouble to make this event possible. We could have made the wedding a smaller celebration in the village."

As the elevator arrived and they all crammed in, Kian wrapped his arm around Syssi's shoulders. "The plans to convert the building from offices to apartments were made long before I decided to host the clan here. Your wedding only hastened the construction, so don't feel guilty about it. I just wish that you could stay in the village during your visit."

Sari shook her head. "I need to be near my people, and they are all staying here. But David and I will come visit the village on Sunday. Miranda can't wait to see it."

"When is she arriving?" Syssi asked.

"Later today." David held the elevator door open until all of them spilled out. "The logistics of bringing everyone here without attracting attention were complicated. Only a small group is arriving straight from Scotland, and not all from the same airport. Others are making stopovers at other major cities, in Europe and in the States, before heading here."

Kian nodded. "We are using delivery trucks to pick them up from the various collection centers they will Uber or taxi to."

Sari winced. "Please tell me those trucks have nice interiors. I don't want my people shuttled in like cattle."

"Of course." Syssi put her hand on Sari's arm. "This is a celebration not an evacuation."

As they started down the corridor toward the corner unit, the door opened and Amanda rushed out. "Sari!" She pulled her sister into a hug. "You look amazing." Amanda smiled at David. "Thanks to you, no doubt." She let go of Sari and hugged him too. "I'm so excited about your wedding. Especially since I didn't have to do anything. Gerard took care of all the details, including hiring the decorators and supervising their work."

Sari shook her head. "I don't know how you managed to rope him into organizing our wedding and Kian's birthday. You must teach me your magic spell."

Amanda pursed her lips. "Got guilt? That's my magic."

"I see." Sari turned to Kian. "Your birthday was supposed to be a surprise, but at some point, it was decided to include you in the plans."

Syssi lifted her hand. "That was my doing. Kian doesn't like surprises, but he loves big clan-wide parties. I figured that he would prefer to be included in the planning, especially since security was a major concern."

"You know me so well." He kissed the top of her head. "Let's not keep Mother waiting."

ORDER DARK POWER UNLEASHED TODAY!

JOIN THE VIP CLUB
To find out what's included in your free membership, flip to the last page.

The Children of the Gods Series

Reading Order

THE CHILDREN OF THE GODS ORIGINS

1: Goddess's Choice

When gods and immortals still ruled the ancient world, one young goddess risked everything for love.

2: Goddess's Hope

Hungry for power and infatuated with the beautiful Areana, Navuh plots his father's demise. After all, by getting rid of the insane god he would be doing the world a favor. Except, when gods and immortals conspire against each other, humanity pays the price.

But things are not what they seem, and prophecies should not to be trusted...

THE CHILDREN OF THE GODS

Dark Stranger

1: Dark Stranger The Dream

2: Dark Stranger Revealed

3: Dark Stranger Immortal

Dark Enemy

4: Dark Enemy Taken

5: Dark Enemy Captive

6: Dark Enemy Redeemed

Kri & Michael's Story
6.5: My Dark Amazon

Dark Warrior
7: Dark Warrior Mine
8: Dark Warrior's Promise
9: Dark Warrior's Destiny
10: Dark Warrior's Legacy

Dark Guardian
11: Dark Guardian Found
12: Dark Guardian Craved
13: Dark Guardian's Mate

Dark Angel
14: Dark Angel's Obsession
15: Dark Angel's Seduction
16: Dark Angel's Surrender

Dark Operative
17: Dark Operative: A Shadow of Death
18: Dark Operative: A Glimmer of Hope
19: Dark Operative: The Dawn of Love

Dark Survivor
20: Dark Survivor Awakened
21: Dark Survivor Echoes of Love
22: Dark Survivor Reunited

DARK WIDOW

23: DARK WIDOW'S SECRET

24: DARK WIDOW'S CURSE

25: DARK WIDOW'S BLESSING

DARK DREAM

26: DARK DREAM'S TEMPTATION

27: DARK DREAM'S UNRAVELING

28: DARK DREAM'S TRAP

DARK PRINCE

29: DARK PRINCE'S ENIGMA

30: DARK PRINCE'S DILEMMA

31: DARK PRINCE'S AGENDA

DARK QUEEN

32: DARK QUEEN'S QUEST

33: DARK QUEEN'S KNIGHT

34: DARK QUEEN'S ARMY

DARK SPY

35: DARK SPY CONSCRIPTED

36: DARK SPY'S MISSION

37: DARK SPY'S RESOLUTION

DARK OVERLORD

38: DARK OVERLORD NEW HORIZON

39: DARK OVERLORD'S WIFE

40: Dark Overlord's Clan

Dark Choices

41: Dark Choices The Quandary

42: Dark Choices Paradigm Shift

43: Dark Choices The Accord

Dark Secrets

44: Dark Secrets Resurgence

45: Dark Secrets Unveiled

46: Dark Secrets Absolved

Dark Haven

47: Dark Haven Illusion

48: Dark Haven Unmasked

49: Dark Haven Found

Dark Power

50: Dark Power Untamed

51: Dark Power Unleashed

52: Dark Power Convergence

The threads of fate converge, mysteries unfold, and the clan's future is forever altered in the least expected way.

Dark Memories

53: Dark Memories Submerged

Geraldine's memories are spotty at best, and many of them are pure fiction. While her family attempts to solve the puzzle with far too many pieces missing, she's forced to confront a past life that she can't remember, a present that's more fantastic than her wildest made-up stories, and a future that might be better than her most heartfelt fantasies. But as more clues are uncovered, the picture starting to emerge is beyond anything she or her family could have ever imagined.

54: Dark Memories Emerge

The more clues emerge about Geraldine's past, the more questions arise.

Did she really have a twin sister who drowned?

Who is the mysterious benefactor in her hazy recollections?

Did he have anything to do with her becoming immortal?

Thankfully, she doesn't have to find the answers alone.

Cassandra and Onegus are there for her, and so is Shai, the immortal who sets her body on fire.

As they work together to solve the mystery, the four of them stumble upon a millennia-old secret that could tip the balance of power between the clan and its enemies.

55: Dark Memories Restored

As the past collides with the present, a new future emerges.

Dark Hunter

56: Dark Hunter's Query

For most of his five centuries of existence, Orion has walked the earth alone, searching for answers.

Why is he immortal?

Where did his powers come from?

Is he the only one of his kind?

When fate puts Orion face to face with the god who sired him, he learns the secret behind his immortality and that he might not be the only one.

As the goddess's eldest daughter and a mother of thirteen, Alena deserves the title of Clan Mother just as much as Annani, but she's not interested in honorifics. Being her mother's companion and keeping the mischievous goddess out of trouble is a rewarding, full-time job. Lately, though, Alena's love for her mother and the clan's gratitude is not enough.

She craves adventure, excitement, and perhaps a true-love mate of her own.

When Alena and Orion meet, sparks fly, but they both resist the pull. Alena could never bring herself to trust the powerful compeller, and Orion could never allow himself to fall in love again.

57: Dark Hunter's Prey

When Alena and Orion join Kalugal and Jacki on a romantic vacation to the enchanting Lake Lugu in China, they anticipate a couple of visits to Kalugal's archeological dig, some sightseeing, and a lot of lovemaking.

Their excursion takes an unexpected turn when Jacki's vision sends them on a perilous hunt for the elusive Kra-ell.

As things progress from bad to worse, Alena beseeches the Fates to keep everyone in their group alive. She can't fathom losing any of them, but most of all, Orion.

For over two thousand years, she walked the earth alone, but after mere days with him at her side, she can't imagine life without him.

58: Dark Hunter's Boon

As Orion and Alena's relationship blooms and solidifies, the two investigative teams combine their recent discoveries to piece together more of the Kra-ell mystery.

Attacking the puzzle from another angle, Eleanor works on gaining access to Echelon's powerful AI spy network.

Together, they are getting dangerously close to finding the elusive Kra-ell.

Dark God

59: Dark God's Avatar

Unaware of the time bomb ticking inside her, Mia had lived the perfect life until it all came to a screeching halt, but despite the difficulties she faces, she doggedly pursues her dreams.

Once known as the god of knowledge and wisdom, Toven has grown cold and indifferent. Disillusioned with humanity, he travels the world and pens novels about the love he can no longer feel.

Seeking to escape his ever-present ennui, Toven gives a cutting-edge virtual experience a try. When his avatar meets Mia's, their sizzling virtual romance unexpectedly turns into something deeper and more meaningful.

Will it endure in the real world?

60: Dark God's Reviviscence

Toven might have failed in his attempts to improve humanity's condition, but he isn't going to fail to improve Mia's life, making it the best it can be despite her fragile health, and he can do that not as a god, but as a man who possesses the means, the smarts, and the determination to do it.

No effort is enough to repay Mia for reviving his deadened heart and making him excited for the next day, but the flip side of his reviviscence is the fear of losing its catalyst.

Given Mia's condition, Toven doesn't dare to over excite her. His venom is a powerful aphrodisiac, euphoric, and an all-around health booster, but it's also extremely potent. It might kill her instead of making her better.

61: Dark God Destinies Converge

Destinies converge, and secrets are revealed in part three of Mia and Toven's story.

Dark Whispers

62: Dark Whispers From The Past

A brilliant scientist and programmer, William lives for his work, but when he recruits a young bioinformatician to help him decipher the gods' genetic blueprints, he find himself smitten with more than just her brain.

A Ph.d at nineteen, Kaia is considered a prodigy and expects a bright future in academia. But when William invites her to join his secret research team, she accepts for reasons that have nothing to do with her career objectives. Wiliam's promise to look into her best friend's disappearance is an offer she just can't refuse.

63: Dark Whispers From Afar

William knows that his budding relationship with the nineteen-year-old Kaia will be frowned upon, but he's unprepared for her family's vehement opposition.

Family means everything to Kaia, so when she finds herself in the impossible position of having to choose between them and William, she resorts to unconventional means to resolve the conflict.

64: Dark Whispers From Beyond

The sacrifices Kaia and her family have to make for a chance of gaining immortality might tear them apart, and success is not guaranteed.

Is the dubious promise of eternal life worth the risk of losing everything?

DARK GAMBIT

65: DARK GAMBIT THE PAWN

66: DARK GAMBIT THE PLAY

67: DARK GAMBIT RELIANCE

DARK ALLIANCE

68: DARK ALLIANCE KINDRED SOULS

69: DARK ALLIANCE TURBULENT WATERS

70: DARK ALLIANCE PERFECT STORM

DARK HEALING

71: DARK HEALING BLIND JUSTICE

72: DARK HEALING BLIND TRUST

73: DARK HEALING BLIND CURVE

DARK ENCOUNTERS

74: DARK ENCOUNTERS OF THE CLOSE KIND

75: DARK ENCOUNTERS OF THE UNEXPECTED KIND

76: DARK ENCOUNTERS OF THE FATED KIND

THE CHILDREN OF THE GODS SERIES SETS

Books 1-3: Dark Stranger trilogy—Includes a bonus short story: **The Fates take a Vacation**

Books 4-6: Dark Enemy Trilogy —Includes a bonus short story—**The Fates' Post-Wedding Celebration**

Books 7-10: Dark Warrior Tetralogy

Books 11-13: Dark Guardian Trilogy

Books 14-16: Dark Angel Trilogy

Books 17-19: Dark Operative Trilogy

Books 20-22: Dark Survivor Trilogy

Books 23-25: Dark Widow Trilogy

Books 26-28: Dark Dream Trilogy

Books 29-31: Dark Prince Trilogy

Books 32-34: Dark Queen Trilogy

Books 35-37: Dark Spy Trilogy

Books 38-40: Dark Overlord Trilogy

Books 41-43: Dark Choices Trilogy

Books 44-46: Dark Secrets Trilogy

Books 47-49: Dark Haven Trilogy

Books 50-52: Dark Power Trilogy

Books 53-55: Dark Memories Trilogy

Books 56-58: Dark Hunter Trilogy

Books 59-61: Dark God Trilogy

Books 62-64: Dark Whispers Trilogy

Books 65-67: Dark Gambit Trilogy

Books 68-70: Dark Alliance Trilogy

Books 71-73: Dark Healing Trilogy

MEGA SETS

INCLUDE CHARACTER LISTS

The Children of the Gods: Books 1-6

The Children of the Gods: Books 6.5-10

TRY THE SERIES ON

AUDIBLE

2 FREE audiobooks with your new Audible subscription!

PERFECT MATCH SERIES

Vampire's Consort

When Gabriel's company is ready to start beta testing, he invites his old crush to inspect its medical safety protocol.

Curious about the revolutionary technology of the *Perfect Match Virtual Fantasy-Fulfillment studios*, Brenna agrees.

Neither expects to end up partnering for its first fully immersive test run.

King's Chosen

When Lisa's nutty friends get her a gift certificate to *Perfect Match Virtual Fantasy Studios*, she has no intentions of using it. But since the only way to get a refund is if no partner can be found for her, she makes sure to request a fantasy so girly and over the top that no sane guy will pick it up.

Except, someone does.

> **Warning:** This fantasy contains a hot, domineering crown prince, sweet insta-love, steamy love scenes painted with light shades of gray, a wedding, and a HEA in both the virtual and real worlds.
>
> Intended for mature audience.

Captain's Conquest

Working as a Starbucks barista, Alicia fends off flirting all day long, but none of the guys are as charming and sexy as Gregg. His frequent visits are the highlight of her day, but since he's never asked her out, she assumes he's taken. Besides, between a day job and a budding music career, she has no time to start a new relationship.

That is until Gregg makes her an offer she can't refuse—a gift certificate to the virtual fantasy fulfillment service everyone is talking about. As a huge Star Trek fan, Alicia has a perfect match in mind—the captain of the Starship Enterprise.

The Thief Who Loved Me

When Marian splurges on a Perfect Match Virtual adventure as a world infamous jewel thief, she expects high-wire fun with a hot partner who she will never have to see again in real life.

A virtual encounter seems like the perfect answer to Marcus's string of dating disasters. No strings attached, no drama, and definitely no love. As a die-hard James Bond fan, he chooses as his avatar a dashing MI6 operative, and to complement his adventure, a dangerously seductive partner.

Neither expects to find their forever Perfect Match.

My Merman Prince

The beautiful architect working late on the twelfth floor of my building thinks that I'm just the maintenance guy. She's also under the impression that I'm not interested.

Nothing could be further from the truth.

I want her like I've never wanted a woman before, but I don't play where I work.

I don't need the complications.

When she tells me about living out her mermaid fantasy with a stranger in a Perfect Match virtual adventure, I decide to do everything possible to ensure that the stranger is me.

THE DRAGON KING

To save his beloved kingdom from a devastating war, the Crown Prince of Trieste makes a deal with a witch that costs him half of his humanity and dooms him to an eternity of loneliness.

Now king, he's a fearsome cobalt-winged dragon by day and a short-tempered monarch by night. Not many are brave enough to serve in the palace of the brooding and volatile ruler, but Charlotte ignores the rumors and accepts a scribe position in court.

As the young scribe reawakens Bruce's frozen heart, all that stands in the way of their happiness is the witch's bargain. Outsmarting the evil hag will take cunning and courage, and Charlotte is just the right woman for the job.

My Werewolf Romeo

The father of my star student is a big-shot screenwriter and the patron of the drama department who thinks he can dictate what production I should put on. The principal makes it very clear that I need to cooperate with the opinionated asshat or walk away from my dream job at the exclusive private high school.

It doesn't help matters that the guy is single, hot, charming, creative, and seems to like me despite my thinly-veiled hostility.

When he invites me to a custom-tailored Perfect Match virtual adventure to prove that his screenplay is perfect for my production, I accept, intending to have fun while proving that messing with the classics is a foolish idea.

I don't expect to be wowed by his werewolf adaptation of Red Riding Hood mesh-up with Romeo and Juliet, and I certainly don't expect to fall in love with the virtual fantasy's leading man.

The Channeler's Companion

A treat for fans of *The Wheel of Time*.

When Erika hires Rand to assist in her pediatric clinic, she does so despite his good looks and irresistible charm, not because of them.

He's empathic, adores children, and has the patience of a saint.

He's also all she can think about, but he's off limits.

What's a doctor to do to scratch that irresistible itch without risking workplace complications?

A shared adventure in the Perfect Match Virtual Studios seems like the solution, but instead of letting the algorithm choose a partner for her, Erika can try to influence it to select the one she wants. Awarding Rand a gift certificate to the service will get him into their database, but unless Erika can tip the odds in her favor, getting paired with him is a long shot.

Hopefully, a virtual adventure based on her and Rand's favorite series will do the trick.

Note

Dear reader,

I hope my stories have added a little joy to your day. If you have a moment to add some to mine, you can help spread the word about the Children Of The Gods series by telling your friends and penning a review. Your recommendations are the most powerful way to inspire new readers to explore the series.

Thank you,

Isabell

FOR EXCLUSIVE PEEKS AT UPCOMING RELEASES & A FREE COMPANION BOOK

Join my *VIP Club* and gain access to the VIP portal at itlucas.com
To Join, go to:
http://eepurl.com/blMTpD

INCLUDED IN YOUR FREE MEMBERSHIP:

YOUR VIP PORTAL

- Read preview chapters of upcoming releases.
- Listen to Goddess's Choice narration by Charles Lawrence
- Exclusive content offered only to my VIPs.

FREE I.T. LUCAS COMPANION INCLUDES:

- Goddess's Choice Part 1
- Perfect Match: Vampire's Consort (A standalone Novella)
- Interview Q & A
- Character Charts

If you're already a subscriber, and you are not getting my emails, your provider is sending them to your junk folder, and you are missing out on **IMPORTANT UPDATES, SIDE CHARACTERS' PORTRAITS, ADDITIONAL CONTENT, AND OTHER GOODIES.** To fix that, add isabell@itlucas.com to your email contacts or your email VIP list.

**Check out the specials at
https://www.itlucas.com/specials**

Printed in Great Britain
by Amazon